Praise for Lorn

"Landvik's characters are generous a... and inclusive. They inspire others, welcome strangers, and appreciate practical things done well."

—*Minneapolis Star Tribune*

"Readers can't help but come away encouraged and even a little in awe of Landvik's wisdom . . ."

—William Kent Krueger

"Wonderful . . . Fun . . . As lovely as anything you're likely to read."

—*Detroit Free Press*

"Smart and sweet, poignant and boisterous, devious and delightful—in short, everything we have come to expect from Lorna Landvik . . ."

—Pete Hautman

"Fun and funny, spiked with tragedy and sad times."

—*USA Today*

LAST CIRCLE OF LOVE

ALSO BY LORNA LANDVIK

Patty Jane's House of Curl

Your Oasis on Flame Lake

The Tall Pine Polka

Welcome to the Great Mysterious

Angry Housewives Eating Bon Bons

Oh My Stars

The View from Mount Joy

'Tis the Season!

Mayor of the Universe

Best to Laugh

Once in a Blue Moon Lodge

Chronicles of a Radical Hag (with Recipes)

LAST CIRCLE OF LOVE

A Novel

LORNA LANDVIK

LAKE UNION
PUBLISHING

Published by Lake Union Publishing, Seattle

www.apub.com

ISBN-13: 9781662506260 (paperback)
ISBN-13: 9781662506253 (digital)

Cover design by Eileen Carey
Cover image: © Gil C / Shutterstock; © winnievinzence / Shutterstock;
© Katerina Arts / Shutterstock; © GoodStudio / Shutterstock;
© Bibadash / Shutterstock; © Sybille Sterk / ArcAngel;
© Carly Allen-Fletcher / Offset; © Jayde Perkin / Offset;
© Helena Perez Garcia / Offset

Printed in the United States of America

For Betsy Nolan
Your friendship and faith in me have been a beacon.

1

Let it be known, there was resistance—and bodily injury. But Edie, understanding that her bloody nose was not due to any maliciousness on her friend's part, accepted Marlys's apology.

"I just got so excited!" said Marlys, who had flapped her hands as if to stave off a gust of heat and in so flapping had clipped the side of Edie's face, knocking off her glasses as well as causing the rhinal bloodshed.

Edie, who didn't like to make a fuss, held a wad of tissues to her nose and assured everyone she was fine.

"And don't worry about those," she said to Marlys, who had offered to replace the glasses, broken in half at the bridge. "They're only readers."

It all started after what had been billed as a "Welcoming and Renewing Friendships" luncheon, although those from All Souls believed it was just another way for Prince of Peace to sock it to them.

The festivities began with a tour of the church's new addition, big enough that All Souls' entire sanctuary could have been tucked inside it like a Russian nesting doll. Three floor-to-ceiling stained glass windows personifying "the glory and wonder of salvation" had been designed by an artist from Santa Fe, whereas All Souls' single stained glass window was a decades-old three-by-four depiction of Jesus as Shepherd; its still unrepaired BB gun damage gave multiple eyes to one lamb and two sheep. (All the more depressing was the knowledge that it wasn't the result of random hooliganism; the sharpshooter was a former clergyman's son, who not only embodied but *quadrupled* the stereotypical rebelliousness of a Pastor's Kid and who many congregants predicted was headed to juvenile hall long before he took aim at Jesus's flock.)

"Now I'm not one to stymie someone's creative impulses, especially a PK's," said Velda, who, when her own children were young, had volunteered, without too much outward resentment, to direct the Christmas pageant. "But I was concerned that the boy wanted to play Lucifer, even after I explained to him the devil makes no appearance in the Nativity story."

Artful floral centerpieces decorated the Prince of Peace tables (All Souls could only afford cheap clumps of supermarket carnations sweating in cellophane cones for its recent Father-Daughter banquet), and a tangy chicken salad was served along with "artisan" bread rolls dotted with assorted pumpkin, flax, and midget sunflower seeds, one of which lodged itself in Bunny's back molar. But what took the cake (the metaphorical one—the women weren't about to let anyone abscond with their slices of a French confection called "dacquoise") was when copies of *Table Blessings*, Prince of Peace's latest church cookbook, were passed around.

"Just a sneak peak," said the woman who had served as the luncheon's emcee. "They'll be available for sale next Sunday. And if you're enjoying dessert, the recipe's on page 203."

"Wow," said Charlene, leafing through the pages. "It's even got colored pictures."

"It looks like something Martha Stewart would put out," said Marlys, "if church cookbooks were a part of her empire."

"They've got a whole section called 'International Favorites,'" said Bunny, reading from the table of contents. "Coq au vin, pad thai, Indian dal . . ."

"Well, we had lefse and Swedish meatballs in ours," said Edie. "They're international."

At the table, a chirpy woman whose chirpy name tape read, "Welcome! I'm Joan!" said, "Our goal is to raise five thousand dollars with these."

Another equally chirpy woman, whose chirpy name tag read, "Welcome! I'm Beth!" said, "Five thousand, minimum! I'm betting these'll bring at least fifteen big ones!"

Driving home in Bunny's SUV on a frontage road whose ratio of potholes to asphalt was about two to one, the women were not as Joan! or Beth! chirpy, what with everyone muttering their grievances against Prince of Peace.

"I thought it was a luncheon," said Edie, fingering the collar of her hand-sewn blouse. "But they were all dressed up like it was a wedding reception!"

"And there was so much air freshener in the ladies' room, I thought I was at a perfume counter!" said Charlene. "Haven't they ever heard of fragrance allergies?"

"Their church motto is *more of everything*," said Bunny. "There were so many diamonds flashing at our table, I thought I was at a light show."

"Too bad they don't put any money into their coffee," said Velda, her purse sliding off her lap as Bunny swerved to avoid a pothole the size of a Hula-Hoop. "Talk about weak!"

"Hot water has more flavor!" said Marlys.

That gave them all a chuckle, as well as a taste for the dark and robust brew for which they were famous (or infamous—the visiting in-law of a parishioner had actually called it "satanic" before adding, "But I mean that in the best way!"), and it was agreed that a pot of All Souls Firewater was just the thing to lift moods that had taken a tumble.

In the church's basement kitchen, they were filled with purpose, making their extra-strength coffee and gathering around a table they had gathered around thousands of times before for prayers and devotionals, for planning, for encouragement, for gossip.

"Do you really think they can raise all that money with a cookbook?" asked Edie.

"If anyone knows how to make money, it's Price of Peace," said Bunny, using one of the (not so) affectionate nicknames they had for the megachurch.

"Unlike us," said Charlene, a pout in her voice. "Look at what happened with our last fundraiser."

Lungs were filled and emptied in a communal sigh.

Hard times had fallen on their beloved parish like a ton of crumbly steeple bricks, and its congregants were having a hard time figuring out how to tuck-point everything back together.

Hopes had been high for the Hot Dish Jamboree, whose theme was "Let's Get Creative!" It was usually a big moneymaker, what with the all-around appeal of a Pyrex dish stuffed and bubbling with the soul-satisfying pairings of ground beef and rice, or tuna fish and noodles, or SPAM and potatoes bound together with sour cream or processed cheese or condensed cream-of-mushroom soup. Marge Johnson outdid herself with her "Everything but the Kitchen Sink" entry, in which she baked, in a 350-degree oven, kielbasa sausage, Tater Tots, canned carrots, creamed corn, and her secret ingredient (pickle relish). Its literal crowning glory was a sweet/savory medley of crushed animal crackers *and* chili-flavored corn chips.

Ticket sales, however, had been down 23 percent, and after the event, the women concluded that when it came to casseroles, tradition was preferable to creativity, as anyone unlucky enough to sample the tofu-okra entry would attest to.

"And our last two 'Fun and Fellowships' were duds too," Charlene reminded them.

It was true. In August, there were only a dozen participants at Ava Martin's Canning & Fermenting seminar, even though sauerkraut was supposedly making a comeback with the underforty set. September's "A Musical Mashup!" was a bold idea, but it only attracted twenty-seven people, and on comment cards, participants stated similar views—they were puzzled and/or put off by singing "I Need Thee Every Hour" to the tune of "Ring of Fire" and thought rapping "How Great Thou Art" might verge less toward the lighthearted than the sacrilegious.

"Sometimes I miss Stella," said Marlys of the retired choir director, whose reliance on old standards and heavy-footed organ playing had caused some parishioners to believe "Abide with Me" was less a hymn than her personal plea.

"Oh, I love Tad!" said Velda. "He's a true visionary!"

If she saw the other women roll their eyes, she ignored it.

For too many years, a girdle had been part of Velda's wardrobe, and it was a day of physical liberation when she tossed out any and all pieces of rubberized, elasticized, and/or boned underwear. It was taking far longer to free herself from the need to conform to others' expectations, and in particular her husband's, even though he'd been dead for over a year. At eighty, she was the group's elder by ten years, but the more she opened her arms (for so long folded in a tight squeeze across her chest) to new experiences, the younger she felt.

"In fact," she added, "I can't wait to see what he does for the Blessing of the Animals service!"

Although there had been murmurings that maybe this new Velda could use a complete medical checkup, Bunny appreciated the changes in her fellow circle member, and laughing, she said, "Maybe he'll do a blues version of 'All Things Bright and Beautiful'!"

"Or how about," said Edie, who always liked to be in on a joke, "how about 'All Creatures of Our God and King?' . . . with a, with a—"

"—disco beat?" suggested Bunny.

Shaking a packet of sweetener into her coffee, Charlene offered a sour smile—her assessment of not just the women's jokes but of the whole day.

She had belonged to the church's Young Mothers group, but as the young mothers got older, some of its members moved away, some dropped out, and some decamped to Prince of Peace. Loyalty kept Charlene at All Souls—loyalty, as well as an unwillingness to join her know-it-all sister-in-law in her defection. Nancy liked to keep her posted (i.e., to brag) about her new church and her involvement in such a "dynamic community," and three years earlier, in response to Charlene telling her she'd joined the Naomi Circle, she had said in a voice honeyed with pity, "Those old ladies? Oh, Charlene."

In its heyday, All Souls, the oldest church in Kittleson, had boasted the Leah and Ruth circles as well as the Naomi, but times changed as well as inclinations to join service/social/spiritual groups that meet in moldering church basements (although the leaky pipe that caused the mildew in the east corner had finally been fixed). Having joined the circle in the early '70s, Velda was the only member to have started out a Naomi. Marlys and Edie joined when they were the only two remaining members of the Leahs, and Bunny signed on several years later when she moved to town.

The Naomis' swath cut wide; the women found themselves volunteering on most committees, including the all-important fundraising one. All Souls needed a new roof, a new carpet in the vestry, and a replacement for the Christmas banner that had hung for thirty years every December in the sanctuary. Since its creator and most gracious church benefactor, Mildred Wattrum, had passed on, the Naomis finally dared consign her five-by-twelve-foot cloth banner to permanent storage. Mildred had a generous and giving soul, but not an artistic one, and her appliquéd depiction of the Nativity scene, and, in particular, two wise men and a camel, was—to quote the children who stood in front of it at pageant time—"scary," "mean looking," and "too lumpy."

"I heard Fred Ellis is going to quit the choir," said Charlene. "That'll bring us down to just fifteen members."

"Fred Ellis is always flat anyway," said Velda.

"Still, that'll only make six men in the choir. Prince of Peace has thirty-two."

"Thirty-two," said Edie. "That's Mormon Tabernacle size!"

Relieved/thrilled when told her sister-in-law couldn't attend the luncheon because of "an *extremely* important sales conference," Charlene found, to her chagrin, that her P of P tablemates liked to modestly boast about their church's awesomeness as much as Nancy did.

"That Jane! or June! or whatever her name was sitting next to me? She just kept going on and on about their choir—about how big it is, about how good it is, about how they've been invited to go on a concert tour of Sweden next summer!"

As the women wrestled with their envy over that bit of news (the last place All Souls' choir had been invited to sing was at Belle Vista Memory Care, and that was only because several of its parishioners now resided there), Marlys offered to make another pot of coffee. All the Naomis loved their brew, but none as much as she. A retired nurse, Marlys volunteered at the local blood bank, but it was rumored she couldn't donate herself because her blood was too full of caffeine.

That her offer was unanimously declined seemed a big sigh ending the afternoon, and, feeling further defeated when Velda reminded them the dishwasher was broken, they were about to gather up their cups and saucers when Pastor Pete entered.

2

“Why so glum, ladies?” she asked. “The luncheon wasn’t *that* bad.”

While their church was of an enlightened Lutheran denomination that had boarded a train leaving others stalled at Patriarchy Station, Mallory Peterson was the first woman to stand at the front of All Souls, and not as a member of the Altar Guild or the choir director. And it was not sexist, just observational, to say that she cut quite a figure in her ministerial vestments, and quite a figure in civilian ones.

Unlike the majority of the Naomis’ footwear, the soles of Pastor Pete’s shoes were not crepe or rubber; her shoes were not sensible at all, partial as she was to heels that raised both her height and some congregants’ eyebrows. And as far as hosiery went, no one knew her preference, as she was a fan of pants, which on this day were black ones, tucked into pointy high-heeled suede boots. Her blonde hair was long and unencumbered by clips or bands, and the sweater she was wearing seemed especially knitted to cling to her curves.

Truth be told, the Naomis had been astounded when she’d accepted the church’s pastoral offer—why would a young, vibrant woman want to take the helm of the leaky old ship that was All Souls?

One reason she voiced was that she and her husband had both grown up in small towns—Mallory in Illinois and John in central Pennsylvania—and the idea of raising their son in a similar environment appealed to them. One hundred miles southwest of the Twin

Cities, Kittleson had a population of almost twenty thousand, and although big-box stores and chain motels lined the freeway to the east, there were still nearby farm fields as well as a ranch offering horseback riding rentals and lessons. Another unvoiced reason was that this particular church had been described to Mallory as an "underperformer" and as a believer in resurrection, she wanted to play a part in the church's.

After almost six months, everyone was still getting used to the youthful youthfulness of "Pastor Pete" (the name Mallory invited the congregation to call her, as "it's just friendlier sounding") and her husband, John, who was unlike their previous pastors' spouses in that he was a man. And a man who, depending on the age of those noticing such things, had the attractiveness of either Liam Neeson or Liam Hemsworth.

"The luncheon was probably better for us than it was for you," said Bunny. "At least we didn't have to sit at the head table with all the Prince of Peace muckety-mucks!"

"Oh, they were all very nice," said Pastor Pete. "I especially enjoyed hearing Mrs. Kindem's stories of her and Pastor Kindem's trip to the Holy Land."

"Which was bankrolled by their outreach fund," said Charlene, whose sister-in-law was *always* happy to share details of P of P's financial might. "We don't even have an outreach fund, and if we did, it would hardly have enough in it to send you and Mr. Pete to Fargo!"

"And while Fargo has its charms," said Velda, a North Dakota native, "it's not exactly a runner-up to the Holy Land."

"We're just feeling a little . . . *dispirited* by their cookbook," said Bunny. "Ours—the one we printed up a couple years ago?—wouldn't have made *any* profit if Marlys hadn't bought four cases."

"I've still got about a dozen copies left," said Marlys. "I've run out of relatives to palm them off on."

"A woman at our table said their cookbook might bring in fifteen thousand dollars!" said Edie. "They've got a marketing staff and everything!"

"We don't call them *Price of Peace* for nothing," muttered Bunny.

Pastor Pete's grin was both appreciative and scolding.

"Well, you don't get to be a megachurch without knowing how to make money."

This rendered the women mute for a moment, not knowing how to respond to Pastor Pete's true—if not very pastoral—statement.

"That might be," began Velda, but she was prevented from further expression by a voice calling out, "Mallory?"

"LeAnn?" said Pastor Pete, jumping up from the table. "LeAnn—in here!"

Within seconds she was racing across the undercroft toward the woman who was racing toward her.

After their long, squeal-filled hug, they came into the kitchen arm in arm, beaming.

"This is my best friend, LeAnn," said Pastor Pete. "I wasn't expecting her this early."

The young woman had glossy black hair and a smile so bright that later Marlys, whose middle son was a dentist, knowingly remarked, "Veneers."

"I went to your house—or should I say the *parsonage*." She wagged her head as she emphasized the word. "John thought it would be fun if I surprised you and told me I'd find you down here."

"I'm so happy to see you!" said Mallory, her arm squeezing her friend's shoulder. LeAnn, noticing the table crowded with cups and saucers, asked if there was any coffee left, as she'd driven all the way from Wisconsin, and she was beat.

No one had to ask Marlys twice to keep a coffee party going, and she happily ground too many beans and filled the pot with water.

With the young women at the table, the dank tarp of discouragement that had descended over the group was shaken off. The kitchen seemed more lit by sun than fluorescence, and the complaints about their underfunded church and P of P's overfunded one were squelched, carried away, as they were, by the giggles and stories of the reunited friends.

"We met at a frat party," LeAnn explained. "But I can't say we were immediate friends, seeing as Mallory had the hots for the guy I was with."

"I did not!" said the pastor, a flush adding a rosy loveliness to her face. "I was just admiring his skill on the football field!" After a moment, she shrugged. "But who wouldn't be interested in Jack Winslow? Not only was he the starting quarterback, he was *cute.*"

The Naomis, all of whom—except Charlene—had entered or passed through that particular pause in their menses, tittered like teenage girls.

"Any man looks cute wearing those stretchy pedal pushers and shoulder pads," said Edie.

"Stretchy pedal pushers?" said LeAnn, and a beat later, their titters expanded, all the more enjoyed by the Naomis as they were laughs shared with women who could be their daughters or, in Velda's case, granddaughters.

"Whew," said Edie finally, lifting her glasses to wipe away the tears that had leaked out of her eyes. "I needed that."

"We *all* needed that," said Velda, and to the younger women, she added, "Thank you for letting us forget our trials and tribulations . . . if but for a brief moment."

Inspired by Velda's dramatic statement, the Naomis unburdened themselves to the young glossy-haired woman, who, to their surprise, seemed genuinely interested in their Price of Peace versus All Souls woes.

"It's really not that bad," Pastor Pete told her friend.

"Yes, it is," Marlys said with a sigh. "We're in a financial hole that's starting to look like a canyon."

Sipping the high-octane coffee she'd been served, LeAnn gave a little shudder and, leveling her gaze at Pastor Pete, said, "I'd say it's time to T-O-T-F-B."

Acknowledging the confusion on the group's faces, the young woman explained, "Think outside the—"

"—box," Pastor Pete interjected. "That was our shorthand for 'think outside the box!'"

"But wasn't there an *F* in there?" asked Bunny, with a feigned innocence.

Pastor Pete looked like a kid not just caught with her hand in the cookie jar, but with crumbs smeared all over her face.

"What can I say?" she said as her blush faded. "It's an expression we came up with when we were young and foolish."

"I distinctly remember *you* came up with it," said LeAnn, and, leaning conspiratorially across the table, she added, "Believe me, I wasn't the only one *shocked* when wild Mallory decided to go to seminary."

"*Wild* Mallory?" asked Marlys.

"Ooh la la," said Edie, intrigued.

"LeAnn is an expert in the art of exaggeration," said Pastor Pete, shaking her head.

"You don't have to apologize for young and foolish behavior around this crowd," said Bunny. "I myself earned the nickname 'The Flasker' at the University of Nebraska because I could always be counted on to spike the punch at any dance or special occasion!"

"We still have to watch her when she chaperones any youth group event," Velda stage-whispered to LeAnn.

"In my senior year, I was part of a sit-in against the war," said Marlys. "The campus police even came to break it up, but I'd already left because I had a pharmacology final."

"And I," said Edie, who didn't have any wild college stories to share because she hadn't gone to college, "well . . . I got a speeding ticket once."

When laughter over their examples of living on the edge had died down, LeAnn asked her friend, "So seriously, Mal. How's All Souls doing?"

Pastor Pete admitted that the church's financial stability wasn't all that stable.

"Although, we do have a bit of a cushion, thanks to the gift of a recently deceased parishioner."

"Tuh," said Velda. "If you're talking about Mildred Wattrum's donation, it's a cushion I would hardly call *plump*."

"And so you want to know how Price of Peace—"

"*Prince* of Peace," said Pastor Pete, correcting her friend.

"—how Prince of Peace," continued LeAnn, "manages to bring in so much money, how they outdo your church in fundraising—"

"—Outdo us in *everything*," said Charlene.

Tapping her long nails, which Edie noticed were made of gel or ceramic or porcelain or whatever material young women affixed to their real ones, LeAnn asked, "So what can you learn from them?"

"LeAnn's in marketing," explained Pastor Pete.

After a long silence—it seemed no one wanted to give credit to their rival church—Marlys said, "Maybe we've learned our cookbooks need a little more zip, a little more zing?"

"Maybe update them?" said Edie. "Less macaroni salads and more pasta ones?"

"Maybe you're thinking old school," said LeAnn.

"Maybe that's because we *are*," said Velda, a little snit to her voice.

"I'm just saying maybe you should step away from a church cookbook. Maybe it's an overdone oeuvre."

"*Oeuvre*," Bunny said, approvingly.

"What else besides recipes do you think the world is hungry for?" said LeAnn, continuing to tap her fabricated nails on the tabletop and looking at each woman like a jury forewoman trying to strong-arm a vote.

Charlene glanced at her watch and checked how many steps she'd taken. Edie fiddled with her locket, the one that held a picture of her husband, Finn, and their daughter, Mary Jo. Marlys, feeling the effects of the luncheon's too-spicy chicken salad, rubbed her solar plexus, and Bunny scratched her knuckles, which were dotted with a recent flare-up of eczema. Velda crossed her arms and stared at LeAnn, her pointed look asking, "That's all you've got, big shot marketing person?"

LeAnn was not daunted by the silence or the old woman's stink eye.

"Come on, ladies," she prodded. "Let's T-O—"

"Yes," interrupted Pastor Pete, throwing her friend a look. "Let's think outside the box."

After a moment, Charlene said, "Maybe . . . maybe we could make one of those inspirational calendars?"

"I get one every year from Abramson's Hardware," said Bunny, with a wave of her hand. "It's got cute pictures of cats and monthly sayings like *Live Your Dream*. Plus I get it for free, with purchase."

"And coming up with twelve inspirational sayings," said Edie. "That might be hard."

"Okay," said LeAnn, rubbing her hands with the can-do attitude that had rewarded her with a promotion just seven months into her new job. "Let's think big. Inspiration is good, but what else do people need help with?"

"Child-rearing?" said Marlys, whose oldest grandson had just called her the day prior asking if there was something wrong with his four-month-old who hadn't yet started crawling.

"Diet?" said Edie, who thirty pounds ago had given up ever reclaiming what she considered her "fighting weight."

"Romance?" said Charlene at the same time both Bunny and Velda said, "Sex?"

The women all stared at one another, taking in the weight of both words.

"Now that gives me an idea," said Pastor Pete, and although *she* didn't rub her palms together, her tone of voice suggested that she did. "When I was in the seminary, one of the most popular classes was 'Healthy, Loving Relationships.' That was sort of a euphemism for 'how do we help our congregants with their love lives?' *So*," she said, drawing out the word, "maybe we could put together a different kind of recipe book—one that has instructions on how to cook up more sex and romance in the bedroom!"

Had Edie not just swallowed her last swig of coffee, it would have sputtered out of her mouth in a surprised cough.

"A book like that would get us kicked out of the synod!" said Charlene.

LeAnn hooted. "Just the kind of controversy that would boost sales!"

"You do realize that we're a *church* circle, right?" Marlys said.

"But a church circle that shouldn't be afraid to forge new territory," said Bunny.

"That's right," said Velda. "A church circle that realizes it doesn't always pay to play it safe."

"But that recognizes when something's totally out of line!" huffed Charlene.

"I'm not talking about anything salacious," said Pastor Pete, although she wasn't exactly sure *what* she was talking about. "I'm thinking of something . . . fun or helpful or—"

"Yeah," said LeAnn, who felt the same excitement she did at a marketing meeting when the air buzzed with ideas and arguments, "something that would make other churches think, 'Why have we been so scared to address what's such a big part of people's lives?' This just takes a different tack—a recipe book for the bedroom!"

"Oh my," said Edie.

"We could call it *Spice It Up*!" said Velda. "Or *A Different Kind of Hot Dish*!"

"*Let Us Play*!" said Bunny.

"Again, it would be fun, not indecent or raunchy," said Pastor Pete, trying to rein things in before they got out of hand.

"And we'd format it like cookbook recipes?" asked Marlys, a far distance from being convinced. "I mean, writing things like 'simmer until hot' or 'turn up the heat until steam rises' might get kind of old."

"Well, we could always make it a guidebook," said Charlene sarcastically.

"Good idea!" said LeAnn. "Something like *An Idiot's Guide to Sex and Romance*!"

"But those Idiot Guides are really thick," said Edie. "I've got one for my computer and I don't know if we have that much to say about sex and romance."

"Speak for yourself," said Bunny.

"We could make it simple," said Velda. "We could write a little primer—something like *Sex and Romance, from A to Z*."

"That'd make it easier," agreed Edie. "There're only twenty-six letters in the alphabet."

"You've got a circle meeting Tuesday morning, right?" said Pastor Pete, and at the women's nods, she added, "So how about if we all think on this over the weekend and get together then to talk more about"—knowing how to hold an audience, she widened her eyes and spoke in a deep, throaty voice—"the fundraising project to top all fundraisers—our *ABCs . . . of Erotica*!"

This was what caused Marlys to flap her hands in excitement, the effects of which were Edie's broken glasses and bloody nose.

3

In the living room of the old brick house that was the church parsonage, a glitter of light rose in the fireplace as John Peterson nudged with a poker the pyramid of burning logs. It was an unusually balmy mid-October evening, and the fire wasn't needed for warmth as much as it was for atmosphere.

"It's just so . . . country cozy in here," said LeAnn, pouring three glasses of wine from the bottle of merlot she had brought. "You should see my new condo—I thought I liked 'industrial,' but really, it's like living in a designer garage. *Brushed concrete floors*." She scoffed. "Next time I'm going to get deep, thick carpeting—or maybe a rag rug like this one."

"A former pastor's wife made it as a gift to the parsonage," said Mallory. "It's not my favorite, but Soren likes driving his trucks over the little ridges."

"Soren," said LeAnn tenderly. "Can't we wake him up so I can play with him some more?"

Getting up from his perch by the fireplace, John plopped himself on a chair facing the couch.

"If you moved here," he said, taking a glass of wine, "you could play with him every day."

"That'll never happen. I could never live in a small town."

"Uh, try bustling community."

"A community that's *really* going to bustle if the Rev here goes through with her fundraising project."

"You were the one egging us on," said Mallory, tipping her glass toward her friend.

John, who'd been updated on the afternoon's events, said, "You really think those ladies are up to it?"

"*Ladies*," said Mallory. "Come on, John."

After tilting his head, as if his words had floated upward and he was studying them, he nodded. LeAnn merely looked confused.

"I didn't like him saying 'ladies' like that," explained Mallory. "The word is just so ageist."

"We're both trying to call one another on stuff like that," said John.

"But you just said ladies," said LeAnn. "You didn't say *old ladies*!"

"But think about it," said Mallory. "There's no male counterpart for that word."

LeAnn rolled her eyes. "Are you forgetting *gentlemen*? As in ladies and . . ."

"Again, it's context. Nobody uses *gentlemen* in the dismissive way they say ladies. You don't hear people say, 'Oh, look at those gentlemen sitting around gabbing' or 'I wonder what crazy idea those gentlemen are cooking up?'"

"Mama!" came a cry from the baby's room.

Mallory rose and so did John.

"I'll take this one," he said. "If I'm not back in a half hour, know that I'm on the hundredth verse of 'The Wheels on the Bus.'"

After John left the room, LeAnn said, "He's such a good man." She sighed. "Do you think I'll ever find a good man?"

"I'm sure—"

"Nah, don't bother," said LeAnn, whose last phone conversation with Mallory had included rants and tears over her latest breakup. "I promised for once I wouldn't whine about what a desperately lonely old maid I am." Seeing Mallory's face, she added, "Kidding! Well, mostly. Anyhow, I don't think John meant any ageism—"

"I don't think *I* intentionally mean any either, but it's so ingrained, we have to make a conscious effort to notice it." Mallory took a small sip of wine. "Now tell me truthfully, what was your first impression when you first met the Naomis?"

"I thought they seemed very nice," said LeAnn, a little snip in her voice.

The two friends looked at one another for a moment before they laughed.

"They did seem nice. But you're right, Mal, what struck me first was . . . they're *old*."

"Same here," said Mallory with a sigh. "Along with all those old-age judgments."

"Judgments like 'Oh, that Velda looks just like my grandma!' Or like 'Hey, Marlys, what's up with your hair?'"

Mallory laughed. "To her credit, she says it's the last time she'll get her hair permed by a 'stylist in training.'"

"But to even get a permanent in the first place! And that red-faced Edie—"

"I can't believe you remember all their names."

"Chalk it up to my brilliant memory . . . and the fact that most of them were wearing name tags."

"Oh, yeah," said Mallory, remembering the luncheon IDs.

"But really, what exactly were those things crawling up her collar?"

"Appliqués. Ladybug appliqués. Edie sews most of her clothes . . . and decorates some of them."

"At least that Bunny's pretty stylin'. I mean, with that white streak in her hair . . . and I'd definitely wear *her* jacket."

"Her husband was a tailor. He made a lot of her clothes. None with ladybugs, as far as I've seen."

"And then that—oh, what's her name? The blonde woman? She doesn't look that old, but she sure acts it."

Mallory wagged her finger and tsked. "I do not," she said, mimicking Charlene. "It's just important to me to always be proper, always be—"

Dropping her hand to her lap, Mallory shook her head.

"Listen to me—mocking my parishioners! Not just laughing, but making jokes at their—"

"Come on, Mal. You know you don't have to be Pastor Perfect with me."

"*Pastor Perfect.* That'd be the day." She studied her goblet, watching the play of firelight on the cut glass. "At least around you I can be my mean old snarky self."

"And I can be my whiny old spinster self around you," said LeAnn and as they toasted their faults, bells rang.

"My boss," said LeAnn, looking at her phone screen. "I should take this."

As LeAnn sought privacy in the kitchen, Mallory settled back on the couch, warmed less by the wine she sipped and the blazing fire than by the love and gratitude she felt for those in the house with her.

Look how far we've come, she thought, remembering LeAnn's shock when Mallory had shared the news that she was going to seminary to become a minister.

"But you're not even religious!" LeAnn had shrieked over the phone so loudly it hurt Mallory's ear.

"I've gotten to be."

"When? Not in college! We always slept in on Sunday mornings . . . although remember, there was that time when you woke me up early to show me the wand that said *not pregnant!*"

"Oh boy, I do remem—"

"—I mean, can we even be friends anymore?"

"LeAnn, of course! How can you ask that? I love you—"

Upset and confused, LeAnn had hung up but called back hours later, apologizing.

"Sorry . . . but the more I think of it . . . well, you could get wild, but you were also the one *always* taking care of everybody else. I mean our dorm room was like a psychiatrist's office with an 'always open' sign and everyone on the floor coming to you with their problems. God, remember Sarah Meyers and her panic attacks and you were the only one who could calm her down? And how Brianna Davies was flunking out and you tutored her for like a whole week before finals? And how you'd hold back my hair when I drank too much and was throwing up in the toilet—"

"Verily, verily," said Mallory solemnly, "for whosoever shall hold back your hair . . ."

They had shared a small laugh before falling into a long silence.

"It's such a big change," LeAnn had said finally. "I mean, it's just so . . . weird."

"I know. But as weird as it is, it feels right."

After getting her degree in business/hospitality management, Mallory had managed a fancy boutique hotel in Chicago and, after two years, was about to relocate to the company's even fancier hotel in Los Angeles when she handed in her resignation, explaining that she wanted to do more.

More turned out to be a stint volunteering as a "community builder" in Ecuador, where the question "How can I help you?" or "*¿Cómo puedo ayudarle?*" was a constant greeting. After leaving the Peace Corps, Mallory landed in the Twin Cities, working for an educational nonprofit, where she met John, who was a board member. On their first date, they put on hard hats and tool belts and helped a Habitat for Humanity crew shore up a sagging bungalow.

"When you told the crew leader you thought the problem was that the pipes were hidden in the kitchen floor joists, well, Mal, that's when I fell in love with you," John had told her later. "I thought, not only is she smart, beautiful, and fun—she knows what floor joists are!"

After they married, John had been supportive of his wife's continued "search for more," and while he didn't shriek when Mallory told him of her plans to enroll in seminary, he did gulp, several times.

"So I'm going to be a minister's spouse?" he said finally. "And do what, hold welcoming teas? Teach Sunday school? Sit in the front pew and beam at you during your sermons?"

As it turned out, he kept his full-time job as a CPA; he served no Earl Grey and scones to new members, nor did he sing "Zacchaeus Was a Wee Little Man" to seven-year-olds. And while he did sit in the front pew on Sunday mornings, he didn't *always* beam at her.

Mallory hadn't asked him to be anything but her sounding board, her complaint department, and her consigliere—all roles he was happy to take on. And the church soon realized that, while Pastor Pete was captain, John Peterson was her first mate, and both of them encouraged their dwindling congregation to "serve our church, our community, and our world in new ways."

Returning to the living room, LeAnn said, "Great news! We've got some clients who are *very* happy with the campaign I worked my butt off on *and* a big international snack-food company wants to meet with us!"

"Oh, LeAnn, that's great. Congratulations!"

Plumping a couch pillow before sitting down, LeAnn said, "Now, where'd we leave off? I know I finished ragging on the circle women for their bad hair and bugs on their clothes, but were you done lecturing me about calling them *ladies*? Which I'm sure I did at some point today, and to their faces, no less."

"Oh, I do, too, and so do they. When women call each other ladies, we're not usually tagging it with that 'old/inconsequential' inference."

LeAnn shook her head.

"So along with figuring out how to relate to these *ladies,* you've also got to figure out when it's okay to call them that?"

"Something like that. But really, LeAnn—and this is the fun thing, the *surprising* thing—the more I get to know the Naomis, the more I'm realizing they're just like us . . . except *older.* Which sounds stupid—"

"But also wise," said John, entering the room and reclaiming his chair.

"Soren's asleep?" asked Mallory.

John nodded. "And it only took about twenty verses of the song—a record." He reached for his wineglass. "So, what do you think? Will the Naomis or will they not follow through on this 'Operation Save All Souls?' fundraiser?"

"Oh, good name!" said LeAnn. "I like the undercover vibe—and *so* inclusive!"

"Whatever we call it," said Mallory, "I doubt anything will come of it. It was just a funny, spur-of-the-moment idea. Really, can you imagine any church circle—no matter how old or young they are—writing a book about erotica?" She laughed along with her friend and husband. "I mean, *come on.*"

~

"Oh, ye of little faith," Velda might have scolded, had she been privy to Pastor Pete's words. Not that she had any idea what she'd write about—the love life she'd had with Merv wasn't going to provide much inspiration—but she was excited to be involved in something challenging and what was sure to be controversial. She was bored—and miffed—by people's low expectations of what she could and should do and was beginning to welcome opportunities to blow a hole through those expectations.

Under the light of a harvest moon, she easily switched from the crawl to the breaststroke as she swam to the center of Henson Lake. It was really a nameless fourteen-acre pond that a half-dozen homes had been built around, but her husband had long ago christened it *their* body of water, although they never shared the name publicly.

Other swimmers found the autumnal waters inhospitable, which might be the reason there were no other swimmers in the water. Velda wore a swimsuit fairly late into the season, feeling that the pond's lower depths held onto the heat of summer, but now she was wearing the wet suit she had bought online. It was a purchase she'd wanted to make for years; if they were lucky enough to have a backyard that sloped down to a swimmable pond, shouldn't they enjoy that pond as long as possible? Merv had claimed the idea "nutty," and thus, it wasn't until the day after his funeral that she decided to gift herself, ordering a dark blue neoprene suit that would allow her pond access until Henson Lake froze over and she used its surface for ice-skating.

The first few stars had been shy, coming out like understudies, unsure of their part in the night sky's spectacle, but now joined by a cast of millions, they twinkled and sparkled and shone, and Velda flipped over on her back and floated, watching the show.

"Bravo!" she said aloud, but not too loudly, as voices carried over the water and she didn't want to disturb her neighbors. Still on her back, she moved her arms in wide arcs, gliding through water that had a thick, velvety consistency. The great horned owl who'd recently taken up residence in the big longleaf pine hooted a few low notes, and a gauzy cloud drifted across the moon. Velda felt as if she were being sung to by nature, by the heavens, and—as a surprise picture came into her head—by memories.

Oh, my, she thought, staring at the twinkling, winking sky, *E might be for erotica . . . but that's not all E stands for.*

~

Bunny, never enjoying a steady relationship with Morpheus, had a rough night. Taking magnesium, drinking chamomile tea, and wearing a black-out mask did little to help her break up with her more constant companion, Insomnia; on most nights she'd hunker down on the couch and watch the classic movie channel whose black-and-white films would eventually lull her to sleep, unless Clark Gable was in one of them. Then she was rapt, and often a little teary eyed, as Mr. Gable's dimples reminded her of her husband's.

Burton, too, had always worn a mustache, which to Bunny was a dash of elegance. More than a dash of elegance were his clothes, which as a tailor he made for himself and wore as well as any movie star, any prince. Her own sense of style was fairly nascent before he began outfitting her, making almost all of her wardrobe (he'd teased that he'd like to sew her underwear as well, but only because he was interested in the measuring). He had introduced her to so many things he loved and that she now loved—jazz, old movies, ballroom dancing, his favorite writer, C. S. Lewis (citing one of the author's titles, he told her, "I'm not as '*Surprised by Joy*' as much as I always expect it!"), and eggs Benedict, which he'd made for her every Saturday morning.

Bunny had marveled that of all the men in the world, she had had the great fortune to find Burton and love him, as she would often tell him, "wildly, madly, passionately!" She still loved him, but in a different way, as he was now a different man, one who for the last two years hadn't recognized the woman he had once called "my honey Bunny."

That afternoon, sitting with him in his room that smelled of sandalwood (Burton had taught her the fine art of celebrating all senses, and Bunny made sure the diffuser she'd brought in was always filled with fragrant oils), she told him about the church luncheon and what had happened at the meeting afterward.

"You should see Price of Peace's new addition. It's like they're trying to be the Crystal Cathedral of the upper Midwest!"

She adjusted the soft wool afghan wrapped around his hunched shoulders.

"Remember how you used to say one of the things you liked best about All Souls was its size? How you said God doesn't need a big space—He only needs a little room in your heart?"

Burton stared at—or through—her, his bright eyes now cataracted with confusion and loss.

Bunny had joked (she had to joke, or she'd go nuts) that if she filed for damages against Alzheimer's for stealing the rare and valuable mind that had been Burt's, she'd be awarded billions.

She told Burton about the woman seated at their table whose diamond brooch was so big that Bunny got a headache from all the reflection and how another woman had a face-lift pulled so tight, her eyebrows touched her hairline.

"That's Price of Peace for you, right? More is never enough."

She pretended his blink was in sly agreement. In all her conversations with her husband now, she had to pretend.

"But I'm saving the best part for last," she said, leaning close to whisper in his ear. "It got us to thinking about All Souls' finances. We're thinking about doing something a little racy to raise money—a book, sort of a little guidebook, on a subject you could have taught a master class in!"

Shifting now on the couch as the images of Jane Powell and Jeanette MacDonald flickered on the TV screen, Bunny sighed.

"Oh, Burton," she said aloud over the actresses' duet, "how could I ever capture all we had with just a couple letters of the alphabet?"

4

Whatever the event—a meeting, a hair appointment, a sale—Charlene Kendrick liked to be first to arrive. It was in her nature not to just be prompt, but to be early. She thought it showed an eagerness to participate, a gung ho spirit, a willingness to jump into whatever it was that had to be jumped into.

"Christ, would it kill you if you were the second person to show up to something?" her husband Charlie had asked that morning. Still in bed, he watched as she scurried across the room, getting ready.

"Don't break the fourth commandment, Charlie," she said and winced as the teeth of her slacks' zipper nipped her waist.

Taking his watch off the end table, Charlie said, "I didn't take the Lord's name in vain. I took His son's name in vain."

"Ha, ha, ha," said Charlene, which more and more she used as a response to his little jokes and jibes; in response to her admonitions and orders, he did a lot of eye-rolling.

After checking her reflection in the vanity mirror, she crossed the room while ticking off chores and reminders like a town crier.

She was the second to arrive at All Souls. The sullen custodian, Godfrey Kowalski, had beat her there; it was, she thought, one of his not-important-but-necessary tasks to unlock the church doors at nine o'clock.

"Good morning, Godfrey!" Charlene's voice was stridently cheerful, a poke at the janitor's usual glum demeanor (exaggerated, she thought, by that smudge of hair under his lower lip).

"If you're meeting in the kitchen, you gotta be out of there by eleven. Got a guy coming in to fix the dishwasher."

Too bad you don't have a barber coming in to cut that hair of yours, thought Charlene, who found the man's long ponytail unseemly. *And we're paying you to take care of the church—shouldn't you know how to fix a dishwasher?*

Aloud she said, "If we go any longer, we'll move to the undercroft."

"Well then, please don't drag your chairs on the floor," said Godfrey. "I just waxed it."

"I'll be sure to tell everyone," said Charlene, her smile as tight as a politician's when forced to attend a town hall meeting with know-it-all constituents.

In the kitchen, she got the coffee started, grinding several fewer tablespoons of the fair trade beans (Pastor Pete had insisted on them) than Marlys did, and sitting down at the same table she'd been at several days before, she tapped on her phone's "Notes" icon. Typed onto its screen was "ABC Book Ideas?" with nothing following.

She was fifty but hardly considered herself old, let alone middle age. In fact, she felt like she was just beginning the prime of her life . . . when she wasn't feeling she was all washed up. One minute she was ready to take on the world and the next minute wondered how, and with what? Her prayers for guidance often came with an apology or were even rescinded; she didn't want to bother God with her problems, puny when compared to those who really suffered. For years she had defined herself as a wife and mother (*a stay-at-home mother* she said with pride or embarrassment, depending on to whom she was speaking), but her kids were grown and didn't need her the way they used to, and Charlie didn't seem to need or *want* her the way he used to . . . and vice versa.

Barring a few wrinkles and a softening jawline, the physical self she saw in the mirror hadn't changed that much, but more and more her interior self was one she hardly recognized. Where had this piousness come from? Why did she feel so uncertain about so many things, and why was it so important to convince everyone that she didn't? In the busy arcade of her mind, she played a constant game of Whac-A-Mole; no sooner had she banged down a doubt or fear than another popped up.

As the room filled with the smell of brewing coffee, Pastor Pete came through the door.

"Hey," she said.

It was sort of a wan greeting, which Charlene answered back with a chipper, "Good morning!"

The young minister was dressed in yoga pants and a sweatshirt, which Charlene didn't think appropriate clergy wear. When did "Casual Friday" become "Casual Every Day"?

Heading straight for the coffee, Pastor Pete said, "I had sort of a rough night last night."

"I know what you mean! I haven't slept well the past couple nights, thinking about"—Charlene offered a little tsk—"*The ABCs of Erotica*! If you ask me, going forward with something like this is just asking for trouble!"

"Actually, it's Soren who kept me up," said Pastor Pete, sitting down. "The little gymnast's learned how to climb out of his crib, and it seemed every hour he was charging into our bedroom."

She took a sip of coffee and, after exhaling a soft sigh, said, "And no worries, Charlene, if you don't want to be a part of whatever this might or might not be. I certainly wouldn't want you to feel pressured."

"Oh, no, I don't feel pressured," said Charlene, blushing, "I just feel . . ."

Pastor Pete wasn't privy to what those feelings were, seeing as the rest of the circle women chose that moment to enter the room on a ripple of laughter.

"Edie was just telling us she did her homework," explained Velda.

"I couldn't believe it," said Edie. "I was always last to hand in my school assignments!"

"She worked on the letter *A*," said Bunny.

"Say no more till we get our coffee!" said Marlys, setting on the table a plate and lifting with a flourish the dish towel covering it. "Donut holes. I made them this morning."

The coffee mugs were filled, and after Bunny dealt out paper napkins like a card shark, the women helped themselves to the arrangement of large-marble-size balls, half of them tawny with cinnamon sugar, half dusted in powdered sugar.

Conversation was limited to *mmm* and "These are so good," about the treats Marlys confessed she had made as a peace offering to Edie.

"For breaking your glasses and almost your nose."

"For a dozen of these, you can smack me anytime," said Bunny.

"Ditto," said Velda. "Or maybe your Danish Kringle. I'd take a punch in the nose for some of your Danish Kringle."

"Let's remember, though," said Charlene before anyone else could say what bodily harm they'd endure for Marlys's baked goods, "we're not just here for a coffee party." She wrapped both hands around her coffee cup, mostly so she wouldn't reach for a fourth donut hole.

"Right," said Pastor Pete, understanding the nudge to get down to business. "Edie, you have something to share with the rest of us?"

The woman's eyes, now magnified behind different readers (she had at least a half-dozen pairs), shone as she took a piece of paper out of her purse and, after snapping it in the air, she cleared her throat and read: "A is for Acting—When you're not all that excited to be on your back, for your husband's sake, ladies: act!"

Her bright smile faded in the silence that followed, and her voice was close to a wail when she said, "You hate it!"

After everyone assured her that they did not, Bunny noted that it was certainly a snappy slogan, and Charlene, confused, asked Pastor

Pete if that was what they were supposed to do, come up with snappy slogans?

The young minister shrugged. "I know as much—or as little—as you do." She smiled at Edie. "But personally, I'd sure like to hear the story behind yours."

Edie admitted to the group that for a while she had not exactly been engaged in what her body was doing when Finn was doing something to her body.

"Not because of my surgery—we got past that ages ago. Instead I was off in my head, going over my to-do lists, or wondering if I should switch over to whole milk now that they're finding skim isn't so hot, or debating whether to use rayon challis or cotton knit for a shirt I was making for Mary Jo, or wondering why there used to be so many soap operas on when I was growing up and how now there are so few—"

"Oh, remember *Dark Shadows*?" said Marlys. "My sorority sisters and I used to watch that!"

"I was partial to *General Hospital*," said Bunny. "All that Luke and Laura drama."

Never having understood the appeal of daytime television dramas, Velda was semisuccessful at keeping the impatience out of her voice when she told Edie to go on.

Things had changed, she told them, when last winter Finn got accidentally locked in his fish house out on Lonely Lake and nearly froze to death, and Edie realized he was not the only one who needed to thaw.

"Just when he claimed he'd gotten all feeling back in his fingers and toes, he came down with the flu and it took him the better part of a week to feel like his old self, which in this case meant his old hot-to-trot self. But I was ready for him."

Taking a time-out from her storytelling, Edie helped herself to a donut hole, then another.

"Now, anyone who knows me knows I'm no baker," she said, brushing a dusting of cinnamon off her chin. "Thank goodness for Sara Lee—and Marlys. But I do like to burn cinnamon and apple-scented candles in my kitchen, so it smells like I've got a perpetual pie in the oven."

"Better than having a perpetual bun in it," said Bunny.

Shaking her head, Charlene offered a little tsk.

"Now why it took me so long to enhance the atmosphere in our bedroom is beyond me," Edie continued, "considering Pal sleeps in our room now that he's gone blind and there's a definite smell of old dog, especially after he's been out in the rain. So I lit a 'special occasion' candle—you can buy them at Jerdes in the housewares aisle—and I arranged myself across the bed in what I thought was a pinup girl pose, and do you know what Finn said when he came in from the bathroom?"

"What?" was the unanimous question.

"He put his hand to his chest and said, 'Aw, geez, you gave me a start!' Then he asked why I was all sprawled out like one of those crime scene bodies, the ones outlined in chalk!"

The women laughed.

"I told him I wasn't aware that I was and then he waved his hand in front of his face and asked what that stink was, and I told him it was a sage candle and he told me to blow it out because it smelled like burning tumbleweeds. And when I put on a Celine Dion CD, he asked if I'd mind turning it off. I told him it was mood music and he said, 'Mood music for what, getting a headache?'"

"So then what happened?" said Marlys, too captivated by the story to refill her empty coffee cup.

"Well, I could fib and tell you that Finn got a second wind and we spent the rest of the night canoodling, but we didn't. But, a couple nights later, after we watched *To Have and Have Not* on TCM, I pretended that I was Lauren Bacall and that Finn was Bogie and I asked him, in my huskiest voice, if he knew how to whistle."

Bunny, herself a fan of the classic movie, clapped her hands.

"So there he was sitting on the edge of the bed, winding the alarm clock, and he just stares at me like I was a stranger who'd suddenly hopped under the covers.

"In a real sultry voice, I told him to smooch up his lips and then blow, and he got all red and smiled, but then he must have remembered he'd taken out his partial denture, so real quick he takes it out of the glass of water on the nightstand and thumbs it back in. He winks then, and whistles—sort of like a cardinal's or maybe it was a blue jay's bird-call. Whatever it was, it got my tail feathers shaking and he was Bogie and I was Bacall."

"Tail feathers shaking!" said Velda.

"Bravo, Edie!" said Bunny. "Bravo to you and 'A is for Acting'!"

Edie might have blushed with pleasure, but it was hard to tell as her face was permanently splotched with rosacea.

"So we can do that?" Marlys directed her question at Pastor Pete. "It doesn't have to be religious, like 'A is for Atonement' or 'B is for Bathsheba'?"

"I don't know that this project—if it *is* a project—has any rules," said Pastor Pete. "Although I think writing about atonement or Bathsheba could make for some interesting stories."

Charlene's spoon clanged against her coffee mug, her sour expression unchanged by the teaspoons of sugar she'd dumped into her coffee. Bunny asked, "You okay?"

"It's just that I couldn't . . . ," Charlene began, her chin quivering. "Well, I don't know if I can write anything that personal! Charlie would have a fit!"

Edie shrugged. "I think Finn'll think it's funny."

Charlene's eyes widened.

"He wouldn't mind if the whole world knows about his sex life?"

"I doubt that many people would be interested! I'll tell him about it, though, and if he's bothered—" She looked at Pastor Pete. "If he's bothered, I can change it, right?"

"Nope, it's set in stone: 'A is for Acting—the story of Edie Hokkanen's big thaw.'"

Taking a moment to realize the minister was joking, Edie offered a weak laugh.

"Well, what about our kids?" said Charlene, her voice sharper than she'd intended. "What will our church's youth think about us writing a book about sex?"

"Actually, I've been giving that some thought too," said Pastor Pete as she pulled a long strand of her blonde hair and began to twirl it around a finger. "About how Soren might react when he's a little older. Would he think, 'Mom, this is gross—what a stupid idea!'"

Marlys thought about the very straightforward birds-and-bees talk she and Roger had given their son Jim, and how promptly he had regaled (and grossed out) his younger brothers by repeating as well as embellishing what he'd been told. Eric, only eight, had burst into tears, demanding to know from his parents, *How could they do such a yucky thing?*

That she was a nurse meant little to her sons as far as her assurances that they could come to her with any questions; the less they had to talk about sex with their mother, the better. Once she'd overheard Jim and his seventh-grade friends joking about losing their virginity, with one boy bragging, "My first time, it's gonna be wham, bam, thank you ma'am—next!" Marlys had been shocked to hear, among the boys' laughter, Jim bray, "Wham, wham, double bam!" Ready to burst into the room and school them all, she saved her lecture about respecting girls and women for Jim alone, who had blushed a deep red and said, his voice cracking, "Geez, Ma, we were only joking!"

"Or," continued Pastor Pete, "would it open up conversations? Would Soren ask, 'Mom! What exactly does "A is for Acting" mean?'"

"Oh, dear," said Edie. "We don't have to use that. I can think of something else for *A*."

"No," said the minister, "it's perfect! That's what'll make this project work—all our different perspectives on a subject that hasn't—at least in church—allowed for many different perspectives!"

Marlys held out the plate, offering the three remaining donut holes to any takers, of which there were several.

"I wasn't too keen on this whole idea," she said, "but I can see it could have value, not just to those boys and girls who might get their hot little hands on a copy, but to some of our church men—"

"Like Bill Hall?" said Edie. "Or Curtis Keeler?"

"I'm not naming names," said Marlys. "But, yes. Like those two and the other men who voted against us bringing in Pastor Pete because, and I quote, 'There weren't any female disciples!'"

Mallory, having scored the last cinnamon donut hole, chewed and swallowed it.

"It's men like that who could really use a book like ours." She took a swig of coffee to help ease the doughy clump down her throat. "The church I was an interim assistant pastor at? There was this parishioner who was a big proponent of 'purity balls'—where fathers and their teenage daughters get all dressed up and the daughters pledge to keep their virginity and the fathers pledge to protect it—"

"—Burton actually had a client in New York who wanted a tuxedo for one of those things," said Bunny, "and when he explained exactly what a purity ball was, Burton said for an extra fifty bucks, he'd sew up a chastity belt for his daughter."

"*No*," said Velda, chuckling.

"I was right there," said Bunny, nodding. "The client got mad and stormed out and Burton said, 'Good riddance.'"

"I couldn't say 'good riddance' to that parishioner," said Pastor Pete, "but I did ask him what I thought was a logical question—if there were purity balls where mothers and sons got all dressed up and the sons pledged to keep their virginity and the mothers pledged to protect it."

The quiet in the room as the women considered the minister's words was broken seconds later by laughter.

"I know . . . it's absurd enough to make us laugh," said Pastor Pete. "No one would stand for a purity ball like that!"

"My sons would have thought I was nuts to even suggest such a thing," said Marlys, who had gone from thinking the ABC book was a silly idea to thinking maybe it was something that was actually needed. "So when's our next assignment due?"

Pastor Pete shrugged. "So, are we really serious? We should move ahead with what John called 'Operation Save All Souls?' Our *ABCs of Erotica* or whatever it might be?"

Each Naomi looked at her fellow circle sisters.

"Why not?" said Velda finally. "Those of us who want to go ahead can go ahead, and if it turns out to be something that's really not appropriate, or that wouldn't help All Souls . . . well, we'll adapt."

"And as far as deadlines go," said Pastor Pete, "I don't think we need to set any. We've got so much coming up with the holidays—for now, how about if we just keep the idea simmering?"

"Don't you mean *sizzling*?" asked Bunny.

"Look," said Pastor Pete, noticing Charlene's expression. "If anyone's embarrassed or worried about revealing too much or getting too personal, well, don't be. This is a project that first and foremost is supposed to be fun, so, like Velda said, you can contribute if you want to and if you don't want to, well, you can help our fundraising effort by increasing your yearly pledge by twenty-five percent."

The women laughed, although Charlene was trying to calculate in her head how much an extra 25 percent would bring her pledge up to.

Having overheard the women's conversation, Godfrey the handyman, who had been organizing the utility closet next to the kitchen, issued a soft whistle.

5

Patting the dishwasher after its successful, nonleaking cycle ran, the plumber packed up his tools. As he reiterated that the problem was with both the strain screen and the door gasket, Godfrey nodded, all the while keeping a sharp eye out, making sure the plumber didn't slip into his overalls pocket some silverware or a handful of the nondairy creamers stored on the kitchen counter in a ceramic bowl shaped like a cow's head.

"Like I said, she's a good brand," said the plumber. "They made these babies to last."

Godfrey took in the information with a slight nod.

"All righty then," said the plumber, an affable sort who liked to converse with his clients and was put off when they didn't like to converse back. "You have a good day, now."

Godfrey's grunt was as loquacious as he was going to get.

The custodian mopped up around the dishwasher, having noticed a drop of grease that might have gone unseen by others. He was thorough, a good trait for a janitor, but he was also agitated by others' sloppiness, which made him overclean. And overdoing anything was pointless and reminded him of a past drug habit, which he had alternated with a past alcohol habit that had made him underdo things.

Replacing a roll of paper towels on the wall holder, he folded its first sheet into a triangle, the way hotel maids folded toilet paper. He didn't know if the old bags who usually populated this kitchen noticed these little touches, but he did.

Ladies, he thought, correcting himself. He had derogatory names for everyone and everything, and it was another bad habit he was trying to change.

When Pastor Peterson (calling her by her more informal title just seemed wrong) had offered him a job, he had blurted, "Is this an April Fools' joke?"

"Uh, it's the middle of April, so no."

"Are you sure?"

"Cross my heart."

"Okay then, why? Why would you want to give a guy like me a job?"

"Maybe because I admire your taste in French pastry?"

The exchange had taken place by the garbage bins in the alley next to Albert's Parisian Bakery.

Having just fished out of the trash a waxed box whose cellophane window revealed a row of croissants, Godfrey's weathered face reddened.

"I can't understand how they ever have any food left, let alone day-old or two-day-old croissants," said Pastor Pete. "They're so good."

Giving his signature nod and grunt, the man turned toward his old pickup, parked in the lot.

"Wait," said Pastor Pete, reaching for his arm. "I didn't mean to embarrass you. I've seen you around, and I just thought you might need some help. Like I do."

He had had some doozies of hallucinations (he had never had a peyote or mushroom habit, although he had certainly enjoyed both once or twice or a hundred times)—was he hallucinating this young woman whose lovely face was framed in fur? (That it was the faux trim from her parka hood was no matter; its effect was snow queenish.) Had she really said she needed his help?

Pastor Pete was apparently not to be run off by his discomfiting stare, which so many took as a threat.

"I'm new here," she had said, and that her voice wavered a bit could have been due to the icy wind that was blowing, even as the calendar said spring had officially started weeks ago. "I . . . just got hired at All Souls Lutheran as their minister—"

After his jaw dropped, Godfrey asked, "Their *minister*?"

"Yes, and the church needs a good spring cleaning, which we're starting this week—and well, if you weren't busy, I'd appreciate your help. We'd pay you, of course."

"How much?"

"How much would you like?"

Squinting his eyes, Godfrey pondered the question for a moment.

"Enough so that I wouldn't have to dumpster dive," he said, and looking at the box in his hands, he added, "The pickings aren't always this good."

The man's hard work had impressed those gathered to give All Souls a sorely needed spit shine, so much so that Art Chelmers, the church treasurer, urged Pastor Pete to offer Godfrey the position.

"We haven't had a regular custodian since Ralph Kleven got a winning pull tab and moved up to Silver Bay," said Art. "That's why All Souls is in such rough shape."

Replacing a broken tile on the stair landing, Godfrey could hardly help eavesdropping.

All souls *are* in rough shape, he said to himself.

"Can we afford it?" Pastor Pete had asked.

"I'm right down here," Godfrey called out. "And I probably wouldn't cost too much."

The pastor and church treasurer racewalked to the staircase to negotiate.

Godfrey Kowalski was forthcoming about his past, at least part of it.

"I'd been sober for two years but then I had a little relapse. Now I've been sober for a year and I know I'll only get to year two by taking it day by day. I used to be a thief: petty, mostly, until I stole a car—a real junker, by the way. Served some time in Oklahoma for that and it was in the slammer that I made a vow never to steal again, especially crappy Corvairs!"

"Have you kept that vow?" asked Art.

"Pretty much." He looked at Pastor Pete. "Dumpster diving's not stealing."

"No, it's not," she agreed.

"Are you a religious man?" asked Art.

He scratched a patch of dried grout on his thumb before he answered.

"Currently, I am my name: God-free."

Pastor Pete couldn't help her yip of laughter, wondering how many times he had made that little joke.

"But that doesn't mean I'm not open to the possibility of something out there," he added.

With the understanding that the first six weeks were probationary, Godfrey Kowalski accepted the terms of employment: a minimum wage salary boosted by permission to park his truck-bed camper rent-free in the RV park outside town that was owned and operated by George and Alena Swenson, longtime All Souls parishioners.

"You can use all hookups and facilities," Alena told him, "and when it gets cold, the guest cottage is yours."

"Shed's more like it," said George. "But at least it's got heat—and a bathroom."

He was also welcome to any food left over from church luncheons, banquets, and coffee hours, as well as from Wednesday's open soup kitchen.

As time went on, both parties thought they were getting a bargain; Godfrey's work marshaled what seemed disparate skills: diligence and speed, and as a surprise bonus, he was artistic. He had painted a new and much improved "Rest Your Wheels" sign for his new landlords and was nearly finished painting a mural on the Sunday school hallway. The one gap in his skill set was in plumbing (hence the call to the dishwasher repairman), but now that he had a library card, he was going to read up on the subject.

~

In front of the full-length mirror attached to her bedroom closet, Marlys Severtson stood the way celebrities did on the red carpet: hands on hips, one leg positioned, toe pointed, in front of the other. As if posing for clamoring photographers, she then fluffed her overprocessed gray curls before turning her head from side to side and pooching up her mouth the way the stars pooched theirs, as if ready to land or give a kiss.

"Grandma?"

Slapping her chest with her palm, Marlys gasped as if she'd seen *and* felt a mouse skitter over her stockinged feet.

"Good heavens, you scared me," she said, leaning against the dresser to steady herself.

"Are you okay?"

"I'm fine," said Marlys, her voice testy. "I just thought doors were for knocking."

"But yours was wide open," said Amelia.

"Well," said Marlys with a little sniff. "Still."

"Why were you making such a mad face in the mirror? And why are you wearing your nightgown in the middle of the day?" As soon as the question was out of her mouth, Amelia's expression changed from bemused to concerned. "Grandma, are you sick?"

The flannel ruffle at the end of her sleeve fanned as Marlys waved her hand.

"No, I'm not sick, and if you don't mind, I'd like my privacy right now."

"Fine," said Amelia in a tone suggesting otherwise. "I'll just . . . I'll just wait in the kitchen."

Watching her leave the room, Marlys thought, *Of course, she'll wait in the kitchen. We had a date.* Trying to winnow out quarts of frozen rhubarb and blueberries from a backyard bumper crop, Marlys had invited her granddaughter to help bake pies.

Almost toppling over on the bed as she struggled with the nightgown she couldn't get over her head, Marlys nearly ripped off the final button, freeing herself. She couldn't get into her navy blue jeggings and Minnesota Lynx sweatshirt fast enough.

"So," said Amelia, setting down the stand mixer, "have I got everything?"

Seeing the containers of fruit, sugar, shortening, and flour, the carton of eggs, tins of spices, sticks of butter, measuring and mixing spoons and pie pans neatly assembled on the countertop, Marlys felt a rush of pride and love for her granddaughter who, at the age of twenty-one, still not only liked to spend time in her grandmother's kitchen but knew what to do once inside it.

"Seems so," said Marlys, and after she got their aprons out of the pantry closet, she selected a CD and loaded it into the player, filling the room with a rueful voice ruminating over "A Fine Romance."

Marlys believed good music and good cooking went hand in hand and, eschewing her grandchildren's offers to load apps into her phone, made daily use of the radio and an extensive CD collection. When she cooked dinner, she was eclectic in her tastes, listening to classical (except for Ravel, who riled her up and made her burn things), Broadway show tunes, bluegrass, '60s R & B, and rock 'n' roll she had listened to as a teenager. But when she baked, she listened only to Fred Astaire's movie music.

"There's just something about his voice," Marlys had explained to Amelia years ago. "His voice and the band arrangements—they just make for a good baking atmosphere."

As Mr. Astaire sang, grandmother and granddaughter measured and mixed, and when the pie dough was chilling in the refrigerator, they sat drinking tea at the granite island that had been installed when Roger gifted her with a kitchen makeover for their fortieth wedding anniversary.

"Do you like it?"

Having studied substance abuse in a sociology class, Amelia had taken to bringing over various teas, hoping to help wean her grandmother off what she thought was a dangerous coffee habit. Today she had made a ginger chai.

Sipping at it tentatively, as if the tea were hotter than it was, Marlys put her cup on its saucer (she always brought out the china for Amelia) and said, "It's different."

Recognizing the noncompliment, Amelia laughed, and, to be a good sport, Marlys took a bigger sip, one that didn't just wet her lips.

"Well, it's better than that putrid green mac—"

"Matcha."

"It's . . . actually not bad. It sure doesn't taste like any tea I've had before."

"It's from India, which is why you should like it, Grandma, because aren't you always saying how good food can take you places—like a good taco can take you to Mexico or a good stir-fry can take you to China?"

"I say that about food. Not beverages. Well, at least not nonalcoholic ones."

Mr. Astaire began a song asking everyone to get together and to step as lightly as a feather, but ignoring his invitation, Marlys said softly, "I'm sorry I yelled at you in the bedroom."

"You didn't really *yell* at me. You just seemed a little . . . *bothered*."

"I am bothered," she said, staring at her cup, unable to look Amelia in the eye.

"About what? Your hair?"

"I was hoping you hadn't noticed," she said, palming her tight frizzy curls.

"How could I not?"

The two laughed.

Marlys could easily say Amelia was her favorite granddaughter because she was her only granddaughter. Not that Marlys didn't love her three sons and her four grandsons (and now a great-grandson), but when Amelia had come along, her glee had been like a shaken bottle of soda pop, ready to explode with sweet fizziness.

As happy as she was for their son Jim's success, when he had told Marlys and Roger that he and his family were leaving Kittleson, as he'd accepted a position at a brokerage firm in Chicago, she couldn't help the "No!" that blurted out of her mouth. Amelia was only thirteen, and Marlys couldn't bear the thought of her granddaughter being so far away, but they'd kept up their relationship virtually and telephonically, with some actual letters thrown in. When Amelia decided she wanted to go to college in Mankato—just forty miles away—Marlys was thrilled, and the two saw each other often for dinners and a bimonthly "Bake Day."

They had always shared a close and trusting relationship with few topics off limits between them, and deciding this one shouldn't be either, Marlys told her of the church women's proposed fundraising venture.

"*The ABCs of Erotica*?" Amelia repeated. "Is it like a jokebook?"

Seeing her grandmother wince, Amelia began to apologize, but Marlys cut her off.

"It might as well be because what do I know about the subject? Your grandfather's and my sex life dried up years ago—when I did."

Their expressions mirrored one another's in astonishment.

"I can't believe I just said that," said Marlys.

"I can't believe I just heard that," said Amelia.

"It's just that I'm so frazzled! To me and the Naomis, All Souls is not just a sanctuary—it's *our* sanctuary! We're trying to raise money for it—but will a guidebook on how to fire up your sex life get us out of our financial hole, or be the final nail in our coffin?"

Amelia was at a momentary loss for *anything*, let alone words, but the pleading look on her grandmother's face begged for a response.

"Okay," she said, after taking a gulp of tea, "just so I understand: you and your circle friends are writing a guidebook on how to fire up your sex life?"

"Well, Pastor Pete is too. And I wouldn't call it a guidebook. And it's more about firing up your love life, I think. Or in my case, what used to fire it up."

Amelia looked as though she wondered how the conversation could possibly get any weirder.

"And even though there are twenty-six letters in the alphabet, I can't think of a single thing to write about—not like Edie, who already wrote about the letter *A*. Edie, who's my age—well, she won't be seventy for a couple weeks—and she's still having sex!" Sighing, Marlys shook her head and said, "I guess we'd better roll out the pie crusts."

They worked quietly, flattening the chilled balls of dough into pale circles. Once in their tins and weighted with dried beans, the pie crusts went into the oven, and while they prebaked, Marlys and Amelia rolled and cut strips of dough.

It was when the crusts were filled with fruit, covered with lattice topping, and put back into the oven that Amelia went to her grandmother's junk drawer. She returned to the island with a pad of paper and a pen.

"This is your old trick, remember? You always used to tell me, 'When you've got a chore you don't want to do, set a timer. Then try to get it done before it goes off.'"

Because the oven timer was already in use, Amelia pressed numbers on her phone screen.

"There. You've got fifteen minutes to write something for your book."

Marlys stared at her granddaughter.

"I don't know what to write."

"Fifteen minutes."

"How about if you write something too?"

"Me? No way! I mean, Grandma, come on. I'd hate to shock you."

"I feel the same way."

They both laughed, and as Amelia got another pen, Marlys opined that she might need more than fifteen minutes and how about if they just write until the pies are done?

"Fine with me," said Amelia.

"Do you have a preference as to a letter?" asked Marlys, and when Amelia shook her head, she said, "All right, since Edie already took *A*, how about I take *B* and you take *C*?"

Amelia picked up her pen. "Go."

B is for Bell

A lot of people don't know this about me, but I used to be shy. Shy to the point where all my grade school report cards had notations on them like, "Marlys needs encouragement in social situations" or "Marlys needs to find ways to get out of her shell." I was never a wallflower because I never went to school dances. Instead,

I stayed home playing Scrabble or watching "The Addams Family" or "The Lawrence Welk Show" with my parents. (Whoop-di-do, huh?) Things changed, though, when a certain boy transferred to my high school. He was seated next to me in homeroom and when Mr. Lee said, "Let's all welcome Roger Severtson, all the way from Fresno, California!" I could tell by his red face and the way he stared at his desktop that this boy was shy too. He was tall and gawky and his blush wasn't the only red thing about him—he wore his hair really short, but you could still see he was a true carrottop. Most of the boys were growing their hair out like the Beatles or the Stones and his crew cut didn't do him any favors—he had a forehead bumpy with pimples, which long bangs could have only helped.

He was in my band class, too, and blushed the same deep red when Mr. Bahn welcomed him to Rancho High (Go Rams!). In the lunchroom, he sat at the end of a table, never looking up as he fiddled with his milk carton or unwrapped his sandwich and smoothed down the wax paper to use as a place mat.

Oh yes, I kept my eye on him. A shy eye (or eyes, I guess) because of course I didn't want anyone—least of all, him—to know that I was watching him, studying him, and, yes, spying on him. (Funny that just one letter separates "shy" from "spy"—I'll bet you James Bond or Mata Hari were shy kids who spent a lot of their time sitting back, watching people!)

This tall gawky redhead's shyness hurt me more than my own—I wanted to grab him by his button-down collar and shout, "Get in the game, Rog!" Of course I, who had a hard time getting in the game myself, didn't grab him by his button-down collar and shout those words; instead, one morning as Mr. Lee wrestled with the windows, I smiled at Roger (hoping my lips wouldn't stick to my teeth because my mouth was so dry) and said, "Does it get as hot in Fresno as it does here in Vegas?"

He gawked at me for a long moment, his skin doing its usual reddening routine, before saying, "Sometimes."

Then the bell rang and he fled the room and I thought that I had blown it, been too pushy.

We hardly spoke in band class, even though we were seated together in the back of the room. All of us percussionists alternated playing instruments, so the conversation between us and Jerry Slyke and Marty Hernandez was mostly putting our dibs on what we wanted to play. Roger had been at school for a couple weeks and before Mr. Bahn announced our first song of the day, Jerry took the snare, I think, Marty took the xylophone, and I was reaching for the kettledrum mallets, when Roger handed me an instrument, and said, "Here, you can ring my bell."

I stared at the cowbell in my hand before I dared look at him, and when I finally did, his face was as red as mine felt. Then we both burst out laughing.

So that's why I picked "B is for Bell." That unexpected racy little joke was the start of everything. Everything.

"Oh, Grandma," said Amelia, after Marlys read it aloud to her. "I know Grandpa plays the drums, but you did too?"

Marlys felt an odd swell of emotion, as if she might cry, but shrugged it away.

"And I knew you guys had met in high school, but I never heard any of the juicy details."

"It's funny what juicy details came back to me, although I might have embellished a little here and there." After a sip of the now tepid tea, Marlys asked, "But 'B is for Bell'—do you think that's dumb?"

Amelia thought for a moment.

"I wouldn't say it's dumb, but from what you wrote, I'd say 'B is for Brave.'"

"Brave?"

"Yeah! Because think about it: nobody gets anywhere, especially in love, without it. You were brave enough to break the ice, and then Grandpa was brave enough to *really* break it."

Marlys beamed. "Good. Then 'B is for Brave.' Now let's hear yours."

Amelia looked down at her paper as if it had just been returned to her by an English teacher with a big red *F* on it.

"It's kind of stupid."

"I'll be the judge of that. Now read."

"'C is for Chin'—"

"Chin?" asked Marlys, not sure she heard correctly.

"I told you it was stupid," mumbled Amelia but she obeyed her grandmother when she urged her to keep reading.

"I was a sophomore in high school, walking down the hallway past this group of senior guys standing by the trophy case (their favorite hangout spot, probably because they were a bunch of jocks), and I heard one say, 'Nice ass.'

"Another one said, 'Nice legs.'

"I felt a weird combo of excitement/embarrassment—these older guys noticed me and liked some of what they saw! Later, I remember sitting in history and while Mr. Bentley droned on about something (the man didn't teach—he droned), I kept thinking about those boys saying those things. What about the other parts of me? I wondered. What's wrong with my breasts, my legs, my face, and all the other stuff guys notice? Later still, when I was talking to my best friend, Makena, who's been like a feminist forever, she said, 'It's gross the way men rate our parts, like they're the USDA and we're pieces of meat!'"

Amelia looked up from her paper and said, "Makena's the kind of person who always knows what acronyms like USDA or amfAR or Mensa mean—she's at Georgetown now, studying international relations, and she wants to go into the CIA."

"CIA. I'm impressed. I'll bet *she* was shy as a kid."

"Maybe," said Amelia, and she continued reading.

"Makena was right, but because I always liked debating with her, I said, 'Well, there are certain body parts of guys that attract me, like narrow hips and little butts,' and she said that everybody has their preferences, but that doesn't mean they have to shout them out as someone walks by.

"Agreed. It's like, what right do they have to do that out loud? It's not flattery, it's more like they're showing off, accosting you, claiming a part of you as theirs.

"But I think everyone has their personal preferences and while I do appreciate narrow hips and little butts, what I'm really finding sexy lately are chins.

"Specifically, the chin of the barista at this campus coffee shop I go to. I like to watch him work—he always has this 'Mona Lisa' smile on his face like he knows the secret to whipping up your latte (the milk really is like velvet foam) and when he calls your name for pickup, he presents your cup with a little wave of his hand, like, 'Ta-da.'

"Not that I'd ever yell out, 'Nice chin!' but his jawline is sharp and tight and angles downward to form this perfect shape that has a deep dimple right in the middle of it. It's sort of like a 'ta-da' itself."

She stared at her paper for a long time, and when she looked up, her face was flushed.

"Stupid, right?"

"Oh, Amelia," said her grandmother, reaching across the counter to squeeze her hand. "I've always been attracted to chins, too, especially when they have a little stubble on them."

Marlys breathed in deeply, the aroma of baking pies filling the kitchen, warm as an olfactory blanket.

"But what do you really think about the whole idea? Will people want to kick us out of church for writing about erotica?"

"For one thing," said Amelia, "what you just wrote doesn't really make me think *erotica*. I mean—" She typed something into her phone. "Listen to the dictionary definition: *sexually explicit written works, art, photos, sculptures, etc., depicting human sexuality* . . . and I can't see your friends writing anything sexually explicit."

"Oh no," said Marlys, her eyes wide. "I couldn't see that either."

After they both giggled, Amelia said, "Actually, what I wrote wasn't exactly erotica either."

"That's true. You wrote what gets your motor running, not the details of the running motor."

Amelia looked at her grandmother and squinted the way a student needing glasses stares at a blackboard.

"So that's what erotica means to you?" she said and repeated slowly, "What gets your motor running, but not the details of the running motor?"

Marlys shrugged. "You're asking me too many questions that I don't know the answer to!"

Deciding to move on to something they knew more about, they cleaned up the kitchen, and when the pies had cooled, Marlys helped herself to a piece of rhubarb and Amelia a piece of blueberry, switching plates midway, sharing tartness and sweetness.

6

Standing in the basement laundry room doorway, Charlene watched her husband at his worktable. They had moved into the house when the kids were just babies, and Charlie had claimed a getaway space near the furnace and water heater, where he built a worktable that spanned the length of the room. His was a neat and efficient area, his tools hanging in their outlined places on pegboard, his table drawers holding partitioned plastic boxes in which hardware was labeled and stored. A classic-car calendar—this month featuring a bright red 1954 DeSoto Adventurer II Concept—was pinned up on the wall above a photograph of Charlie and his bride cutting their wedding cake, Charlene's head tilted back, a bit of frosting as well as glee smeared on her face.

Charlene felt a little buzzy, and at first attributed it to the strong "ocean fresh" scent of fabric softener wafting from the basket of laundry she held in her arms, but the longer she studied the rear view of her husband, dressed in a white T-shirt and khakis, the more she recognized a feeling she often stifled before it went anywhere: the sight of her husband was turning her on.

Sanding something—Charlene never knew what project he was working on—his right arm was flexed, both his forearm and bicep bulging. Charlene breathed in a quick puff of air, admiring the wide span of his shoulders.

Hearing her little gasp, Charlie started and turned around.

"Hey," he said, and when his wife didn't answer, he added, "You all right?"

As if her neck were a spring, Charlene nodded wildly, and after a long moment, Charlie said, "Do you need help? Want me to carry the laundry up?"

"Oh," said Charlene, his words acting like smelling salts or snapped fingers. "No. I was just . . . just admiring you."

"Admiring me?" asked Charlie, long pauses between each syllable.

Her initial reaction, and one she normally would have acted on, was to say "never mind" and flee up the narrow, carpeted steps.

"It's just that . . . well, you just look so nice. So muscly. You've . . . you've got a good physique."

Charlie coughed out a laugh, as if not believing what he was hearing, but then seeing a cringe of embarrassment on his wife's face, he brushed the sawdust off his palms and was ready to go to her. As much as Charlene wanted to drop the laundry basket and take her husband in her arms, she scurried up the stairs instead, claiming the need to "fold all this before it wrinkles!"

That night, after a chaste good night kiss, Charlie had turned in and Charlene, curled up on the den sofa, opened the new journal whose cover, in swirling calligraphy, read "Deep Thoughts." She had bought it months ago, but the title had intimidated more than inspired her. Now, after staring at the blank first page, she began writing.

C is for Compliment

It's easy to take your spouse for granted—especially if you've been married for longer than the honeymoon period is supposed to last. (And how long is that, really? Two weeks? Six months? A year?) It's easy to let the "did yous?" take over your marital conversations: Did you call your mother? Did you pick up the dry cleaning? Did you make that appointment with our financial guy? Or maybe I should say it's easy for me, because I think of all the times I say "did you?" instead of "you are." And not like "You are thoughtless!" or "You are sloppy!" or "You are reckless with our nest egg!" What I mean is following "you are" with more uplifting words, more grateful ones, and, yes, sexier ones.

For years, while I was saying things like, "Did you fix the garbage disposal?" my husband was saying, "You are so beautiful."

"Did you check the kids' homework?"

"You are such a good mother."

"Did you shovel out the driveway?"

"Your body is amazing."

He played offense, throwing a million "you ares," only to be tackled constantly by two million of my defensive "did yous?"

The weight of the words she'd written made her sit back. Charlene was a good person; it was important to her to be a good person, and yet . . . why was it so hard to say something nice to her own husband? It hurt her to remember the look on his face when she told him he had a good physique; he had been so surprised, so delighted. And she, unable to keep the momentum of their emotions going, had skittered upstairs, afraid. Afraid of what a mere compliment might lead to.

She capped and uncapped the pen, thinking for a moment before writing.

Was it all my "did yous?" that made me one day have to ask, "How could you?"

A tear splatted on the paper, blurring the question mark.

Charlene was an early riser and considered it a sign of if not superiority, then at least above averageness. After all, didn't the early bird get the worm? Charlie had gotten up at 6:00 a.m. for years, but when he opened his own car dealership and realized that as the boss, he could set his own hours, his alarm began to ring at 7:30 a.m., which was two hours later than Charlene's internal wake-up call.

She loved the changing light, how in the summer the sun would already be up, painting the sky's edge pink, and she could weed her flower garden before the mosquitos got busy. On dark winter mornings, the kitchen would be cozy with lamplight and she'd fill in the paper's crossword and sudoku puzzles. This time for her was both productive and meditative, but when Tyler and Tammy went off to college and the morning's quiet time seemed more oppressive than inspirational, Charlene had started walking, a phone app keeping track of steps taken and calories burned.

Occasionally she'd run into Velda, who was also a morning walker, and while the women would exchange pleasantries, neither extended a "Join me!" invitation, preferring to exercise both their bodies and minds alone. Besides, Velda kept up a pace that Charlene was not interested in matching.

However, this morning, still rosy from the newly awakened sun, this chilly morning whose dewy grass dampened both Velda's old Clarks walking shoes and Charlene's new Skechers, was different. Seeing the older woman stretching her torso over the leg she had propped up on the fence surrounding the high school's football field, Charlene trotted across the street.

"Velda! Velda, I wrote about the letter *C*!"

Letting go of the toe of her shoe, Velda straightened up and, after easing her foot off the fence, did a deep knee bend. She was very proud—and who wouldn't be?—of her agility and joints that still did their job (often audibly with creaks but with only occasional twinges of pain), but the exaggerated exercise was to bide her time as she had no idea what Charlene was talking about.

"Oh!" she said, after her brain whirred, rifled through files, and brought up pertinent data. "Our sex book! So what'd you decide—'C is for Cunnilingus'?"

If a roving photographer had been at that particular corner of Smith Street and Hyland Avenue and pressed the shutter button, she would have captured two women—one wiry and white haired, the other softly curved and salon highlighted—staring at one another, a smirk on the older woman's face, an open-mouthed gape on the other's.

"No!" Charlene finally sputtered. "No, I didn't . . . but uh, thanks for the suggestion!"

Watching her fellow Naomi flounce away, Velda's smirk dissolved into a frown. What she had meant as a risqué little joke came off as a rebuke, her tone suggesting that of course Charlene would never think of such a thing, because Charlene was too uptight to think of such a thing.

It was so hard to be a Christian when you didn't like someone, thought Velda, but no, it wasn't exactly that she didn't like her, it was just that Charlene reminded her of herself, the self she used to be when what everyone else thought of her was more important than what she thought of herself.

While aging was a factor, it was her fairly recent widowhood that was helping her move backward (but ultimately forward) to that wild and free girl who had not yet picked up all the baggage adolescence brings with it—the girl who not only completely accepted herself but would never think to question that acceptance. Mervin had been a mover and shaker in Kittleson. He was a man used to being the boss, not just of the high school but of boards, committees, and their household, and the certain decorum he expected of Velda was the certain decorum he got.

Pumping her arms as she increased her pace, Velda thought of her friend Sally, a longtime Naomi who'd died several years ago.

"I'm passing you the torch," she had said from her hospital bed.

"What torch is that?" Velda had asked.

"The torch that'll help shine a light for all the younger women."

"Shine a light! Shine a light on what?"

"On everything. On what you've learned. On what's helped and what hasn't." And because Sally had been an English teacher who had faithfully deposited sonnets and poems into her memory bank, she was able to withdraw words of Robert Frost. Velda wished she could remember the exact quote, but it was something about the afternoon knowing what had not yet occurred to the morning.

Walking as fast as a person can without breaking into a jog, Velda felt ashamed of her poor torch bearing. Still, how much light was she, despite her many afternoons, supposed to shine when she still so often stumbled around in the dark?

I will be nicer to Charlene, she vowed. A car, full of teenagers on their way to Mervin's old high school, passed her, and even though the windows were up, she could hear the radio's thumping, throbbing bass.

Or at least I won't purposely try to shock her.

The thumping beat faded as the car turned into the corner by the football field.

Then again, why should "C is for Cunnilingus" be so shocking?

~

Several hours later, in a Kittleson Elementary classroom, Edie was relaying to a group of first graders that according to Dr. Seuss, *C* stood for—

"*C*!" said a boy named Chue. "That's my letter!"

"It certainly is," said Edie. "You and Cassandra and Corey! All your names begin with *C*!"

The enthusiasm in her voice was equal to a sportscaster announcing a World Series grand slam, but she couldn't help it; the children in Miss Klinger's class never failed to delight her.

She, along with Marlys who was next door in Miss Horn's second-grade class, was a weekly "Reading Fairy," picking up selected books from the school librarian and reading them aloud to a rapt audience who, per teachers' instructions, sat in a semicircle with their hands in their laps, listening carefully and not bothering their neighbors.

Chue's claiming the letter *C* inspired the other children to shout out their own names. When Edie read about a character named Icabod being itchy, Isabella cried out "That's my letter!" And even as Edie had to explain what exactly a necktie and a nightshirt were, both Ned and Nuala were happy to put their dibs on *N*.

When the thirty-five-minute reading session was over, the children would swarm around the little varnished wooden chair on which she sat, thanking and hugging "Miss Edie," and she always left as rejuvenated as if she'd been to a spa rather than a classroom.

In grade school, it was determined she was "a problem reader," or worse, "slow." Teachers at that time didn't fully understand dyslexia, and Edie was forever grateful to her forward-thinking sixth-grade teacher, Mr. Angelos, who gave her homework—lists of words that she was to type out carefully on her mother's portable Royal.

Searching for the correct keys and typing over and over words like *won* and *now* or *felt* and *left* helped her to unscramble the part of her brain that scrambled words, and while the letters of some words still occasionally rearranged themselves, their mischief was more an aberration than a constant. She often wished Mr. Angelos had been her teacher in an earlier grade so that she might have avoided the pain that haunted her elementary school years—of being the dumb kid for which reading out loud was an exercise in shame and humiliation. Even as she grew to love reading and maintained a B- average throughout her remaining school years, the taunts of "dummy" were a stain in her psyche, one that had mostly been scrubbed out but whose faint residue remained.

"How'd it go?" the librarian asked as the Reading Fairies returned their books.

"Great," said Marlys. "I loved that you picked out some classics—*Little Toot* was one of my boys' favorites, and the kids loved everything, especially *Sneakers, the Seaside Cat*."

"And we had a lot of fun with the Dr. Seuss book," said Edie.

"You had a Dr. Seuss book?" asked Marlys. "Which one?"

"His ABC book."

Wiggling her eyebrows, Marlys said, "Imagine *his* take."

Not having any idea what struck the women so funny, the librarian, to be polite, joined in their laughter.

7

Outside her office window were lilac bushes that had long ago lost their flowers and were quickly losing their leaves, and Mallory stared at them as well as her own reflection. Wearing a long white cassock, she adjusted the fringed, embroidered stole draped around her neck so that it hung evenly on each side, and before walking through the side door into the sanctuary, she whispered words that had become her mantra/cheer/hope: "You can do this."

Kathy Knudsen had been asked to sing Joni Mitchell's "River," and listening to the plaintive, wishful words and tune, Evan Bates, the church's oldest congregant at ninety-three, was not alone in feeling tears rise, although he was the only one to dab at his eyes with a monogrammed handkerchief rather than a tissue.

Right before she was to speak, Mallory swallowed hard, needing the tamping down of emotions for which swallowing seemed useful. She hoped her clerical collar gave her neck enough coverage so that the congregation wouldn't be distracted by the bobbing in her throat, and she swallowed one final time before stepping behind the pulpit and looking out at the mourners. She raised her arms slightly and said, "The word of Grace."

Pastor Pete didn't know Zac Donovan, the twenty-two-year-old son of Larry Donovan, head usher and frequent volunteer at All Souls. Larry had been widowed when Zac was thirteen, and in the anguished two-hour talk Mallory had had with him in the man's kitchen, which managed to be both spare and messy, he said his son had never been the same after.

"How could he be? He was a mama's boy!" Larry had said, his voice twisting octaves. "He loved his mom—Carol was a wonderful mother—and she thought he was the most perfect boy in the whole world! Which he was, but then, oh man . . ."

He told the young pastor about the horror of watching his energetic, beautiful wife getting eaten up by cancer, about how Zac, their only child, pleaded with God in loud and tormented prayers to please save his mother.

"After Carol died, we stopped going to church for a while," said Larry, his fingers combing his snarl of dark hair. "It was Zac who decided to go back his junior year of high school, and I could hardly let him walk back through the doors alone."

Larry offered a crooked, apologetic smile.

"Turns out it sort of brought us back to life. It wasn't because of the uninspired pastor at the time—if he heard the call to serve, it wasn't very loud," he said, and Mallory welcomed the shared little laugh, "but the fellowship! People had reached out to us all along, but if you never return a call or write a thank-you for a hot dish left on your steps for the tenth time, people tend to think, 'Well, maybe they just want to be left alone.' But when we came back, everyone welcomed us in and All Souls got to be not just a Sunday stop, but a place Zac would go for youth group, for choir practice, for basketball games in the parking lot. That's one good thing Pastor Wiggans did—put up a basketball hoop!"

He told Pastor Pete how it wasn't just in basketball that Zac was rebounding.

"He could talk about his mom without crying, with laughing even! And he had so many friends and the girls loved him! He did well in school, in sports—he was a star center on his hockey team, he danced on the ice more than skated—and when he went away to college, it was on an *academic* scholarship! Everything was great, until that stupid car accident."

He had broken his back in that stupid car accident, one that was truly an accident and caused by trying to dodge a tire that had rolled off the bed of the truck ahead of him. He'd swerved to avoid it, but another car blocked the swerve, and there was a crash and a rollover, and Zac wound up with a broken back and an addiction to pain pills, and then heroin.

"He tried so hard to fight it," Larry said, his voice clogged with emotion. "He went to rehab twice! And then last year, we all thought he was finally free and he was, for about six months . . . until he OD'd."

Pastor Pete's hands had surrounded the tight knot that was Larry's folded ones and she'd prayed her constant pastoral prayer: *please help me help*.

Now, at the young man's funeral, she listened as his college friend gave a heartfelt eulogy—about how the deceased was such a ladies' man.

"And he had the wildest imagination—he'd make up hilarious little stories about everything from the cafeteria mystery meat to this real boring TA being a former spy—and was so fun and energetic that anytime he showed up at a party or a gathering, everyone called it a 'Zac Attack!'"

From a chair off to the side of the pulpit, Pastor Pete smiled sadly, thinking how much she would have liked to have known this young man, and when it was time for her sermon, she made it as personal as she could, ending it by referencing something Larry had told her about Zac's boyhood dream.

"He wanted to be an astronaut when he grew up," she said, "because he wanted to know what was beyond the sky." Mallory swallowed again and waited a moment until she was sure she could speak.

"While on Earth, Zac Donovan didn't get to explore what's beyond the sky, but I believe he gets to now. Fly high, Zac, on angels' wings."

"Beautiful service," wrote Evan Bates in the church bulletin. A former newspaperman, he still took notes as if he were planning to file a story. "And what music!" he wrote as the congregation joined Kathy Knudsen in singing John Lennon's "Beautiful Boy."

There wasn't a lot to clean up after a funeral; it wasn't a movie theater after all, where crumpled boxes of Dots and Jordan almonds and scattered kernels of popcorn had to be swept up, but still, there was detritus. Godfrey began in the choir loft (one of the second sopranos, whether singing at a wedding, baptism, or funeral, *always* left an empty plastic box of Tic Tacs on her chair) and worked his way downstairs, weaving in and out of each row, picking up wadded-up tissues that pom-pommed the floor, pushing up the occasional kneeler, and returning hymnals splayed on pews to the racks next to the pledge cards.

Since coming to Kittleson and All Souls, he'd made it a point to sit in the back row at funerals (serving as sentry and observer), which introduced him to more of Kittleson's parishioners, albeit posthumously.

This funeral was rough, and more than once Godfrey had felt the sting of tears in his eyes. Rarely released, his tears really *did* sting, as if a corrosive rust from disuse had built up in them. He wondered how a supposedly loving God could give up on a man—no, a boy—of twenty-two, whose wrong choices weren't really his fault. He'd broken his back for Chrissake! And he was given those damn prescription drugs by medical professionals!

Sighing, Godfrey picked up a crumpled pledge card from the floor. It wasn't filled out with the promise of a monthly tithe. Instead someone had drawn a big heart, and inside it, written over and over, were the words *Luv U Zac!*

Returning the single glove, two scarves, and a pair of sunglasses to the lost and found box in the coat room, Godfrey heard the murmur of voices coming from the undercroft, where the postfuneral luncheon was being served, and although he had planned on going, he didn't descend the staircase but walked through the narthex and to the Sunday school classrooms.

From the teachers' supply closet, he got what he needed and, out in the hallway, unfolded the step stool and unpacked his supplies from a wooden orange crate.

Leaning against the wall opposite, he studied his nearly finished mural like an art critic debating whether to heap upon, or deny, praise.

He uncapped tubes and squeezed dollops of paint onto the wedge of cardboard that served as his palette. He dipped his brush in the swirls of color and, for the next hour, he deepened shadows, enhanced highlights, and slightly altered expressions, stepping back now and then to survey his progress. Satisfied with his work, but not the mural's entirety, he reached up and began painting, surprised by the red bird in flight that emerged from under his brush. Birds—in flight or at rest—hadn't been planned, but it now seemed they belonged. His plan to add another one changed, however, when he saw the tube of paint he rarely used.

His brush filled with silver, he got up on the step stool and painted a tiny figure, positioning it above a cloud. On the stool and up close it was detailed and obvious, but when he stepped back to the floor, it was hard to tell what it was, which was exactly what Godfrey wanted. For the first time that mournful day, he felt himself smile, and after wiping his brush clean, he filled it with blue and began painting another bird in the sky.

"Oh, that looks great."

Startled, the handyman's brush jerked downward, giving the bluebird what looked like a compound fracture.

"Oh, sorry!" said Pastor Pete. "I didn't mean to sneak up on you."

"No problem," said Godfrey, wiping away the malformed wing with a wet rag.

"Soren left this in the nursery Sunday." She held up a stuffed bunny. "He's pretty cavalier with it, but when he needs Fuzzy, he *needs* Fuzzy."

She stared at him for a moment.

"Do you always paint in a shirt and tie?"

Looking down at his church-attending clothes, Godfrey shrugged.

"I don't know if it's a weird talent or what, but I never seem to get paint on myself."

"*This* isn't a weird talent," said Pastor Pete, gesturing at the wall. "It's beyond what I hoped it would be."

When she had conferred with Godfrey about the mural, she had recited the lyrics to an old Sunday school song ("although I won't do you the disfavor of singing them"), emphasizing the first and last lines.

"Jesus loves the little children, all the children of the world," she had repeated, asking that he focus on the word *all*.

And Godfrey had, painting against an azure sky a dozen children of varying ages and ethnicities, their expressions and clothing reflecting disparate nations and classes: a skinny, smudged-faced child in rags, a teenager smiling at her cell phone, a boy holding a small child in one arm and a bundle of clothes in the other.

"I did hear Curtis Keeler say it was 'a bit overdramatic,'" said Godfrey.

He would, thought Mallory, but said aloud, "I think it's perfect. And I love those birds you've added and . . ." She squinted. "Is that a balloon?"

Pushing the step stool toward her, the artist said, "Take a closer look."

Mallory climbed up, and in a small voice, she said, "Oh. It's an astronaut."

"I . . . I started painting the birds in Zac's honor," said Godfrey, a warble in his voice. "Then I remembered what you said he wanted to be when he grew up." He looked at the floor, also free of paint droplets. "I just . . . feel so bad about him."

"Me too," said Pastor Pete, and because she didn't know what else to say, she asked him if she could watch him paint for a while.

"Be my guest," said Godfrey. "Although I'm just about finished." He let out a sharp "ha!" and stared at the splotches of paint on his palette before adding, "That's not the first time I've thought that."

"What do you mean?" asked Mallory, holding Fuzzy in a hug as she leaned against the opposite wall.

Stepping up onto the stool, he said quietly, "I mean, there've been times I thought I *was* finished . . . with my *life*."

He was surprised and slightly embarrassed by his admission. He had never been in a confessional booth, but as he began repairing the bluebird's wing, the old church hallway took on the atmosphere of one, in that he began confiding to a cleric. Granted, he considered Pastor Pete his employer rather than his spiritual guide, but that she was there and that his back was to her made it easy for him to talk, telling Mallory that if *he'd* ever been prescribed an opioid, it for sure would have shoved him into more dangerous addictions.

"I was in a haze—or maybe I should say maze—for a long time, but weed and alcohol never killed me, obviously. Sure, those little monkeys on my back stopped me from having a certain life, but it didn't *stop* my life like it did that Donovan kid's."

He told her about his ex-wife in Phoenix—"Well, common-law ex: we never had our union 'sanctified' by the church or state"—and how their eight years together were "less 'Archie and Betty' and more 'Poison Ivy and Batman.'"

"Can you tell I was a big comic book fan?" he asked, squeezing from a tube a curl of white onto the palette. "I would draw for hours, first copying the panels and then making up my own." He swirled another brush in the paint. "Anyway, Jeanine and I caused a lot of damage together, not just to each other but to my brother and his wife.

They have a ranch in northern Arizona and any time we'd visit, we'd abuse their hospitality by, oh . . . plowing their car into a big ponderosa pine, or setting their microwave on fire, or running off with one of their credit cards and ringing up about six hundred dollars on it. The credit card thing sort of ended all further invitations."

Reaching high, he almost set his brush on the wall before reconsidering its placement, and Mallory watched his hand move his brush as intentionally as a conductor moves his baton.

"I finally left Jeanine, but the problems I had with her I still had with myself. Man, I kicked around for a long time, drunk, stoned, jailed—I told you about that—you name it." He stood back for a moment. "Does that look like a dove or a duck to you?"

Having watched a white bird take flight under his brush, Mallory cocked her head and said, "A little like a duck."

"Anyway, I finally got so sick of my sick self that I crawled back to my brother's ranch, banging on his door, begging for help."

A dove emerged as Godfrey turned its bill into a beak, and he told Mallory of his sibling's graciousness, even as he was dealing with the death of his beloved wife.

"I didn't even know Eve had died! Of an aneurysm, of all things! I felt like such a shitty—uh, lousy—brother, but Chauncey—yeah, you can imagine how well those names served us as kids . . . *not*. Anyway, Chauncey took me in, under a couple conditions."

Godfrey had to attend daily AA meetings as well as pay back the money he'd stolen by working on the ranch. He'd be beat from digging irrigation ditches or putting up fences, but his sunset rides with Eve's old horse, Agnes, were sacrosanct—his therapy, as important as his meetings.

"Every evening, me and Agnes would amble along in that air that smelled of mesquite, watching the sky turn colors. I'd bitch and moan to her, and every time she'd look back at me or whinny, I'd pretend she was asking me things, and I'd repeat her questions out loud, like: 'Why keep up something that takes away more than it gives? Why do you need to be high or numb in this life—what's so bad about life that you can't just be in it as you are?'"

After six months, the two brothers fit their lean frames together in a long hug filled with regret and hope, and Godfrey set off, seeking his new life.

In the three years since he'd left the ranch, he had traveled to eleven states, working odd jobs, doing some painting, falling in love a little but never enough to keep him in one place.

"Until Sioux Falls," he said. "I fell hard for a woman, and we had an *unforgettable* month together until her big shot international-banker husband—I didn't even know she was married!—came back from some big shot international trip, and Noreen broke things off. My mature reaction? 'Hey, let's go on a bender of historic proportions!'" Satisfied with his soaring dove, he wiped his brush. "Somehow, I got back on track and the bender didn't turn into a lifestyle, and a year later, I wind up here. Working at a church. Go figure."

As he began his cleanup, Mallory said, "Thanks for sharing your story with me, Godfrey."

"Well, not all of it," he said, embarrassed. "Just the parts I thought you could handle."

Even as she thought, *My job is to handle things,* she said, "We are our stories—good, bad, and in between."

"We just don't want them to be short stories. Like Zac's."

Mallory nodded sadly, her chin rubbing against the stuffed animal's soft fur.

When he finished packing up his equipment, Godfrey said, "Zac's friend who gave the eulogy? He did a good job. 'Zac Attacks!' Imagine being the kind of person who had the reputation of livening up a party so much!"

Following Godfrey down the hallway, Mallory agreed he sounded like a special young man.

"Man, the whole afternoon, I've been so down . . . and then I had this funny thought. I wondered what a kid like Zac, with his hilarious stories, might have contributed to that little book of yours."

Pastor Pete stopped as if a turnstile suddenly blocked her path.

"Little book . . . ," she sputtered. "What little book?"

Opening up the supply-room door, Godfrey gave her a wry smile.

"The little book you and the Naomis are working on."

"How do you—where did you—"

At the small sink, he began rinsing his brushes.

"You forget my office—a.k.a. the utility closet—is next to the kitchen, and if I'm there, or working anywhere in the basement, well, it's not like you gals exactly whisper. To tell you the truth, I hear all sorts of things in this church. I go about my work and people tend to forget I'm there."

He dried his brushes and replaced them in the coffee can in the wooden crate. "Anyway, it's interesting to wonder what a 'ladies' man' with a 'wild imagination' might have added to your erotica book."

"Godfrey," muttered Mallory, feeling her face flush. "It's not really erotica . . . we don't really know what it is, but for now . . . please keep it to yourself."

"My lips are sealed," he said.

"Okay then," said Mallory, realizing she'd been hugging poor Fuzzy so hard that if he were a real rabbit, he'd be in need of resuscitation, "the luncheon's probably winding down, but if you hurry up, you still might score some turkey buns or coleslaw."

~

"So that was rough," said Bunny, smoothing the loosely crocheted afghan that covered her husband's lap. (It was a gift from Edie, who'd splurged on cashmere yarn, knowing that Burton would appreciate it.)

"Remember Zac in the youth choir? He always soloed and you said, 'That boy could be the next Pavarotti.'"

Bunny smiled. "I believe I disagreed with you on that one. I thought he had a good voice, but it certainly wasn't operatic."

She held her left hand, its knuckles patched with red, in front of her husband's face.

"Look, my eczema's back. I've got a little spot on my foot, too—what do you suppose makes it come back where it comes back?"

Her dermatologist couldn't answer the question, and she certainly didn't expect one from Burton, but talking to him was like talking to herself. She recapped the funeral for her husband and had to switch topics, worn out as she was with sadness.

"But you don't want to hear about funerals or my skin troubles, do you? Let's talk about . . ." She paused for a long moment, searching for conversational inspiration. "Hey, there was a guy sitting in the lobby with these great slippers—big furry things that looked like bear paws."

Bunny pulled up the afghan, revealing Burton's stockinged feet.

"You, sir, need slippers. You can't dance in your socks!"

Squeezing his toes, she began to massage his feet, and as he gave a wan, reflexive smile, Bunny felt a catch in her throat and whispered, "Oh, Burt, you know what D is for?"

D is for Dancing

Ah, the Foxgrove. It is my opinion that every town and hamlet should have a supper club like the Foxgrove that not only features relish trays on every table and an All-You-Can-Eat Friday Fish Fry, but a whole separate room reserved for a five-piece band and a big dance floor.

There was a rock club near campus that we college kids would go to and do our head bobbing and arm flailing, but when I met my husband—my senior by almost ten years—he introduced me to a different kind of dancing, one that inspired me to ditch my jeans and T-shirts and finally (finally!) put on a little dress, pantyhose, and heels to do the cha-cha, the rhumba, the quickstep, the jive. My husband was so light on his feet that if he ever stepped on mine, I never felt it, and was such a gentleman that whenever I stepped on his feet (something I did a lot when he was teaching me), he'd hide his grimace with a smile.

Burton felt the music as if it were pulsing in his bloodstream, as if he'd synced his heartbeat to that which the drums played.

Thanks to TV, ballroom dancing is a lot more popular now than it was when I was young, but the twentysomethings at a wedding I was at recently hadn't gotten the memo, doing nothing more rhythmic than swaying, and I thought, "Where are the dips, the slinky steps, the trust that the person holding your hand and back is going to move you into a place you haven't been before?"

When Burton pressed my body to his, and we'd step back, forward, back, back, forward, and I'd inhale the Rive Gauche cologne (he had French tastes) on his clean-shaven jaw and the band would play "Tennessee Waltz" or "Sweet Caroline" or "Volver a Verte," well, I could not imagine any other place I'd rather be than in his arms. And isn't that the definition of erotica—wanting to glide, slide, and move with a partner?

8

As decades-long members of AAA, Velda and Merv had collected their share of free maps, and when the cherry blossoms on her breakfast nook wallpaper began to look a little wilted, she told Mervin she'd like to paper the walls with them. It was another of her ideas that he dismissed with a joke, asking her what she wanted to turn their kitchen into, "a Rand McNally atlas?" She took on the project after his death, humming as she ironed out the creases of the folded maps, slathered on paste, and hung them so that clean, unused state maps checkerboarded with ones spotted with coffee and routes marked up in red ink. A map of Wyoming reminded her of the family's RV trip through Grand Teton National Park, in which a mama bear and three cubs had sat on the side of the road, watching the parade of vehicles pass by, and how Wayne, her youngest, had frantically waved at them, shouting, "Look, everybody! It's a Teddy Bear's Picnic!"

The map of South Carolina had reminded her of another RV trip, this one when the kids were older and a bit less enamored of travel with their parents. When they pulled up to a little crab shack that was listed as a "must visit" in the tourist brochures Velda collected, fourteen-year-old Pam decided she'd rather stay in the RV and finish the bag of Cheetos she'd bought when they were gassing up in Myrtle Beach. It was the first of her refusals to join her family for a restaurant dinner, a policy that lasted two whole days, until she saw two cute guys enter the Greenville Cracker Barrel that was their destination.

Velda had cut with an X-Acto knife maps to fit around her windowsills and above the baseboards; she had smoothed out every air bubble and wrinkle so that in the end, the walls looked papered by a professional. She was pleased with her work and pleased that every morning she might learn something new when looking at her walls—"Oh, New Hampshire really does look like a triangle!"—and pleased how much ground the family had covered during all those summers, even though Mervin had always decided their vacation spots.

They had never visited New York City, Merv preferring national parks and monuments, and so there was no map of the place that had meant the most to Velda: Manhattan.

"E is for Eloise," she typed, the keys of her old Selectric not quite clattering, but still making a satisfying, industrious sound. She was a typing wiz whose speed reached nearly one hundred words per minute, and while she did a lot of utilitarian things on her computer's keyboard, she fired up the Selectric when she wanted to *write*.

> I could probably think of something erotic for each letter—but the letter for me that I want to put my dibs on first is E, and this is why. Her name began with it. Yes, I know, to all here at All Souls, I am the widow of Mervin Henson, long-term principal of Kittleson High. We were a "power couple," as they say, always at the head table at whatever school/political/business banquet was being held. Merv liked that, that acknowledgment of his big voice in the community, and I suppose I liked it, too, even as I thought, Hey, what about my voice? I knew I was just as smart as Merv (I could decimate him at chess, which so irked him that several times this grown man "accidentally" upended the board) but I was, unfortunately, A WOMAN, with a voice that, despite how loud I might scream, wasn't heard.

I had gotten my teaching degree out of practicality more than a passion that drives good teachers, and I was fine acting as a sub, choosing when I wanted to work . . . mostly choosing not to. My plan, once our own kids were in school, was to devote my time to my art, but Merv's reactions to the ink and watercolor paintings I showed him were so relentlessly dismissive—"my little artiste," he'd say with a snide little chuckle—that I put down my pen and brushes for good.

But I'm getting off track, or maybe I'm not. Maybe I want to write about another track that I've recently been thinking a lot about, wondering where it might have led me.

Gathering her thoughts, she paused, fixing her gaze on the marked-up maps of Texas (visiting the Alamo, Merv had bought Wayne a rubber Bowie knife, with which he'd tormented his sister, until Pamela managed to grab it and hurl it out the car window) and Florida (in Disney World's EPCOT Center, they'd seen Carl Sagan talking to a robot). After one glimpse at the map of Pennsylvania, she returned to her typing.

Eloise. We met each other at Bryn Mawr, class of '61. Even though I was a country mouse from North Dakota and she was a city mouse from Manhattan, we were both art and literature lovers, which to us meant we experienced life far more deeply, far more purely than the rest of the world's vermin. (Ha ha.) We would take the train into Philadelphia and, over coffee, have long, passionate discussions about Jackson Pollock and Georgia O'Keeffe and Sylvia Plath and Emily Dickinson, and one night, riding the train back in an empty car, Eloise leaned toward me and I leaned toward her and we kissed. (K has to be for kiss, right? Because when two pairs of hungry, searching lips meet and realize they've found what they're hungry and searching for . . . well. Bells don't just ring—they clang, clang, clang.)

For the next year, Eloise and I were a couple—not to the world, which couldn't/didn't want to handle us as a couple—but to each other, which was all that mattered.

Her single dorm room was now most often a double, with me sharing her bed, her touch, her body. Her hands and tongue were like powerful updrafts, lifting me to altitudes that made me gasp for air. We were almost always naked—it made us feel powerful and free—whether we were in bed or writing term papers or holding silly little contests, like who could stand on one leg the longest. Being naked started feeling natural, but being naked was not tolerated in my own dorm room, which I shared—when I couldn't be with Eloise—with an econ major from Colorado Springs.

"Put some clothes on or I'll report you to the RA!" she threatened, this young woman who wore long underwear under her nightgown.

Eloise had dark stick-straight hair that refused to take a curl and three beauty marks on her face. "They're moles," she said the first time I made mention of them. "If they're beauty marks, they're on the wrong face."

Once, when her parents were off vacationing somewhere exotic, we stayed for two weeks in their Fifth Avenue apartment.

By day, we walked all over Manhattan, eating gelato in Little Italy, window shopping at Bergdorf Goodman's, sailing little paper boats in Central Park. At night we'd go to Greenwich Village clubs, laughing at comics, listening to poets and jazz combos, and drinking coffee and eating bagels at an all-night diner.

On our last night together in her parents' apartment, we were of course naked, and she took my bare foot in her hands and said, "I am the famous explorer Eloise de Leon, and I'm charting the map of the Body Velda." She kissed my instep. "This is the Velda Foot, known for its high arch and symmetrical toes. This is the Velda Ankle," she said next and kissed my ankle bone. "Slim yet strong, supporting the lean and supple expanse of the Velda Calf."

That thorough surveyor explored every nook and cranny of the Body Velda, and I shivered and spasmed when her lips pressed down on each part named and conquered.

The rush and clarity of memories stunned Velda, and she slumped in her chair, as if she were inflatable and someone had pulled the stopper and let the air out. She stared at the paper under the typewriter's platen and then at her hands, which now lay in her lap palms up in shocked surrender. How could she ever, *ever* show anyone the words she had just written?

~

Two-year-old Soren Peterson didn't just get a second wind, he often got a third, and most often it was when his parents had settled themselves on the couch, content to spend the rest of the evening hours reading or, on this night, watching a Netflix documentary on corporate greed.

"Mommy! Daddy! Hi, hi, hi!"

As cute as he and his enthusiastic greetings were, neither Mallory nor John applauded his entrance, as he had already made several earlier ones, having recently learned how to climb out of his crib.

John, who was leaning into the pillowed comfort of both the couch cushions and his wife's body, straightened and stood up.

"Come on, bud," he said, holding out his arms to the toddler, who took the gesture as an invitation to play tag.

"Catch me, catch me!" Soren shouted, racing around the couch and into the kitchen.

The game was like a sprint—explosive and quick—and after the squealing and running amok, Soren had burned through several hundred calories and his parents' patience. He finally allowed himself to be caught, collapsing in his father's arms and murmuring, "Ni night," when placed in his crib.

Feeling a weary sense of victory as he left the toddler's room, John was startled when a hand bumped against his shoulder.

"You're it!" said Mallory. "Chase me, chase me!"

And he did.

Wound up by their son's wound-uppedness, the couple raced through the hallway, across the living room, through the dining room, and into the kitchen, their laughter propelling them like turbines.

"I got you!" said John, tagging his wife as he raced past the refrigerator, gleefully switching from the chaser to the chased.

Mallory, who'd been a star on her college track-and-field team (but for a quarter inch, she would have broken the high jump record) gave John a good running start, but catching up to him by the fireplace, she could hardly *not* tag him.

"You're it!"

"I'm glad!" said John, and, confusing the rules of the game, he grabbed her, pulling her onto the couch.

He kissed her as if there were a fire on her mouth and his job was to put it out, and she kissed him back the same way, even as other fires were being ignited in their bodies.

They laughed as they tore off clothes and Mallory grabbed the remote, cutting off the real estate developer's denial that he was a slumlord. John reached back and jerked the old lamp's metal bead chain. With the room now only lit and shadowed by the waning flames in the fireplace, they stared at one another before they began to kiss each other again and Mallory's brain deferred to her body, but not before she knew what one of her ABC entries would be. The next morning, right before she wrote her sermon, she wrote:

F is for Fun

There's no sonorous sergeant-at-arms announcing, "Sexual Congress is now in session!" Baboons' bottoms turn red, peacocks fan their feathers, and humans floss their teeth, cue up a John Legend song, and let the good times roll. Sex can be many things, including a lot of fun. Chase each other around the living room once the kids have been tucked in. Play strip poker as if you mean it. Feed each other ice cream—while wearing blindfolds—and clean up any mess with your tongues. Just lighten up. Make up phrases that only the two of you understand, for instance: the trap's set. (And no, I'm not going to tell you what that means.)

Wear a ski hat and swim fins into the boudoir. Riff on TV commercials as come-ons, "I'll give you something better than a Coke and a smile."

Or just flop back on your old mattress, tell a knock-knock joke, open your arms, and say, "C'mere."

~

Years ago, Edie had sewn birthday vests for herself and her family, and even if she couldn't button it now, she wore hers, whose neckline was appliquéd with little balloons and presents.

"You look beautiful," said Finn, lighting the candles on the cupcakes he'd bought at Albert's Parisian Bakery. "Now before you make your wish, let me just tell you what mine is. That tonight you be Joan Collins and I'll be the rich guy."

Edie giggled. After letting Finn read her short "A is for Acting" entry, he had been giving all sorts of suggestions of personas they might take on. Back in the '80s, she'd been a big fan of the television show *Dynasty* and had occasionally been able to entice him (usually with a batch of Jiffy Pop) to watch an episode with her. That he remembered those characters, or at least semiremembered, touched her.

She took a deep breath and extinguished every single flame. It didn't take much lung power; the cupcakes held only two candles, shaped like numbers: one a seven, the other a zero.

Her daughter, Mary Jo, wasn't at the "party" but promised to FaceTime her mother from London, where she had lived for fourteen years, after a study-year abroad during which she'd fallen in love with both Britain and a boy named Nigel, whom she had met in a pub called the Cock and Bull.

"How about a little estrogen in the name?" Mary Jo had said to Sandy, her roommate from Baltimore, who was always up for exploring the nightlife in Bath.

Love was in the air for both the American students and the cousins Nigel and Ian Williams, and a double wedding would occur just a year later.

"Can you believe it?" were Edie's first words to Sandy's mother, Donna, when they met for the first time at the rehearsal dinner.

Laughing, Donna had shaken her head.

"We told Sandy a year abroad would be life changing, but we didn't know it would be *this* life changing!"

Edie and Donna had kept in touch for years, the latter sending the former pictures of Gregory, her first grandchild, then Millicent, her second, then Oliver, her third, and Edie sending photos of herself and Finn posed with Mary Jo and Nigel in front of the Tower of London, or Finn and herself posed with Mary Jo and Nigel in front of Buckingham Palace or Finn and herself on a boat with Marlys and Roger, Finn reeling in a sunnie. There was never a grandchild in these photos, seeing as Mary Jo and Nigel didn't want to have children.

After hearing her mother gasp over the long-ago, long-distance phone call during which she apprised her mother of this decision, Mary Jo had said, "Mom, I know it's a disappointment," to which Edie had wailed, "*Disappointment*'s not the word I'd choose!"

Aware of the international phone charges, Mary Jo broke the silence that followed and said, "We both think we can contribute more to the world as *people*, not parents."

"Parents *are* people," said Edie, cutting the call short before she burst into tears.

Despite Finn's faux-outraged jokes about "that damn kid forgetting we're in charge of her life, not her," Edie allowed herself to stew in sadness for a whole day, but because she truly did value her daughter's happiness, she called Mary Jo back to let her know that she'd always support her.

"And I'm glad you and Nigel are in agreement. I'd imagine it would be difficult if one of you wanted kids and the other didn't."

"Thank you, Mom. Thank you for understanding."

And Edie did, she supposed. She had played with baby dolls as a girl, but not with the intensity of her friends, who couldn't wait to grow up to be mommies. And yet, at thirty-two, when she became pregnant after nearly ten years of marriage, she thought, *of course this is what I want.*

When Mary Jo was born and she was floored with a maternal tsunami of love, she wanted to have another baby as soon as possible, and another one after that, but Fate arranged no further assignations between her eggs and Finn's sperm. While that was disappointing, Mary Jo was not, and Edie threw herself fully and joyfully into being a mother of what would be her only child.

That she wasn't going to have a grandchild hurt, but it wasn't a gaping wound. She had a daughter she loved, and that daughter was childlessly happy—what could she do? That's the way the cookie crumbled, the dice rolled, the ball bounced, ad infinitum. Edie could rage, rage against the dying of the light, or she could screw a long-lasting LED into the socket and get on with things.

On her FaceTime birthday call, Edie told her daughter about *The ABCs of Erotica.*

"Is it a sex book like the one Madonna wrote?" said Mary Jo between hoots of laughter. "Or are you going to pose naked like those Calendar Girls?"

Edie didn't reply, her virtual image on the computer screen tight lipped.

"Remember," said Mary Jo, "they were those older women who took off their clothes to raise money? They made a movie about them, starring Helen Mirren?"

"Guess I didn't see that one."

Edie valued her daughter's opinion but had hoped for a little more validation and less heckling, and it didn't take Mary Jo long to realize her mother was failing to laugh at her jokes.

"Oh, Mom, I'm sorry. I was just teasing. Tell me more."

Daydreaming about spring, Edie browsed through an online gardening catalog as she wondered which figurine she might add to the gnomes and trolls already overpopulating her backyard. She jumped when a chirp announced a FaceTime call, and when she accepted it, the faces of her daughter and son-in-law filled the screen.

"Is everything all right?" Edie asked—a perfectly sensible question, considering she had just spoken to Mary Jo the night before.

"Everything's fine, Mum E," said Nigel, using his pet name for her. "I'm sorry I couldn't be on your birthday call, but here I am now, with a belated gift!"

"I told him all about what you and the Naomis are doing," said Mary Jo, "and he couldn't wait to talk to you about it!"

Oh, goodie, more jokes, thought Edie, her smile stiffening.

"And I say 'Bravo!'" said Nigel. "If more churches did things like that, more people would want to go to them!"

Unsure if this was just a prelude to sarcasm, Edie's smile didn't completely relax.

"Really, the vicar in the church I grew up in was so stern and dour that the biggest lesson I learned was, 'This is not a place I feel good in, let alone uplifted!'"

Ambling into the kitchen to refill his coffee cup, Finn joined his wife at the computer.

"Hello, kids!" he said, pressing his cheek against Edie's so they both were in camera range.

"Dad, Nigel was just saying—" Mary Jo smiled at her husband. "Well, he was just saying what a good idea he thinks Mom's circle project is."

"Right!" said Nigel, as enthusiastic as an ad man at a client meeting. "God gives the gift of sex to people and what does the church do? The church makes it sinful and dirty or gives restrictions as to how and when and with whom to enjoy it—well, bloody hell! And what church celebrates the undeniable fact that God has a fantastic sense of humor? Sounds like Mum E and her church friends do!"

"I agree," said Finn. "I'm even thinking of writing something up for it."

"Brilliant," said Nigel. "Let the men have a say too!"

He clinked his wineglass against Mary Jo's—while it was coffee time in Kittleson, it was happy hour in London. "In fact, if my beautiful wife and I were to contribute, we'd pick the letter *F*."

"For flirting," said Mary Jo, giggling. "He was as good a flirt—"

"As she was," said Nigel. "And it's our flirting that led to everything."

Nigel began to recount their first meeting. He told them how he'd always claimed he smelled the woman who was to become his bride before he saw her. How he'd been sitting at the bar with his cousin, commiserating over their studies, when his nose was suddenly tickled by a floral scent (bergamot and rose, among others, he learned later) and, swiveling around, he saw two girls had entered the small pub. Both he and Ian, his cousin, sat up straighter.

"Where are they off to?" Nigel had asked one of the girls, pointing to the reindeer dancing across her Christmas jumper.

"The South of France," said the girl. "Where it's warmer."

"Do they have visas?" asked Nigel.

"Reindeer don't need them. They fly off the radar."

"Are you American?"

"What gave it away—my accent or my good teeth?"

"Both," said Nigel. "Although, don't fall for the stereotype that all Brits have bad teeth."

"Prove it," said the American, and when he gave her a full-on smile, she staggered, pretending to be dazzled.

Nigel told her he didn't have to pretend.

"Two questions. One: What's that you're wearing?" He had taken her wrist and pressed it to his nose. "And two: What's your name?"

"In answer to number one: Shalimar. In answer to number two: Mary Jo."

"The Shalimar is positively intoxicating, and so are you, Mary Jo."

"And so is this," she said, reaching over to lift his nearly empty pint off the bar. "Are you sure that's not what's doing the talking?"

"What do you think?"

"I think you look like a more handsome Hugh Grant."

"I think you look like a more beautiful Julia Roberts."

The old Wings song "Band on the Run" came on over the jukebox, and he'd asked, "Do you want to dance?" and she'd said, "Do I ever."

When the younger couple finished telling their story, the older couple applauded, and all four faces on screen beamed as if the computer's brightness key had been tapped and tapped again.

9

For years (*so many years,* Charlene thought) she and Charlie had had dinner the last Sunday of the month at Nancy and Rick's house. Charlene was always happy to bring her homemade rolls and a side dish, until Nancy began calling her on Saturday and telling her what sort of side dish to bring so as not to clash with the entrée.

"Well how about we just have the dinner at my house, since I make so much of it anyway?" Charlene had wanted to say but, as was often the case with things she wanted to say to her sister-in-law, didn't.

Nancy and Rick had certainly moved up in the world—Rick was a bank president and Nancy was a fancier version of an Avon lady, selling expensive creams and lipsticks and elixirs at house parties, where wine and rumaki were served instead of coffee and Fig Newtons.

Their kids were close enough in age that those Sunday afternoon dinners had been something everyone looked forward to: the cousins sitting at their own table, joking, boasting, holding burping contests; the adults joking and boasting as well (Rick and Charlie were competitive brothers) but keeping the burping to a minimum. For the first couple of years, the men's parents had regularly joined them, but the day Richard Senior retired was the same day he and his wife, Polly, bought a condo in Hilton Head, South Carolina, and their visits back north, especially in the winter months, were few and far between.

Charlene wished she and Charlie had an excuse to occasionally decline the open invitation—or at least be able to host it—but no; the last-Sunday-of-the-month dinner at her in-laws' was not just inked in on their calendar but practically etched.

Fun had flattened into obligation around the time Rick became the chair of the Downtown Kittleson Development Committee and Nancy's cosmetic saleswomanship earned her an all-expenses-paid trip to Lake Tahoe, which was also around the time they left All Souls for Prince of Peace.

"We're upgrading," Nancy had told Charlene.

"Upgrading to what?"

"We just want to belong to a winning church."

"Winning at what?"

Shrugging, Nancy said, "At everything."

Charlene grinned and bore the table conversations, *bore* being the operative word, as it would be difficult to be entertained by Nancy's recounting of how much their new Jacuzzi cost or how hard it was to find a good tile man, with Rick piping in, "Lots!" or "Craftsmanship's a lost art!"

On and on droned Nancy and Rick during those dinners, and now that the kids had flown the coop, there were just the four of them, which for Charlene upped the tedium factor tenfold. Her jaws ached from the interested smile she forced her mouth to make over news of Rick's big investment coup or Nancy selling more matte foundation than anyone in the tristate area. Her jawbone was given a break, however, when the talk shifted to church; she was not about to fake a smile when anyone denigrated All Souls.

At their most recent dinner, Charlene's famous cloverleaf rolls (like buttery clouds, they were so light and fluffy) and garlicky Szechuan green beans had supplemented Nancy's dry, bland pot roast and slightly undercooked potatoes au gratin, and it was while eating dessert that Nancy prattled on about how Prince of Peace had started a lecture series and how they'd already signed up a theologian from St. Basil's Cathedral in Moscow and how a prizewinning interior decorator had completely redone the church's education wing and now they had problems with children not wanting to leave!

"Well," said Charlene, "you should see the mural our custodian painted on the Sunday school hallway! It's—"

"Your custodian painted a mural?" Nancy shook her head, her face pressed in an expression of pity. "No offense," she continued, even though Charlene could count on the next thing coming out of Nancy's mouth being offensive, "but you won't even need a Sunday school with the way people are leaving All Souls. Pretty soon you'll have to change the name to No Souls!"

Resisting the temptation to reveal the nickname the Naomis had given *her* church, Charlene looked at the half-eaten (definitely store-bought) brownie on her plate and, deciding it wasn't worth finishing, she patted her mouth with a napkin.

"You know," she said, "All Souls is doing some big things too."

Nancy's professionally threaded eyebrows and lip-lined mouth crinkled into a simpering expression.

"And what might those be?"

"I'm not at liberty to say."

Nancy made a dismissive *tuh* sound.

"What, are you thinking of making your Hot Dish Jamboree a biannual event? Or maybe have your Christmas carolers go door to door passing the hat? Or maybe you could start charging for baptisms!"

Nancy's laughter over her boundless wit ended when Charlie stood and, holding out his hand to his wife, said, "I think it's time for us to go."

Charlene's eyes widened.

"Charlie?" asked Rick, confused.

"Thanks as usual for dinner," said Charlie, "and weren't Charlene's rolls and Chinese string beans wonderful?"

Hand in hand, and surprising themselves as much as their hosts, the couple strode out of the dining room, their feet leaving tracks in the thick, newly installed Saxony carpeting.

Thanks to Charlie's dealership, every year they got a new Honda—this one a silver Acura—and on the ride home, Charlene breathed in the leathery new-car smell, which really was Charlie's smell. Neither of them spoke for a while, until Charlie turned left at a corner where he usually turned right and said, "Let's go to Tacy's, before it closes for the season."

A carhop—one of the many grandchildren of Bud Tacy, the drive-in's founder—clamped the tray holding two root beer floats on the driver's side half-open window, and Charlie counted out bills in her open palm and added three extra ones, telling her to keep the change.

"*Thank you,*" said the teenager, whose Sunday service so far had only brought forth tips ranging from 10 percent to nothing.

Neither Charlie or Charlene partook in much of the dried-out brownies Nancy had served and now eagerly slurped and spooned up their root beer floats, relishing the smooth tastes of sassafras and vanilla.

There was a loud gurgle as Charlene sipped up from her straw the last inch of root beer.

"Ahhh," she said.

"You beat me," said Charlie, taking a final sip of his own and placing both empty vase-shaped glasses on the window tray.

Facing the big menu painted on the drive-in's wall, Charlie said, "'Caribbean Shrimp Basket.' I wonder what makes shrimp Caribbean."

"Probably the spices," said Charlene. "Garlic, ginger . . . and that jerk stuff."

Moving his gaze to the steering wheel, Charlie said, "I'm the jerk. Sorry about the dinner."

"Oh! Oh, no, it was . . . fine."

Charlie's raised eyebrow expressed doubt.

"Well," said Charlene, "it's just lately that they—well, especially Nancy—seem so, I don't know—"

"Assholey?"

With a little laugh, Charlene said, "I guess you could say that," even though she never would herself.

Dangling from his key chain was a miniature silver car, and with one finger, Charlie batted it back and forth.

"So what did you mean when you said All Souls is doing some big things? The things you're not at liberty to say?"

Charlene's bottom teeth scraped her upper lip as she scrambled for something, *anything* to tell him.

"The Naomis," she said finally, "well, we're writing a book about erotica."

"Say again?" said Charlie.

"We want to bring in the kind of money Price of Peace does with their fundraising projects, but instead of a recipe book—you should see theirs, Charlie, it has color pictures and everything and we can't afford anything like that—we decided to write about erotica. Sort of an ABC guide."

After the words tumbled out of her mouth, Charlene wanted to tumble out of the car, but instead returned her husband's stare, hers so alarmed that his puzzled one softened as he smiled.

"What exactly do you all mean by erotica?"

Flushing, she wished she could erase all conversation that had followed their discussion of what made a shrimp Caribbean.

"I don't exactly know," she squeaked more than said. She cleared her throat. "It's not going to be anything pornographic . . . although I haven't read anything Velda's written."

They allowed themselves a small laugh before Charlie asked, "Have you written anything?"

Tears—from embarrassment and she didn't know what else—filled Charlene's eyes.

"I did. I wrote about *C* being for compliments."

"Compliments?" said Charlie, and he nodded, not so much in agreement but as if trying to understand her. "Would you like me to read it—"

Charlene's quick shake of her head stopped his words.

"Okay," he said finally. "I'll read it if and when you want me to."

As a car pulled in next to theirs, its newly licensed teenage driver braking hard several times before lurching to a stop, the long-married couple continued to stare at one another. Then Charlie, like millions of boys in cars parked in drive-ins, leaned toward the girl in the passenger seat.

Her husband had the most beautiful smile, and Charlene's inner stoplight, so often red (in her mind, justifiably so), flickered yellow before switching to green, and she leaned toward the boy in the driver's seat.

Theirs wasn't a deep kiss, or a long one, but when they both sat back in the car seats, Charlene felt a little light headed, remembering how her husband had stood up for her at her in-laws', how he hadn't dismissed their project or demanded that he read what she wasn't yet ready to share, and Charlene thought, *G is for Gallantry.*

~

After meeting Tad Schell for the first time, Mallory clearly wondered, *Is he for real?*

The young man wore his dark hair slicked back so that it shone like patent leather, and his plaid bow tie matched his plaid suspenders, but it wasn't that he looked like an old-fashioned general store proprietor that Mallory found so striking; it was his personality. His enthusiasm and energy were cranked up to just about parody level . . . and he smelled like apples.

"It doesn't come from a bottle—it comes from our family apple farm!" he said when Mallory complimented him on his cologne. "Schell Orchards: We're in the Business of Sweetness!"

When she asked him why he wanted to be their church's music director, his ardor had practically raised him off his chair.

"Because music is as mysterious as faith! Because it's magical and mystical and can lift up people—can lift up all souls, if you'll excuse the pun!"

Tad knew some found his exuberance off-putting; during choir practice, he could count on at least a half-dozen eye rolls from Stu Mansfield, his best male singer (best voice would go to Kathy Knudsen, no contest), for his direction: "Sing like trumpets here, altos! Like you're making an announcement!" or "Come on, basses, it's you who'll make the pews shake!"

For a man whose childhood had been battered by bullying and name calling, and whose adult life (at twenty-eight he lived with his mother) gave fodder to those who embraced gossip—the once-removed form of bullying—Tad had a bounty of self-confidence that came from knowing exactly who he was. A man who loved music. Who wanted to make music. Whose keyboards and composer's notebook he couldn't wait, every day, to touch, to write in.

He also believed in sharing both his time and talents and was a regular volunteer at Wednesday's soup kitchen, that evening having contributed, as usual, a box of Schell Orchards' top-selling Honeycrisp apples.

While Tad ladled out the soup kitchen's offering of bland split pea or watery broccoli cheese, a man with a long gray beard had said to him, "Ever see *The Little Rascals*? You look just like Alfalfa!"

Tad laughed; he did, in fact, know who Alfalfa was, having watched the reruns of *Our Gang* that would play on Clancy Carney's Saturday-morning kids' show.

"Except Tad doesn't part his hair in the middle," said Bunny, serving next to him. "And he doesn't have that weird piece of hair sticking straight up in the back."

"I always thought it was like an antenna," said the man with a laugh. "Like Alfalfa was receiving signals from another planet."

At the end of the evening, most guests gave sincere thanks for the meal (except for the woman who took Pastor Pete aside and said she had eaten vichyssoise at a Parisian four-star restaurant and therefore knew good soup, which the broccoli cheese was definitely not), and after the volunteers bussed and cleaned and reluctantly took home leftovers, only Tad, Bunny, and Pastor Pete remained in the church kitchen.

Their conversation had been of the easy, unmemorable sort that accompanies putting dishes away and wiping down counters, until Bunny told Tad about the Naomis' fundraising project.

"A book about erotica?" he had said, the syllables of the last word like weights his mouth hefted up and down. "And the members are okay with this?"

"It's not exactly public knowledge right now," said Pastor Pete, stifling the urge to say, *Thanks a lot, Bunny.* "It's just an idea the Naomis and I have been tossing around."

"But we're open to submissions," said Bunny with a wink.

"Oh . . . well!" said Tad, hoping his face wasn't as red as it felt. "Oh!"

What he didn't say/shout was, "What could I possibly write about?"

If they wanted to write an ABC guide about apples, he could easily run through the alphabet, maybe even twice. And there were so many subjects about which he could have contributed—music, positive thinking, Alexander McCall Smith novels, fashion, politics, teaching methods—but erotica? How could he explain the love affair—albeit a sexless one—he had with life?

"Umm," he said, scrubbing the counter as if his goal were to take off the finish, "I'll definitely give it some thought!"

At the Blessing of the Animals service, whispers of "Awww" and "Aren't they cute?" accompanied the march of nine children and two adults to the altar. A French bulldog snarled at a calico cat, and a boy's stumble up the chancel steps nearly evicted three goldfish from their bowl, but no actual fur or fins flew.

Evan Bates leaned toward his brother and asked, "Remember Shirley?"

Eldred thought for a moment before nodding.

"Best darn dog in the world," he said, and both men smiled, remembering the burr-riddled, emaciated mutt who'd slunk into the farmyard looking for food and died thirteen years later, well brushed, well fed, and well loved.

After the congregation sang "The Creatures We Love," Eldred Bates sighed and slowly sank, like a deflated tire, against the pew. It was only when he failed to accept his brother's proffered stick of Juicy Fruit that Evan realized something was wrong.

"Eldred!" he called out, loud enough to cause a golden retriever to bark in response and to stop Pastor Pete's blessing of the animals.

The younger brother of All Souls' oldest parishioner, Eldred had been visiting from Williston, North Dakota, where decades earlier he had staked his claim on two hundred acres of arable land as well as one Avis Pallenberg. He and his wife had not been blessed with children, but their marriage had been long and good, until emphysema had taken Avis away three years earlier.

"I don't know why she couldn't have smoked filtered cigarettes like me!" Eldred had cried to his brother Evan when he reported Avis's death. "But no, she just couldn't give up that 'pure unadulterated flavor'!"

Because of their physical distance, the brothers had communicated mostly by phone, giving Evan the freedom to roll his eyes at the many eye-rollable things his brother said. Still, they were close (closer, no doubt, thanks to their physical distance), and now that they were both single (Evan never having married), they visited each other every few months.

There had been four other *E* siblings—Emma, Evangeline, Elmira, and Ernest—but Evan and Eldred were the only ones remaining on Earth. Seven years separated them, and Evan the elder had assumed that he would beat his brother to the grave, but no, Eldred was dead before they carried him out of church, joining his family members in that ultimate *E*—eternity.

"They never taught us this in the seminary," Mallory said to John that night when, exhausted but wired, she fluffed/punched her bed pillows, trying to get comfortable. "What to do when someone dies in the middle of the Blessing of the Animals."

"You followed the exact protocol a minister's supposed to do in a situation like that," said John, leaning comfortably against his own pillows, his hands folded over his bare, hairy chest. "At least that's what *Ministers' Weekly* said in a fascinating article I just read."

"*Ministers' Weekly*?" said Mallory, smiling. "Is that a magazine you're reading when you're not doing the puzzles in *Highlights for CPAs*?"

John accepted her kiss and said, "Actually, it wouldn't be a bad idea to plan ahead for those kinds of contingencies in a church service—like what to do if someone goes into labor, or has a mental breakdown, or pulls out a gun—"

"You were cheering me up," said Mallory, feeling the claws of a headache settling in. "But you're not now."

John turned on his side to face her. "I want you to feel better, but I also want you to be prepared. You handled Elvin—"

"Eldred."

"—Eldred dying right there in the middle of a church service really well—you were calm and assured—but what *would* you do if someone started shooting up the place?"

"I don't even want to think about that."

"I know, babe. But these days, you have to."

Mallory wanted to roll over, wanted to turn off the lamp on her nightstand, signaling an end to the conversation, but she knew if she did, John would turn her around to face him and answer the question.

"Maybe," she said after a long moment spent staring into her husband's eyes, "maybe I should hold a meeting. Decide on a plan. Like the fire drill we practiced with the Sunday school kids."

As John nodded, Mallory felt tears well in her eyes.

"I hate that we even have to think about what to do if there's a shooter in church."

"I know. But being prepared doesn't mean you're inviting trouble."

"Thank you," she said, giving him a quick kiss.

"You're welcome," he said, giving her a longer one.

She had thought she only wanted to pull the covers over herself and her long, hard day, but it was easy to settle into that kiss, easy to let the tension drain out of her body as her husband enveloped her in his arms, easy to think maybe she wasn't so tired after all.

Their kisses quickly advanced from languid to excitable; both pairs of hands were like Leif Eriksson exploring the terrain, and just as Mallory climbed on top of her husband, they heard a wail from their son's bedroom.

As Mallory rolled off him, John said, "No, you stay here. It's my turn."

He got out of bed to console whatever made Soren inconsolable, and grabbing his robe off the door hook, he turned to blow Mallory a kiss.

Pretending to catch it, she said, "Hurry back," and as John padded off, she smiled to herself, imagining the delights to come, and it occurred to her that *H is for Hurry Back*. A moment later she added, and *all the help you give me*.

10

“Is that a peace sign?” Axel asked.

Squinting, Megan shook her head.

“Looks like a smiley face with a long nose.”

“No,” said Amelia. “It is definitely a peace sign . . . listen to the song they’re playing.”

It was by a favorite of her grandmother’s—Cat Stevens—and she explained they were listening to “Peace Train.”

The three friends had joined a smattering of students in the football-field bleachers and were watching the marching band practice. It was a bright, crisp autumn day, with the sun shining in a full blue sky, and Amelia was glad she had roused herself from the nearly irresistible temptation of sleeping in.

How could both sleep and wakefulness be so delicious? And yet how was it, if you slept too much, you felt draggy and grumpy, knowing you’d missed out on *life*, and if you were awake too much, you felt wiry and grumpy and couldn’t wait to leave the real world and surrender to the dream one?

“What are you thinking about?” asked Axel, pronouncing *what* as *vhat* and *thinking* as *sinking*.

“Oh,” said Amelia. “Sleep.” She smiled at her new friend. “How do you say *sleep* in German?”

“*Schlafen.*”

"Schlafen," repeated Amelia. "It sounds like a pillow."

"Yeah, where's my schlafen?" said Megan, rising up and patting her backside. "These seats are hard."

The band ended its practice by forming a moving lasso as they played "Happy Trails," after which Axel said, "So much sitting. Who would like to *spazieren gehen*?" To both Amelia's and Megan's questioning looks, he added, "A walk. Anyone like to go for a walk?"

Inspired to show around this student new to America, Amelia said, "I've got a car. How about we all go to Minneopa?"

"Minneopa?" said Axel, pronouncing each syllable carefully.

"A state park," said Amelia. "It's really pretty, and it's only a couple miles away."

Megan telegraphed with her eyes that this was a bad idea—she had been hoping she and Axel might *spazieren gehen* back to her dorm room (her roommate was gone for the weekend)—but Amelia didn't receive, or chose to ignore, the message.

"Look at those heads!" Axel said with a tourist's excitement. "Look at those horns!"

Holding his phone out the car window, he snapped picture after picture.

"My parents will love these! They will think I really am in Cowboy Country!"

His enthusiasm was catchy, and Amelia and Megan called out "yippee ki yay" and "yeehaw!" at the furry bison lumbering in their enclosure.

After Amelia parked the old Camry she'd inherited from her brother, they began their walk, Axel continuing his exclamations over the view, the waterfalls, the windmill.

The first time Axel said, "*Sehr schön*," Megan asked what he meant.

"Very nice, very pretty," he said, repeating the words at least a dozen times, taking pictures of a rock, a rush of water, a bush whose leaves were a patchwork of color.

While the trio explored, what had been a blue sky was painted over by gray clouds and a pleasant breeze cranked up into a forceful wind.

"Should we turn back?" asked Megan, who always chose style over function and was not dressed for the dropping temperatures.

"Here," said Axel, taking off his heavy sweater and handing it to her. "This will keep you warm."

With its gold buttons and corded piping, the sweater was hardly fashion forward, but it did what Axel promised.

They continued their *sehr schön* hike, but when the wind further riled up the air and a cold drizzle began to fall, they turned back and were just inside the car when the drizzle turned into a hard sleeting rain.

"Whoa," said Amelia.

She turned on the windshield wipers, but they didn't clear away water as much as push it around.

Sitting in the back seat, Axel leaned forward and with awe in his voice said, "It's a deluge."

"I don't think I should drive in this," said Amelia. "Do you mind if we sit here for a while?"

"Just as long as we're home by tonight," said Megan. "There's a party at Delta Chi."

"Do you have fraternities and sororities in Germany?" Amelia asked Axel.

"Some. But they are not such a big part of our university life, although parties are! In fact, my parents—hey, this will keep you warm," he said, picking up the folded stadium blanket off the floor and passing it to them.

"No, you keep it," said Megan, climbing into the back seat. "You already gave me your sweater."

Following her lead, Amelia climbed over, and as rain pounded the car, the three snuggled under the blanket.

"What was it you were saying about your parents?" she asked Axel.

Axel told them how his mother and father, both studying music at a Frankfurt conservatory, had met at a party where a violinist got into a fight with a pianist, but both were so nervous about hurting their hands that they undid their ties and slapped one another with them.

Laughing, Megan asked, "How would you know who'd won?"

"Guess they'd have to call it a tie," said Amelia to deserved groans.

Megan's parents met at a laundromat.

"And listen to my dad's pickup line—"

"Pickup line?" asked Axel.

After they explained the words' meaning, Megan said, "So my dad comes up to my mom, who's just taken her laundry out of the dryer, and he says, 'If I helped you fold those jeans, would you hold them against me?'"

Outside the wind howled; inside the car, they did the same, riffing on pickup lines they might use in some of their classes: Can I be your lab partner because we've got phenomenal chemistry? I'm majoring in physical therapy—wanna have some? Will you be in my human-sexuality study group?

As the weather continued its tantrum, Amelia told them about the fundraising project of her grandmother's circle.

"What is a circle?" asked Axel.

"It's a group, almost always women, I think, who do things for their church . . . have bake sales and talk about God and stuff like that."

"Stuff like writing about erotica?" said Megan. "Ewww! If my nana was part of a group like that, well, *hurl* . . . big time!"

"So they are old people writing an alphabet book about sex?" asked Axel. His English was excellent, but sometimes he wasn't quite sure of what he heard.

"They're not necessarily writing about sex," said Amelia. "They're writing about what's *sexy*—or at least what they think is sexy."

"Like I said," said Megan, "Ewww. Or should I say, 'E is for Ewww.'"

"Or," said Axel, "*eklig*. Which means, I think, the same thing as *ewww*."

He and Megan high-fived, and although Amelia laughed with them, Axel sensed it was not quite genuine.

"My apologies. I have offended you."

"No, no. I'm not offended. It's just that . . . well, don't you plan on having sex when you get older?"

Axel's face colored, and after Megan barked out a laugh, she asked, "Who said I wouldn't?"

"Well," said Amelia, "you act as if the idea of your grandparents having sex—or even being interested in it—is gross."

"It is! I mean, those old saggy, flabby bodies . . ." Too disgusted to finish, Megan exaggerated a shiver as she shook her head.

"We're all going to have old saggy, flabby bodies one day," said Amelia.

"Not me. I'm going to die young, leaving a beautiful corpse behind."

"You would rather die young than have your body get old?" Axel asked, surprise in his voice.

Megan scoffed. "Of course not, I was *joking*. But I tell you what—I'm not going to let my body get old! I'll die in my nineties, either at my spin class or in the weight room. And I'll be just as hot in the bedroom as I am in the gym!"

"What you are saying, then, is that when you are in your nineties, you will still be interested in having sex."

Megan stared at the exchange student for a moment.

"Yeah, but remember, I'm not going to let my body get old."

"Good luck with that," muttered Amelia, and seeing that the rain had lightened up, suggested they get going; she had to study for a psych exam.

"And I for my statistics class," said Axel.

"And I," said Megan, who thought studying on a Saturday night made a mockery of collegiate life, "have to get ready to *par-tay*!"

In the early evening, just as Amelia turned her phone back on (she had learned in high school the perils of trying to study while looking at shoes on Zappos or checking her social media feeds, and more and more she was appreciating the freedom of not always being "connected"), there was a soft knock on her dorm-room door. She was surprised and pleased to see who it was who'd knocked.

"I'm not meaning to interrupt you," said Axel. He was wearing the old-fashioned cardigan sweater he'd loaned Megan, as well as a sheepish smile.

"No, no, not at all. I'm all done reading what I needed to read."

After a moment when they stood facing one another, smiling but silent, Amelia asked if he wanted to come in.

"I could make some hot chocolate—my grandma gave me a big tin of this powdered mix that she makes herself. It's really good and—"

"For that invitation, I would like to take up one of your rain checks," Axel said, "but for now, I have more studying to do. I see you later!" Thrusting a piece of paper at her as if it were a relay baton, he continued the race by scurrying down the hallway.

Back under the covers of her dorm bed (her favorite place to study), Amelia unfolded the paper and read, in Axel's precise penmanship, "I is for Imagination."

"Oh," she said aloud, with the same tone of voice people use when watching a cute kitten or baby video.

On the semi-rainy drive back to campus, Amelia had told her friends about how she and her grandmother had taken on the alphabet book challenge.

"Chin?" Megan had said. "That's all you could come up with for the letter *C*?"

Ignoring her friend's snideness (to be Megan's friend, she *had* to ignore the snideness), Amelia said, "My grandma was happy with what I wrote—in fact, she said their erotica book could use some young people's ideas. So if you find yourself looking for something to do, feel free to write something down."

After Megan responded with a dismissive "I'm sure," and Axel laughed, Amelia thought that was the end of that.

But it turned out it wasn't, and she read on.

"I choose I for Imagination because I am thinking imagination is the start of all good things. (And yes, some bad, too, certainly.) I am not saying I am Herr Casanova, but I am finding that it is always a 'turn-on,' as you say, when a partner takes time and efforts to use her (in my case) imagination to surprise you. Last winter, walking with my girlfriend, she quite suddenly tackled me into a snowdrift and said I was not to worry, she would keep me warm. And her kisses did—the snowflakes seemed to sizzle (I had to look up the word for brutzeln) when they touched my face. HanneLore will also do such things as packing a picnic lunch with some sandwiches and beer, but also with a book—once a copy of The Taming of the Shrew and we read from a few scenes—but here is the surprise: HanneLore asked that I read Katherine's part and she read Petruchio's! It made us laugh and also made me think in a different way, and by the end of our playacting, I could not believe there was anyone more special, more desirable than HanneLore. She inspired me to bring more imagination into our relationship, and therefore, one night I told her we were going to make up a love language and we could communicate only with noises. I will tell you that we got to understand what this grunt or that whistle or hiss meant! Now that we are far apart, she will send me little gifts through the post—just yesterday I received my favorite Toblerone candy bar with a note attached that read, 'Du bist süßer' (you are sweeter). A gift does not have to be something physical that needs unwrapping, like a necklace or a music box, but can be something like doing a stripping dance to oompah band music or taking all the raisins out of her bowl of muesli and replacing them with cinnamon red hearts. To me, nothing is more sexy than someone using their imagination to surprise and delight me, and me returning the favor!"

Amelia studied the piece of paper for a long time, wondering all sorts of things: what did HanneLore look like (what a pretty name she had); did she and Axel read Shakespeare plays in English or German; what would Shakespeare sound like in German; and what exactly was an oompah band? (Later she would google it and listen to a YouTube video, laughing as she imagined anyone doing "a stripping dance" to the tuba-heavy music. Then, remembering Axel had mentioned while they watched the marching band that he himself played the tuba, she wondered if it had been to his accompaniment that HanneLore stripped.)

She had seen Axel at several gatherings before, and while she thought he was nice enough and cute enough (with a great accent), she only thought of him as another friend to add to her ever-expanding circle. But after spending the day with him and reading what he'd written, she found herself envying HanneLore for having him as her boyfriend. Would she ever find a guy who'd want to take the raisins out of her muesli (she'd googled that as well) and replace them with candy hearts? Not that that was especially erotic, but it sure was romantic.

Okay, you had I, she thought. *I'll take* J. Reaching across the bed for her laptop, with little hesitation she typed, "J is for Jokes," but after staring at the sentence for what seemed minutes, she deleted it and wrote, "Jewel."

Hey, why am I thinking of you when I was going to write about the importance of humor in a relationship? From what I saw in your "relationships," they were the opposite of funny.

Remember our very first weekend of freshman year and you brought a guy to our room and were hooking up in your bed, which was only about ten feet away from mine?

Amelia's fingers dashed across the keyboard, trying to keep pace with her thoughts.

I didn't know anyone yet to go knock on doors, asking if I could sleep on their floor, so I just stayed there, practically suffocating under the pillow I used to muffle all the moans and groans. The next day I said it sure sounded like you were having a good time last night (slightly passive-aggressive, I know) and didn't you mind that you had an audience?

You asked me if I got off being a voyeur . . . yeah, our roommate friendship was sure off to a great start.

You were pretty studious during weekdays, but when the weekend came around, same old thing: party in your bed. One time I was woken up not with the usual moaning and groaning, but with you whimpering, saying, "Ow, that hurts," and I got scared and asked if you were okay.

The guy swore and so did you, before you told me to mind my own fucking business! (Sad little pun there, huh?)

Wrapping my quilt around me, I grabbed my phone and stumbled out of that room (I was afraid to turn on a light) as fast as I could. Fortunately, by then I had made a friend two doors down, and Gina let me sleep on her floor.

The next weekend was quiet, because—relief!—you weren't in our room until Sunday afternoon. I came home from watching a Vikings game in the commons and opened our dorm door to see you standing in front of your dresser mirror.

We both gasped, and you scrambled to pull up your bathrobe, but too late—I had seen the bruises you'd been examining on your chest and upper arms.

And then a couple weeks later I came to our room to find your bed stripped and your closet empty. You didn't bother to let me know where you'd gone, but I heard you'd moved off campus with some guy. Then I read in the school newspaper that you got a big undergrad math award, but then at the beginning of sophomore year I heard you'd left school.

I hope you've transferred to some place like MIT or Princeton—I know you were a math wizard—and I just want to apologize for being too scared/dorky to help you more. And I sure hope you aren't with anybody who hurts you.

It's kinda weird how I'm writing "J is for Jewel," but shouldn't you—shouldn't everybody—be treated like you're precious? And treat the person you're with like they're precious too?

Amelia closed her laptop and sank under the covers, as exhausted as if she'd written a term paper for a class she hadn't yet taken.

11

Edie had thought life was over—at least life the way she wanted to live it—when her colon cancer diagnosis had resulted in an ileostomy. Everything that needed to be flushed out (literally) would be flushed out the end of her small intestine through her stoma, a hole made in her abdomen, and into a bag attached to it, one she'd have to replace . . . when needed. This was not good for someone whose gag reflex had kicked in every time she'd changed Mary Jo's diapers, who once threw away, rather than clean, shoes whose treads were filled with dog poop, who thought passing gas was less a natural bodily function than a moral failing.

"Edie," Finn had said in the hospital when she had cried and apologized for this new accessory to her body, "I love this bag. I love anything that helps you stay alive."

He had lifted her patterned cotton gown and leaned down, seemingly poised to kiss the flaccid plastic sack that lay against her belly.

"Uh, guess not," he said, reeling back. "After all, I don't know where it's been."

They'd gotten a laugh out of that, which, more than the nurses' TLC or her doctor's optimistic prognosis, Edie needed.

That had been a dozen years ago, and Finn had made it clear, by words and action, that he was in love with Edie, no matter what medical procedures / medical accoutrements had been done/added to her. She had been in good health since, and on every anniversary of the surgery that had rerouted her digestive highway, Finn bought a quart of her favorite butter-pecan Häagen-Dazs (it was, to her mind, a luxury item worth every penny) and two dozen yellow roses, because he thought yellow was the color of hope and healing.

"I didn't know hope and healing had a color," Edie had said the first year he presented them to her.

"It's the color of sunshine," Finn had said, his voice choked, and Edie's hand went to her chest, as if pressing the words into her heart.

Now he wondered aloud if he should stop by Fiona's Floral to buy his own bouquet of yellow roses.

"Oh, honey, don't worry," said Edie, squeezing his hand. "The doctor himself said everything should be fine."

She was not used to his worry and agitation; Finn's was an easygoing amble through life's ups and downs. He was a man whose mantra was, "Everything's copacetic."

"But the side effects of surgery!" he said, wringing his big hands and shaking his head.

"Honey, the doctor didn't say anything about surgery yet! It's stage one; we're in a wait-and-see period, remember?"

She pressed a button on her key fob and their Buick, parked across the street, emitted a little chirp.

Finn Hokkanen was a big, barrel-chested man who, as a building contractor, had hefted and carried two ninety-four-pound cement bags on each shoulder; who didn't scream but only said, "Uff!" when his partner's nephew wielded his nail gun in the wrong direction and shot an 8d nail into Finn's left foot; who, as a fisherman, had whistled during his fight reeling in a near-record-breaking sixty-pound muskie. As big and strong and in control of his body as he was, he easily surrendered to his emotions, and now tears streamed from his blue, blue eyes.

"But what if I can't . . . you know, do it anymore? What if I can't give you pleasure?"

Edie stared at him until the car that had stopped tooted politely, reminding them that street crosswalks weren't meant to stand in the middle of, but to cross.

They had fevered, yet tender sex that night, with whispers and declarations of love, and when Finn and his ruffly snores let her know he had entered Dreamland, Edie slid out of bed and into her robe and tiptoed into her sewing room.

Home economics had been taught in her seventh-grade sewing class, where she'd learned how to thread a machine and sew a straight seam, how to backstitch and how to make the class project: a pocketed apron. Her work was above and beyond her classmates', and that she'd only gotten a B+ had more to do with Mrs. Strom's rigid standards (legend was that she'd only ever given one A, and this was to a girl who eventually became an assistant to Bill Blass) than Edie's skill. She continued not only to sew but to design her two (junior and senior) prom dresses *and* her own bridal gown. She made all Mary Jo's clothes until her daughter rebelled in middle school, demanding her wardrobe come from the River Hills Mall.

Scrounging through rolled-up pieces and folded rectangles of silk, satin, and chiffon in the top drawer of an old dresser (in it, she stored fabric by weight—the middle two drawers were filled with cottons, linens, and rayons, and the bottom with corduroy, denim, and pleather), Edie took out a half yard of red satin—a leftover remnant from a doll's dress or Christmas decoration—and with her always-sharpened scissors, carefully cut out a shape.

Switching on her Bernina (to her mind, the Cadillac of sewing machines), she placed the fabric under the needle and, pressing the treadle with her foot and to the accompaniment of a soft *whrrr*, began sewing. When she finished her straight, even seams, she turned the satin right-side out, stuffing cotton batting into the end she'd left open, and when it was full, she took a needle and thread and hand sewed the opening shut.

It was a big letter *K*, and, propping it on the bed (the sewing room doubled as the guest room), she whispered, "K is for Knight."

In bright shining or rusted creaky armor, Finn was her knight.

They had met on the crowded midway at the Minnesota State Fair when the big, tall blond noticed an obviously distressed tiny brunette and asked what was wrong.

"I lost my friends!" Edie had said.

"Here," said Finn, squatting down. "Get on my shoulders."

Edie couldn't say why she didn't immediately turn and run far away but instead whispered, "Okay," and, putting her hands onto his shoulders, boosted herself up. As he rose, she repositioned her hands on her thighs and thought, *Wowie!* She was used to being eye level with people's chests; now she was looking down at tops of heads.

Finn stood for a long moment facing one direction, asking "Anything?" and when Edie answered no, he'd slowly pivot. While she was unlucky at finding her friends, she was enjoying the view of not just the mass of people, but the rides, the games of chance, and the food stands.

"Anything?" Finn asked a final time, and when Edie, disappointed for several reasons, said no, he bent his knees, lowering himself so that she could climb off.

Back on the ground, she felt a sudden claustrophobia, and her face must have shown it because Finn took her hand, leading her through the crowds and over to a bench by a cotton candy stand.

They spent several hours "looking" for her friends, which meant going on three rides; wandering through the swine and cow barns; sharing one foot-long hot dog, a bag of mini donuts, and a funnel cake; and watching a horse-jumping competition.

Along with the person he had come to the fair with—his father, who volunteered in the Veterans' Building—Finn gave Edie a ride home.

That she lived nearly an hour out of their way didn't seem to bother him or his dad, who insisted on taking the back seat "so you young folks can talk" and conveniently fell asleep.

That was the first time he'd come to her rescue, but certainly not the last, and the red satin *K* that she'd place the next morning in the center of their bed's pillow pile would remind Finn that he was her knight and that she was his. A knight on a racing steed, lance held high and with precise aim, ready to slay all dragons, fears, and prostate-cancer cells stupid enough to invade their love territory.

~

I'm surprised they don't enforce a dress code, thought Bunny of the new and swanky supermarket that had recently opened. The displays of fruits and vegetables in the produce aisle looked like movie-set props; not that she'd ever been on a movie set, but still, there was something that seemed fake about the perfection of the pink grapefruit pyramids, the blooms of emerald-green broccoli, the stacked oblongs of glossy purple eggplants.

She chided herself over her bedazzlement—of course this store, part of a national chain, had marketing experts who knew how to display food; how to play soft but slightly energizing Muzak; how to have sample ladies doling out little paper cups of prosciutto or lobster mac and cheese or 70 percent dark chocolate truffles. That its highway exit ramp was the same one used for Price of Peace further galled her—of course that church would be near this paean to grocery store excess! The family-owned Jerdes, the neighborhood grocery store that had been in Kittleson since the '50s, was smaller and shabbier and certainly lacking a "French Pastry Café" or a chef who, in an "open classroom," taught a small group how to make a Malaysian stir-fry.

Smaller, shabbier, with no special perks, thought Bunny, *just like All Souls.*

Sighing, she headed toward the sandwich shop, stationed next to the deli section's pizza parlor, which was next to the Spanish tapas counter, and ordered a "Ham & Swiss Delight," which included artichokes, horseradish mayo, and caramelized onions, although all she really wanted was a simple ham and cheese.

Outside, she raced to her SUV. It was cold; October had tiptoed in, but now almost over, it was in its stomping here's-what's-coming-next phase.

"Miss me?" she asked Burton. Although he wasn't ambulatory, Bunny had still felt delinquent leaving him alone in the car, even for a few minutes.

She turned the car heater to seventy-two, adjusting the vent, and as the warm air flowed onto his face, Burton made a sound that Bunny pretended was a chuckle.

"Feels good, eh, Burt?" she said and, unwrapping her sandwich, offered him a bite. Not expecting, or getting, a response, she wolfed down half of her sandwich (the other half would be her dinner) before easing out of the parking lot and driving several miles until the residential/business landscape turned rural.

"Look to your right, Burton. See those fields? Aren't they pretty, with that stubbly shorn wheat? Ellison's all done with his harvest—remember Leon Ellison? Remember that good apple crisp his wife would make, and how he'd drop it off now and then as a thank-you for *quote* making him the best-looking farmer currently farming? And that time we ate it while we listened to one of your Miles Davis albums?"

She didn't really expect Burton to nod and offer further recollection, so she did it herself.

"And as Miles was tearing up a trumpet solo, you said something about the precision and surprise of his timing matching the precision and timing of the apple-crisp recipe."

Bunny blinked back tears. Sometimes in urging memories out of her memoryless husband, ones came back to her, as new as just-opened presents.

In the passenger seat of the SUV that smelled of deli ham, Burton stared out the window, seeing what Bunny could only guess at.

At least twice a month, she took him on a road trip, driving anywhere that led them away from Belle Vista.

"I have circle meeting tomorrow," said Bunny now. "We're getting ready for our Halloween party, and then we'll start planning our Thanksgiving outreach. Remember those?"

Where their conversations had once been filled with *Let's—*, or *How about if we—*, or *What do you think about—*, now Bunny prefaced nearly everything she said to her husband with *Remember*?

"Anyway, as usual, church members will be making up Thanksgiving baskets to be delivered, but we've also been trying to think of another form of sharing, one that doesn't make the recipient feel like, well, a charity case. Which is what no one wants to feel, right? But really, why have the words *charity case* gotten such a bad rap? Who's against kindness and compassion? So anyway, after we figure out how to bring more cans of cranberry sauce to the needy—"

Burton, who'd always laughed at his wife's flippant comments, said nothing.

"—well, then maybe we can concentrate on our plans to bring erotica to the masses!"

Driving west, the sun was an egg yolk on the horizon, its yellow slowly melting, and Bunny imagined what Burton, in his right mind, would have added to that particular conversation.

He had introduced her to so much. They had met in the late '70s, when she was in her sophomore year at the University of Nebraska and on her very first—and last—acid trip.

On a cold winter's night, Bunny had huddled with her friend Jann on a bench in the Old Market, watching people stream out of the theater across the street. Jann *oohed* and *aahed* at a woman's purple coat—"I didn't know purple could be that purple!"—while Bunny expressed her sorrow for the curbside slush.

"Tossed aside, like snow's scorned lover," she said.

"That is the most beautiful thing I ever heard," said Jann.

They sat for what seemed to be an hour inhaling and exhaling the frosty air until Bunny said, "My breath is a cold smoky poem to the unspoken."

"No it isn't," said Jann, watching as vapor streamed out of her own mouth. "Because you just spoke."

This struck them both as the funniest thing ever, until Jann's mirth veered into concern. Tears welling in her eyes, she turned to Bunny and asked, "Are they really?"

"Huh?"

Jann pointed at the theater marquee, which read, **BUTTERFLIES ARE FREE.**

"Monarchs are," said Bunny with authority. "But not their subjects."

Jann nodded at her friend's wisdom, and after a moment asked, with some urgency, "Are we in the same time zone?"

Bunny pushed down her mitten and stared at her wristwatch.

"Doesn't matter," she said finally. "All that matters is it's time to eat. Preferably pancakes."

Jann, who was from Arkansas, got excited by a sidewalk chalkboard easel.

"I reckon this is even better than pancakes!"

The sign read "Tonight: Hot Po'Boys!" Bunny asked what they were.

"Really big, really good sandwiches," said Jann, pushing her friend toward the door.

A wailing saxophone greeted them as they entered the darkened room.

"Hey, music," said Bunny perceptively.

"Can I see your IDs?" asked a woman sitting on a stool.

"Why? We didn't do anything wrong!" said Jann.

"We just want some pancakes," said Bunny. "Although my friend here says hot po'boys are even better."

"Are you serious?" asked the woman, but seeing no guile in the girls' faces, she nodded to her left and told them that the Hot Po'Boys were onstage.

"And I need to see your IDs because we serve liquor here."

"How about pancakes?" asked Bunny.

"Just peanuts. But only for paying customers. Cover charge is five dollars—but first I need to see your IDs."

A man shrugging into his coat bid a "Good night, Deirdre" to the gatekeeper on the stool, and to the young women, he said, "There's a coffee shop just down the street. I'm actually headed there myself."

Deirdre nodded to the girls and said, "He's cool."

Bunny smiled at the memory and to Burton said, "You were, thankfully. More than cool. *Nice.*"

He had sat with them in a booth, and while Bunny and Jann inhaled pancakes, the nicely dressed, mustachioed man had an order of toast. When Bunny wondered aloud if there were sparks coming from her fork, Jann confided to Burton that they'd taken LSD.

"I assumed you'd taken something," he said, "although I didn't know people took acid much anymore. That's something we took in college."

"How old are you, anyway?" asked Jann.

"Thirty."

Both girls gaped at the dapper man, in both dress and manner so different from the college boys they hung out with.

"Really?" said Bunny finally. "I thought you were at least fifty."

"I thought about a hundred," said Jann.

Burton laughed, and after he paid the check, asked them how they were going to get home.

"'Home or our dorm home?'" Jann asked.

"You live on the U of N campus?" asked Burton. "Or Creighton?"

"We live everywhere," Bunny said.

"But also at the U," said Jann.

Smiling, Burton took a ten from his wallet.

"I'd give you a ride, but I'm going in the opposite direction. Call a cab—there's a phone booth right outside—and have a good, *safe* night."

Several days later, possessing all her faculties, Bunny had been on Harney Street when she passed a storefront whose window was adorned in gold script, "Burton Barone, Custom Tailoring."

Pushing open the door whose bell announced her presence, Bunny wondered, *It couldn't be, could it?*

It could; the man who emerged from a curtained back room, his neckwear not a tie but a measuring tape, was indeed the man who had treated them to pancakes and given them cab fare.

"Bunny?" the man asked, surprise lifting the last syllable of her name.

Spreading her arms wide in a ta-da! pose, Bunny said, "None other."

"Are you . . . okay?"

"Okay? Sure! I just saw the sign on the window—Burton Barone—and I remembered, hey, *your* name was Burton, and so I just thought I'd come in and see if it was you . . . and it is. So anyway, thanks for helping my friend and me!"

"You're welcome. And it's Baron-*ee*," he said, pronouncing the long *e*. He ran a hand through his dark waves of hair. "So you got home all right? You weren't seeing sparks in the cab?"

"Just the ones shooting out of the driver's ears."

Burton swiped at his mustache with his thumb, a gesture Bunny would come to see over and over. It was a prelude to his laughter, and he laughed now, as she did.

"And do I still look fifty?" he asked.

"Did I say you did?" asked Bunny, not altogether cognizant of everything she said or did while under the influence.

"And I believe your friend said I looked a hundred."

Bunny tilted her head, surveying the compact (he was the same height as Bunny, but at five foot ten, she considered anyone who wasn't over six foot two short), handsome, hazel-eyed man.

"You don't look either."

The doorbell jingled.

"Signore Barone!" said a customer, and as Burton greeted him and ushered him into a back room, Bunny busied herself looking at the suits and shirts on display. Not a person interested in fashion (she got most of her clothes at the Goodwill, not for their vintage/retro factor but for their price tag), she still could recognize quality and craftsmanship.

"This man should be on Savile Row!" said the customer to Bunny as he left, carrying a garment bag over his shoulder.

Burton gave her a tour of the shop, showing her the backroom shelves stacked with bolts of fabric, a mannequin wearing a partially finished suit coat marked up with chalk, a cutting table and two sewing machines, and by the ironing board, a small table on which sat the first espresso machine Bunny had ever seen.

"Clients often bring someone along when they're choosing fabrics or trying something on," said Burton, leading her into a smaller room and gesturing to two velvet chairs outside of the curtained dressing room. It was there that Bunny sat and sipped her first cappuccino out of a small white china cup. Such an odd experience for her—normally when she drank something with a guy, it was beer out of a red Solo cup at a frat-house kegger.

"Remember our first official date after that coffee, Burton? You took me to the symphony, and I had to borrow one of Jann's dresses because I didn't have one of my own and you—"

Burton's snore stopped her words. His head had lolled to the side, one cheek smooshed against the seat belt harness. Even though his conscious state wasn't much different than his unconscious one, she knew he enjoyed their road trips, but now that he was sleeping, she turned around and headed back home.

She turned the radio on and felt a little jump of excitement because just the right song came on, as if a DJ, sensing her mood over the airwaves, had put a 45 on the turntable with the message, "This one's for you."

"Turntable," Bunny muttered. "As if they even have 45s in radio stations anymore. As if they even have turntables."

The song was "In a Sentimental Mood," one she and Burton would always consider one of "their songs" because of what it had accompanied.

They'd been seeing each other for two months, and after a night of dancing, Bunny accepted an invitation to Burton's apartment (she had been as impressed by its neatness as its sophisticated decor—not a dirty sock, orange crate, or floor mattress in sight), and on his stereo turntable, Burton had put on a Duke Ellington and John Coltrane album, and, as the tease between piano and saxophone began, he turned to her.

Her last boyfriend thought dressing up meant changing T-shirts (and truth be told, she pretty much thought the same thing), but Burton, Burton was always dressed like an Italian movie star.

His smile was like an invitation to everywhere she wanted to go, and as he took off his tailored (of course) sport coat and tossed it on the couch, Bunny felt her heart thump. He approached her like a tango partner, and Bunny felt as if a swarm of butterflies had been let loose in her pelvis.

The sky was darkening, and in the car interior's soft gray light, Bunny turned to Burton, not seeing the slumped, slack-jawed, snoring old man, but her very own Marcello Mastroianni, on that night when his hand worked and loosened the knot of his gray silk tie. Her heart had stopped thumping and began banging as he slowly slid the tie through the channel of his collar (Bunny was sure she heard the fabric swish) and twirled it before tossing it over his shoulder.

When the final notes of the song on the radio ended, Bunny sighed, thinking, *L is for Loosening.*

12

"Your numbers are as good as ever," said Dr. Nguyen, scanning her laptop computer.

"Nothing's elevated, nothing's too low or high; all blood work's completely normal."

She closed the computer and smiled at her patient.

"Whatever you're doing, keep doing it."

"So you're giving me permission to keep up the booze and the dope?" said Velda. "Thanks, Doc!"

Dr. Nguyen picked up a pen and prescription pad on her desk and began writing.

"Booze, dope, and whatever else you're taking to stay in such great shape.'"

With a flourish, she tore off the piece of paper and handed it to Velda, who laughed, reading the words the doctor had just spoken.

"I wonder what my pharmacist would say if I gave this to him."

"Sure, put my medical license in jeopardy."

That Velda always got good reports was one of the reasons she liked her doctor so much, the other being their teasing rapport. Standing up, Velda thanked her for her time, and Dr. Nguyen honestly told her it was always a pleasure and stood politely as the older woman headed toward the door.

Velda's hand was on the doorknob when she turned and, her words coming out in a rush, said, "Dr. Nguyen, how did you know you were a lesbian?"

Having seen and heard many things in her medical practice, the physician still was taken aback.

"Oh, I've embarrassed you," said Velda.

"No, no," said Dr. Nguyen, even as her face felt it was parboiling. "It's just . . . I was just, surprised is all." She shook her head as if aligning her thoughts. "I have a few minutes before my next patient. Would you like to sit down, and we can talk a bit?"

Velda, wringing her hands, nodded and sat.

"I only ask because, well, I think I might be part . . . lesbian."

It took all Dr. Nguyen's very practiced control to not laugh, but she wasn't entirely successful, a small little "ha!" sneaking out.

"I'm sorry," she said, seeing Velda's expression. "That was just a surprised reaction." She twisted her ring, a nervous tic. "You're full of surprises today!"

Dr. Nguyen waited for a moment, but Velda sat ramrod straight with her hands folded in her lap, saying nothing.

"First of all, we're learning more and more about the complexities of sexual orientation. Rather than being 'part' lesbian, it may be that you're bisexual." Dr. Nguyen made a conscious decision to stop twisting her ring and, like her patient, folded her hands in her lap. "As for me, I think I always knew I was attracted to my own sex, even when I was little. But I fought those feelings for the longest time and didn't get honest with myself until my last year of medical school."

Velda remained silent, but her nod urged the doctor to continue.

"That's when I met Kirsten, during my clinical rotations. She worked in administration and one day in the cafeteria . . ." Dr. Nguyen colored again, a small smile gracing her face. "Well, she asked, 'Is this seat taken?' and it obviously wasn't—I was sitting alone at a table for four—and she sat down and the rest . . . well, the rest is history. But . . . what makes you think you might be 'part lesbian'?"

"Because I think I was in love with a woman in college! I think she was in love with me too!" Tears formed in the old woman's eyes. "But it was . . . you know, the times and all. It wasn't as easy as it is nowadays to love someone who goes to the bathroom the same way you do."

Again, Dr. Nguyen squeaked out a laugh, but instead of apologizing, she shrugged.

"You do have an interesting way with words."

"But I loved my husband too!" said Velda, yanking a tissue from the box.

After a moment, Dr. Nguyen said, "As I said, it may be that you're bisexual, drawn to both men and women."

Dabbing her eyes, Velda said, "The truth is . . . well, the truth is that I don't think I ever loved Merv as much as I loved Eloise. I tried—and I thought I was successful at—burying my feelings for her years ago, but lately, they've popped up." She hung her head, as if its weight had suddenly doubled, and Dr. Nguyen reached out and squeezed the woman's hand.

"Do you ever think of contacting her?"

"I'm too afraid to. I'm sure she wouldn't remember me—or if she did, she'd probably think what we had was just some silly schoolgirl-crush sort of thing."

"But what if she did remember you, and what if what you had meant more to her than some silly schoolgirl crush?"

"And what if money grew on trees?"

Dr. Nguyen flinched at the sharpness in her voice, and if Velda's legs weren't crossed, she would have kicked herself, but before she could apologize, Dr. Nguyen said, "Acting on our true feelings is always a big risk. But I've always thought the bigger risk was not acting on them. Not acting on them and instead being shadowed by regret, asking that terrible question, 'What if?'"

"I've had a life of 'what ifs.'" The words surprised Velda, but more so saddened her.

A good doctor, Jenna Nguyen always thought, was a good psychologist, able not only to listen to her patients' complaints but to their hopes and fears. Many patients couldn't—or wouldn't—share their feelings (and yes, the majority of those tight-lipped ones were men), but it was always easier to treat the ones who did. It felt more like teamwork.

"Everyone has regrets and 'what ifs,'" she said. "But if there's time and a real desire to change those, my prescription is, *go for it.*"

Velda stared at her hands, and as she did every time she saw the crepey, spotted hands of an old woman, she thought, *These can't be mine!* She knew she was old in years—eighty-one her next birthday—but young at heart and yet, why couldn't her exterior reflect that? Then again, she appreciated the protection that age gave her; if she did something rash or stupid, she wouldn't have decades to stew about it.

A soft buzz issued from the desk telephone as a little square lit up. Dr. Nguyen picked up the receiver and listened for a few moments, and when she hung up, she began, "Velda, my eleven o'clock—" but the woman had already stood.

"Thank you for your time, Dr. Nguyen. You've been a big help."

"I hope so."

"Don't hope, know it," said Velda, striding out of the office as if she'd just been infused with an energy drink and vitamin B shots. "Toodle-oo!"

Dr. Nguyen stared after her, even as Velda had exited and there was nothing more to stare at than the anatomy chart tacked onto the door.

Velda had a rarely used Facebook page Merv had set up for them years ago, thinking that it was a good way to "keep up with how Wayne and Pamela are doing." He sent his son and daughter quotes on success, news items, and his political views, but Velda considered its public forum an invasion of privacy.

On her kitchen table, in the nook with her homemade map wallpaper, she sat staring at her laptop. It hadn't taken her long to find the Eloise Y. McWilliams (thank goodness for that middle initial!) she was certain was *her* Eloise Y. McWilliams, and on her Facebook page, she made a friend request.

Too nervous to wait for any kind of response, she went for a long walk, and when she returned, she vacuumed the first floor, which didn't need vacuuming, as she had run the Bissell just the day before; straightened out her junk drawer, whose junk was already organized; and polished her already gleaming stove top. Cleaning was therapy for her, and conversely, she couldn't immerse herself in it because her house was always clean.

Finally, after snacking on buttered crackers and half a can of peaches and washing and putting away her dishes, she opened up her computer.

There was not just the acceptance of her friend request, but a message, which read:

> Holy %$*@#!!—Velda, Velda, Velda! To say it's a treat to hear from you is an understatement. Here's my phone number—call me, asap!

Staring at the message, Velda felt as if she were a turbo-charged engine whose ignition switch had just been turned. Her body revved and thrummed as she reached for her phone, and she had to wait for a moment before dialing to still her shaking fingers.

Putting her phone on speaker, she listened to it ring once, twice, three times before it was picked up and a bright voice said, "Hello?"

Stifling an impulse to hang up, Velda instead said, "Hi, Eloise, it's me, Velda. Velda Henson, well, formerly Trygstad."

Eloise's delighted laugh filled the kitchen as Velda thought, *M is for . . . Maybe.*

~

Concerned that she hadn't seen him since his brother's death during the Blessing of the Animals service, Pastor Pete paid Evan Bates a visit and was relieved that the person who answered the door wasn't a disheveled and depressed old man wearing a fuzz of white whiskers and a stained bathrobe, but a bright-eyed and smiling nonagenarian sporting, over his pants and shirt, a crisp white apron.

"Pastor Pete, come in, come in!" he said, enthusiastic as a Walmart greeter just back from break. "You're just in time!"

"Time for what?" asked Mallory.

"Time for a sample!

"But please, first sign the guest book," said Evan and she did, wondering why the custom had gone out of fashion; it was flattering that someone wanted your presence noted.

"Well, come on," he said, beckoning her with a wave of his wooden spoon, the smell of chocolate intensifying as he led her into the kitchen and invited her to sit at a small table covered in old-fashioned oilcloth.

"I was thinking of truffles," he said, pushing a plate toward her, "but I decided to downshift to fudge."

"Yum," said Mallory after her first bite. "I was expecting something more—"

"Creamy, not crumbly, right?" said Evan. "I prefer fudge that has a little more texture."

Finishing her first piece and helping herself to a second, Mallory said, "Where did you ever learn to make fudge like this? It's *so* good."

"I took a candy-making class years ago, and I've faithfully practiced the craft ever since. So, of course, I'm delighted that you chose to drop by on a day I can offer you a sample of my confectionery skills."

Mallory apologized for dropping by unannounced.

"It's just that I've been worried about you. Not seeing you in church and never getting an answer when I telephoned—"

"I was out of town until yesterday. Up in Williston. I brought Eldred's ashes back and then stayed up there to take care of his business."

"And you're . . . you're doing all right?"

"Swell!" he said with a cackle. Seeing the minister's look of surprise over his exuberance, he added, "It's easier to mourn a brother when he's lived a long life. And I'm sure he was happier to join his wife in heaven than he was missing her on Earth."

The telephone rang, and after a brief conversation, Evan replaced the receiver on its old-fashioned wall mount.

"I've got a guest coming," he said, explaining that a "sweetheart" was coming by. His *heh-heh-heh* was a dry little chortle. "Not that kind—a candy groupie. You're welcome to stay and meet her."

"No, I've got a meeting too," said Mallory, rising. "I'm glad you're doing well, and I'll see you in church next Sunday?"

"You certainly will," he said and as he showed her to the door, Mallory couldn't help smiling as she thought, *A candy groupie?*

~

Godfrey was setting potted evergreens on the front steps when Marlys arrived for circle with a covered dish in hand.

"Oh, so now you're a landscape designer too?"

"As a matter of fact," said Godfrey, brushing his palms, "I was thinking of digging up the parking lot and turning it into a sculpture garden."

"Wouldn't affect me since we walk to church."

"That's how I go about doing anything around here. Asking myself, 'How will this affect Marlys?'"

"You mind passing on those words of wisdom to Roger?"

They both chuckled, enjoying their banter, and before Marlys entered the church, she held up the dish she was carrying and said, "Gingersnaps. I'll leave some on the counter for you."

Godfrey liked Marlys, in fact he liked every one of the Naomis with the exception of Charlene, who he found uptight to the uptightest degree.

He'd never had the opportunity or impetus to hang around women who had aged themselves out of interest to him, and kidding around with the older church women had made him realize the folly of his judgment that the opposite sex was of value to him only when it concerned sex.

When did I get so obtuse? he had asked himself several Sundays earlier, when Bunny had whispered, "Can't you mute his mic?"

They'd been sitting next to each other in the back row, listening to a soloist who'd flown in from Pittsburgh. He had actually flown in to visit his sister who attended All Souls, but when said sister told Tad, the choir director, that her brother had once performed with the Albanian Opera, arrangements had quickly been made for the tenor to sing during the service.

Higher notes and better days had been left behind, and when the tenor warbled through "I Need Thee Every Hour," Godfrey had whispered to Bunny, "How about every second?" And when he searched for a key that might unlock the song "O Lord We Praise You," Bunny had whispered to Godfrey, "Only if you stop singing."

In adulthood, he had based his friendships on who could get him what substance, and while Godfrey still looked back on his life and its many missed opportunities, he was trying to loosen the iron grip of regret and learn to be grateful for what was in his life *right now*. And right now, he was enjoying the friendship of older women.

"So, tell me what I can expect at the Halloween party," said Pastor Pete, opening her iPad as the women gathered at the church's kitchen table, mugs of coffee in hand, remnants of cookie crumbs on their plates. "All I know is that Godfrey's volunteered to do some decorating and Doug Eastman and Bonnie Anderson are the hosts?"

"They do a bang-up job," said Edie. "Bonnie owns Gourmet Popcorn on Main and they donate all these little bags of pumpkin-flavored popcorn. It's to die for."

"It's a very popular event," said Velda. "We get All Souls' families of course, but lots of other people, too, and in fact last year, two mothers who brought kids to the party joined the church. Julie Enger and Faith Geye?"

"We don't actively recruit people," said Marlys, "but it's just so fun. Doug always thinks up really good games and we give prizes . . . well, if I were a nonmember, I'd want to come back to check this place out!"

"Unfortunately, we do get a lot of moles from Prince of Peace," said Charlene.

"Moles?" asked Pastor Pete.

"You know, spies. They come here and steal our good ideas."

As was often the case, one of Charlene's pronouncements, as true as it might be, took the mood of the group down a notch.

"Well, that's flattering, don't you think?" said Pastor Pete after a moment. "Anyway, I look forward to Halloween and also to Thanksgiving because"—she scrolled down the screen—"because we've already got twenty-three people signed up to donate food baskets. That's already nearly half our goal!"

"That's encouraging," said Velda. "Just make sure that the Men on a Mission—they're the usual delivery crew—know to 'edit' the Emslanders' basket. They always donate things like cans of chili and jackfruit. Who eats chili on Thanksgiving?"

"Who eats jackfruit at any time?" said Bunny.

"What *is* jackfruit?" said Edie.

After every topic she had wanted to discuss had been checkmarked, Pastor Pete closed her iPad and smiled/grimaced at the five women.

"Well, I guess it's time we talk about what we all really want to talk about. Are we still on board for our little fundraising book? Has anyone got anything to contribute?"

It was as if a floodgate had been opened, and had they not been firmly seated, everyone would have been washed out of the door on the crest of a wave, through the undercroft, and up the stairs into the narthex.

As everyone talked over one another, Pastor Pete called for order and, laughing, called for order again as the chatter continued. When the group finally quieted and she asked who wanted to start, Edie raised her hand.

"First of all, I've got to say the idea struck Mary Jo as pretty funny."

"She's Edie's daughter, who lives in England," said Velda, who liked to act as Pastor Pete's unofficial social secretary, helping her keep straight all her parishioners and their families. "Married to a Brit."

"Which I have to admit sort of hurt my feelings," continued Edie. "Not Nigel's being a Brit—I love him—but the fact that Mary Jo thought the idea was so funny. It didn't take her long to come around, though, and she and Nigel even picked a letter and told Finn and me the story behind it!"

"Same thing with my granddaughter," said Marlys. "First she teases me and then we both wind up writing pieces! She's even talking to a couple of her college friends about contributing something so there'd be some younger voices in the mix!"

"I've been working on a couple of things," said Bunny, her usually animated voice suddenly shy. "I was sitting with Burton the other day and suddenly the letter *D* came into my head and I remembered what a smooth operator Burt was on the dance floor, and I thought, *D is for Dancing.*"

"That's what's happening to me!" said Velda. "I thought of a letter and a name instantly popped up."

"M is for Merv?" asked Marlys, who, as a past president of the high school PTA, had had many dealings with Velda's husband, the principal.

"Didn't get to *M*," snapped Velda.

"Sorry, Vel," began Marlys, "I was just—"

"I'm just a little touchy," she said, with a wave of her hand. "This whole thing has . . . well, it's brought up a lot of *stuff.*"

The room went silent, except for the radiator, issuing a sloshing sound followed by a hiss.

"I agree," said Charlene after the heater clunked. "I mean, I was sure this was something I wanted no part of and yet it's been making me think . . . about a lot of things."

The women waited expectantly for her to elaborate, and when she didn't, Bunny offered a helpful, "And?"

"Well, this is the thing," she said, staring at her nails, ten perfectly polished pink ovals. "I was raised by a mother who taught me that sex was a bad thing—so bad she couldn't even say it, she'd spell it! She thought *s-e-x* was something not to be enjoyed, but . . . withstood. And only withstood once you were married.

"But this, this project, or whatever it is, has made me wonder about a lot of things . . . like why did I listen so much to my mother when my husband, when my body was telling me differently? How could something that can feel so good be so bad? I mean, if you look at all of God's creatures who have sex—and they all do, even if it's just to reproduce—"

"Actually," said Velda, who had a decades-long subscription to *Popular Science*, "there's parthenogenesis, or asexual reproduction, in the animal kingdom with some insects, birds, reptiles—"

"And why is there so often shame attached?" continued Charlene. "Is it because the parts we use for sex are parts we use for other things, like a man uses his penis to urinate or—"

"Oh!" said Edie, as if she had just sat down on a tippy chair.

"I get what you're saying," said Bunny. "Think about the euphemisms—*get down and dirty, doing the dirty deed, doing the nasty*—do we say those things because a woman's vagina is between two openings used to—oh, let's call it what it is—poop and pee?"

Volunteering in the church nursery, Marlys had often heard the words *poop* and *pee* but never in a circle meeting.

"So wouldn't you think," Bunny went on, "that in designing our bodies, God could have come up with more parts less associated with . . . waste removal?"

The women around the table looked dazed, their words like boxing-ring blows knocking them into a silent stupor.

"Really," said Pastor Pete finally, "it's a pretty economical design. Elegant even. I mean, do we really need any more extra parts when the ones we have are so multipurpose?"

"That was a conversation I sure didn't expect," said Marlys, refilling her cup with the last of the coffee. "And definitely not from you."

"I know," said Charlene, with a smile that managed to be both shy and sly. "I mean, I'm not dense, I am aware I tend to keep my emotions buttoned up."

"But not your opinions," Bunny teased.

Instead of a testy denial, Charlene further surprised them by saying, "I guess opinions are easier to express than feelings. But maybe it's time to unbutton my emotions a little."

Although they might have said it differently, all the women's thoughts shared the same sentiment as Velda's: *As I live and breathe.*

"Now, I don't even know if this counts as 'erotica,'" Charlene continued, "but this is what I came up with."

She told them the story of her husband sticking up for her at the home of her Price of Peace in-laws.

"Charlie is a big family man, and he loves spending time with his brother, Rick. But he could see, despite my always putting on my 'everything's fine' face, that everything wasn't fine . . . and he stood up for me. Plus he didn't laugh when I told him about our project." Charlene smiled—she was a fan of at-home teeth-bleaching strips, and they served her well—and softly added, "So that was my idea of erotic—his gallantry. 'G is for Gallantry.' And I've also written a little piece about the letter *C*—"

"Oh no," said Marlys, turning to Pastor Pete. "Amelia wrote about the letter *C* too."

"Well, we're not assigning letters, so there's bound to be some overlap," said the minister. "But that brings up a good question—*should* we assign letters?"

The consensus was no.

"I say we keep writing about whatever letters inspire us," said Velda. "Because even writing about the same letter, our entries would be different because we all have different ideas about what touches us, what moves us, what—"

"Gets us hot," said Bunny, and amid the women's laughter, Pastor Pete stood up.

"Ladies, I'm so sorry," she said, "but I have another appointment. I'll leave it to you to hammer out any further details."

That was something the Naomis were good at—hammering out details. The sooner money could be raised for the church, the better, but also noting they were heading into a busy holiday season, they gave themselves a deadline: all entries for the project would be collected before the State of the Church meeting in January.

"That'll start the new year off with a bang," said Bunny.

You got that right, thought Godfrey, who having finished his outdoor chores had heard the tail end of the women's conversation on his way to the utility closet. Tempted to pop his head in and ask if submissions were open to everyone, he chuckled, certain that his own ideas as to what was erotic wouldn't wind up in their little church booklet.

13

Dear Bro,

Never expected to get a condolence card for a horse, but thanks! I've got to tell you, saying goodbye to Agnes was like saying yet another goodbye to Eve. My beautiful wife loved that old nag and thought that if there were IQ tests for horses, Agnes would be a Mensa member!

Anyway, I was glad that old horse meant a lot to you too. I remember the first time you took her for a ride, and you were so slumped over I thought you were going to fall off. But day by day, you sat up a little straighter.

Three stuttering breaths rose from Godfrey's chest as he lifted his gaze to look out the window, and in his mind's eye, he saw himself astride Agnes, silhouetted against a red sunset. He blinked once—hard—and continued reading his brother's letter.

Other exciting news? Well, I drove into town and picked up some fertilizer. Stopped and had coffee at Ornery Bob's—you remember that little café where the help lives up to its name? Still, I'd wager no one makes a better waffle. Anyhow, Dave McAndrews was there, bragging about getting over two hundred "likes" on one of his stupid Facebook posts. If those damn posts are anything like the stupid stuff he says in person, I can't imagine how anyone would like them. World's full of all kinds of stuff, including morons.

So that's my (maybe not so exciting) news. Love hearing about that strange new life you're living!*

Chaunce

**strange in a different way*

Godfrey's hand moved back and forth on the lined paper, as if he were petting his brother's handwritten words.

Strange in a different way is right, he thought. As proud as he was of his sobriety, he was more proud that he was starting to like himself in his sobriety. It had taken a while, and not that he was suddenly Mr. Nice Guy, but for sure he wasn't as big an asshole as he used to be. He could even feel some compassion for his ex, Jeanine, until he'd remind himself what a real asshole *she* was.

Returning his brother's letter to its envelope and placing it in a shoebox under the narrow twin bed, he had to laugh to himself, thinking the old Godfrey would have never been so sentimental as to save his brother's letters. Then again, the old Godfrey wouldn't have started up a written correspondence, one that Chauncey, thankfully, reciprocated. As short as their letters might be, they seemed to say more than they could manage in their monthly phone calls.

His landlords, the Swensons, were right—the little cottage on their RV property was cozy, and after Godfrey heated a cup of water in the microwave and bobbed a Lipton bag in it (tea!—now he was drinking tea!), he helped himself to the gingersnap cookies Marlys had left for him and turned on the little portable radio that only got two stations. Fortunately, one of them, when it wasn't blabbing ads for home security systems or bundled insurance, played classic rock.

A couple of weeks after he'd left his brother's house, Godfrey had landed in Roswell, New Mexico. He had money from working at Chauncey's, but until he found a place he wanted to land, or a vehicle he liked and could afford, he wanted to hold on to as much of his cash as possible.

After a bus ride and several hours of frustrating hitchhiking (the longest ride he'd been able to score was thirty-five miles with an arborist, who'd alarmed him with tales of emerald ash borers and spongy moths), he had to walk several miles into town, which didn't improve his already bad mood. Staking a claim to a temporary homestead, he was about to spread out his sleeping bag under a highway overpass when a tiny woman with a huge puff of hair accosted him.

When he wanted nothing more than to be left alone, a simple "Hello!" was enough for Godfrey to feel accosted, and his annoyance was only slightly tempered when the woman gave him a bag lunch she withdrew from her backpack as well as a business card.

"I'm Necia, and if you need a little R & R, my husband, Ned, and I run this halfway house," she said and, in a voice that could only be described as jolly, added, "Half shelter and half spa! It's called Bo's Place and it's just down the road!"

Not waiting around for an RSVP, she left Godfrey to enjoy one of the better tuna sandwiches he'd ever had in his life and a Rice Krispies bar big as a brick.

Stubborn as he was, it took Godfrey several hours before he left the slope of concrete for what he hoped were softer accommodations, and he entered the old Victorian house just as people were gathering around a big round table.

"Hi, I'm Ned," said a man who looked like he knew his way around a gym, and specifically, the weight room. "I'll get another plate!"

Godfrey agreed with the seven other guests—all veterans—that it was the best spaghetti *ever* and listened to a volley of jokes and stories as platters of garlic bread and extra sauce were passed around. He spoke only when spoken to.

"No, I never did serve."

"No, I didn't come to Roswell hoping to see a spaceship." (An eye roll accompanied his answer to this question.)

"Don't know where I'm going yet, just going."

Through the less taciturn people at the table, Godfrey learned that his hosts had started Bo's Place in honor of Necia's father, a Vietnam veteran who'd suffered from PTSD.

"He went to war one man and came back another," she said.

"Didn't we all," said Terry, who'd had two deployments to Iraq.

"Isn't it funny," said Necia, her tone implying that it was not, "that we haven't figured out how to *not* send our men—and now our women—to war? To let them be everyday heroes in their own lives, their own homes?"

Ned, the buff man, said, "Necia wants there to be a constitutional amendment against all wars."

"An *international* constitutional amendment," said Necia. "But I can't get any world leaders to take my calls."

After dessert (a peach pie, which was tasty, but not up to the "best ever" standards of the tuna fish and spaghetti), cleanup duties were democratically and quickly handled. The group then dispersed; a few people went to the TV room and several, including Godfrey, to the porch.

He and a man named Fred settled themselves on rocking chairs, and when Fred lit a pipe, Godfrey was relieved to smell the flare of tobacco rather than weed. Although he had put in calls to his sponsor, he hadn't been to a meeting since he'd left his brother's, and while he was certain he'd say no to an offered toke, he wasn't *absolutely* certain. Two other guests on a porch swing communed with their phones, Jerilyn chuckling as her finger scrolled down the screen, Javier scowling as he pecked out a text.

That nobody cared to continue the dinner table conversations was fine with Godfrey. It wasn't that he was antisocial; he just hadn't been in that many social situations—while sober.

The evening darkened, lit only by a dim streetlight and the glowing rectangles that were cell phones, but after a few stars began twinkling, it was as if a night-sky switch had been turned on.

"And that's why," said Fred, breaking the long silence, "aliens like to land in Roswell—they can navigate by all the starlight."

"What I heard," said Javier, "is that aliens land in Roswell because of sympathetic gravitational coordinates."

"Really?" said Jerilyn.

"Nah. I just made that up."

The group chuckled before taking a poll as to who believed in aliens and who didn't. It was unanimous, all of them did, although Godfrey was the only one who thought they hadn't yet visited Earth.

"That's because you haven't been in the military," said Fred.

A sudden twang of notes, of guitars being tuned, stopped their conversation on the many things civilians have no clue about, and Fred, laughing at the look on Godfrey's face, whispered, "Ned and Necia." With his thumb, he pointed over his shoulder. "Around the corner, on the back side of the porch."

"They've both been taking guitar lessons," said Javier, "because Necia says the key to happiness is to keep learning."

"She's not bad," said Fred, "but Ned is."

"To say he has a tin ear would be to dis tin," said Jerilyn.

"My cue to go to bed," said Javier, rising.

As the tuning gave way to slow strumming and attempted chord changes, Fred and Jerilyn joined Javier inside the house and, left alone, Godfrey quietly rocked in his chair, listening.

"My fingers can't make that jump," said Ned, interrupting his strumming to move to a C chord.

"Sure they can," said Necia, whose fingers navigated the fret board with more dexterity. "We just have to practice. Now come on—three chords and we've got this song."

One guitar played, and Godfrey presumed it was hers, as there weren't long pauses moving from G to C to A, and when Ned joined in, each new chord was preceded by his soft entreaty, "Wait."

Minutes passed as they strummed and played, Necia offering words of encouragement when Ned's transitions became a little less jerky.

"You're Guitarzan! Now you've got it! Beautiful!"

Necia's high, sweet voice rose up and Ned's deeper, atonal one joined in as they matched the words of "Blowin' in the Wind" to the chords they played.

The air was redolent with music and the smell of blue-hill meadow sage, and Godfrey rocked back and forth, for a change not in a hurry to say good night to reality for the easier state of subconsciousness.

In that cottage whose space heater coils glowed red, as he finished the last of Marlys's cookies, Godfrey thought of the couple and their "half shelter / half spa." Although he'd been told the welcome mat was out for as long as he needed, it seemed his ability to accept kindness had a cap and he stayed only two nights.

Watching the way Necia and Ned interacted—was there some magnetic connection going on that made it impossible for them to pass one another without kissing or touching?—Godfrey felt like a D student in a class whose subject, married love, would drop his grade even lower. His own parents had been more adversaries than allies, fighting the civil war that was their own union, until his father went AWOL, leaving the family when Godfrey was ten. He had no doubt that Chauncey and Eve had had a loving relationship, but unfortunately, was never sober enough around them to notice.

The last morning Godfrey was at Bo's Place, Jerilyn announced during breakfast that she was giving free haircuts—"Don't worry, I went to barber college before I joined the army"—and while Fred and Terry agreed to take her up on the offer, Godfrey was not willing to say goodbye to his long hair, feeling it gave him some kind of protection. Against what, he wasn't exactly sure, but he liked the weight of his ponytail against his neck.

"How about you, Necia?" asked Jerilyn.

"Oh, no," said their host, patting her nearly foot-high afro. "This gives me extra height."

"She doesn't understand that in most people's eyes, and certainly mine," said Ned, pulling his aproned wife to his lap, "she's a beautiful and mighty Amazon."

Necia kissed him and said, "Thank you, sir," and to the others at the table, she stage-whispered, "He'll say anything for the last waffle."

"Let's Get It On" by Marvin Gaye was on the radio, and Godfrey's thoughts turned to Noreen, the woman he had been convinced was going to be the love of his life, and not just thirty days of it. That particular song hadn't been playing the night they were in her backyard hot tub, but its invitation reminded him of the look on Noreen's face, of the way she licked her lips, of her beautiful breasts glistening with water.

N is for Noreen was the thought that popped into his head, but then Billy Joel's "Just the Way You Are" came on and Godfrey thought of the tall buff man pulling the petite woman to his lap and their playful banter, thought of that starlit night when the veterans' talk of UFOs was interrupted by the amateur yet loving guitar practice of the couple who were so kind to one another, to him, to everyone, and the surprising thought came to him: *N is for Necia and Ned.*

Godfrey's next thought, accompanied by both a shake of his head and a smile was, *I've been around those ladies too long.*

14

"I really hadn't even wanted to go," said LeAnn, "I mean, I've had dinner with these kinds of clients before—they come from Chicago or New York and expect us to woo and coddle them, which we do of course, I mean they bring a lot of money and prestige to the agency—but wooing and coddling takes a lot out of a person!"

Mallory kept in touch with most of her friends with texts and emails, but she and LeAnn had always enjoyed long, old-fashioned telephone conversations.

"I'm going to put you on speaker, okay? I'm trying to get some lunch in Soren and he's being a little fussy."

To prove her point, the two-year-old threw his spoon over the high chair tray, laughing maniacally.

"Great," said LeAnn, "because I don't want you to miss a single word of what I'm going to tell you."

"Ooh, the intrigue," said Mallory, setting the phone on the table as she stooped to wipe up another splat of food her son had flung to the floor.

LeAnn's amplified voice instructing Soren to eat his lunch like a good boy had the wondrous effect of making him do just that, and Mallory clapped her hands as he dipped a piece of peanut butter toast into his cup of fruit cocktail and took a bite.

"Good boy!" she said to Soren, and into the phone, she instructed LeAnn, "Tell me more."

A girlish giggle came over the speaker.

"I've been dying to!"

Even as she wiped up a puddle of milk and pried a squished maraschino cherry off the floor, Mallory found herself grinning; for the longest time she had listened/counseled/comforted her friend as she raged against her bad luck with men. Now LeAnn was claiming that she may have *finally* done the impossible: met the man of her dreams.

"Well, I really shouldn't say that; I mean, I'd avoid like hell any man who was in one of my weird dreams, but . . . oh, Mallory."

While dining in the swanky steak house with clients ("Mal, this company is convinced their microwaveable snack is going to make chips obsolete") LeAnn had noticed him, this "hot male-model guy" surrounded by a bunch of young women in a corner booth. He'd noticed her, too, enough so that when she emerged from the restroom, he slipped her a business card with a handwritten message on the back: "You miss 100 percent of the shots you don't take."

"What does that even mean?" asked Mallory. "And why was he surrounded by a bunch of young women?"

"It's a Wayne Gretzky quote! Owen—that's his name, isn't that a great name?—anyway, what Owen meant was that he wasn't going to miss out on the chance of getting to know me by not doing anything at all!"

She further explained that he was a DPT—a doctor of physical therapy.

"The women he was with—they're Badger hockey players! He's their athletic trainer!"

After Soren finished depositing 80 percent of his lunch in his mouth and 20 percent on the floor (*not a bad ratio,* Mallory thought), she lifted him out of his high chair, listening as LeAnn gushed about their first date: it was as if the large pepperoni pizza they'd shared had been hand tossed in a Napoli trattoria by the inventor of pizza himself, as if the cruise they had taken was on a luxury yacht to Capri rather than one that took them, in Owen's Dodge Durango, alongside Lake Mendota.

"Oh, Mal, he's everything I've ever wanted! Smart! Funny! And did I mention what a babe he is?"

"A couple of times," said Mallory as Soren wriggled out of her arms and raced to the living room toy box with a high-pitched squeal.

"I could mention it ten times more, but okay, your turn. What's happening with the Naomis? Still going ahead with the ABC book?"

"I don't really see how we can," said Mallory, as Soren dumped a plastic box of LEGOs on the floor, "and yet, everyone's really into it! I don't know how much has been written, and I'm sure there'll be a lot of overlap with letters and—"

"Hey, I've got something to contribute."

"Oh?"

"*O* is right!" said LeAnn with a laugh. "O is for Owen!"

~

Never having flown on Halloween, it was a treat (how apt!) for Velda to be served coffee and a mini bag of cheese crackers by a flight attendant wearing Mickey Mouse ears.

"We used to be able to go all out," said the woman after Velda complimented her getting into the spirit of things. "But then new management decided one of the first things to go—along with pillows and blankets and our union—was fun."

As the trudge of passengers left the plane, one pilot had put on googly-eye glasses and stood near the exit door bidding them a happy Halloween.

"Hope you weren't wearing those in flight!" said the passenger ahead of Velda.

"Just during takeoff and landing," said the pilot.

Having been given thorough instructions, Velda walked through the terminal and to the baggage claim, even though she had only brought a carry-on. By the escalators, her heart hammered as she saw a sign with her name on it.

"That's me," she said to the sign's holder, whose hands dropped the paper so that her arms could encircle Velda.

"Oh my gosh," said Eloise. "It's been so long."

It had all happened so fast. Velda had anticipated a long, reacquainting conversation, but they had only exchanged brief biographical information when Eloise asked if Velda wouldn't rather catch up in person, and when Velda agreed that she would, an invitation to Boston was issued. An unexpected, almost rash invitation, thought Velda, but one that she accepted.

It didn't take long to reach her host's home in the Charlestown neighborhood, and when Velda walked into the saltbox house, she said, a touch of awe in her voice, "Eloise, this is so you!"

The entryway had leopard-print wallpaper, and its coat rack didn't have hooks so much as branches.

"Wait'll you see your room," said Eloise. "All I can say is, I hope you like Warhol."

Every room was a salute/shout-out to a particular animal or art movement. Dozens of paintings and photographs of elephants filled the gray walls of the living room. The bases of its end tables were carved-wood elephant legs, and its couch and chairs were adorned with elephant-shaped pillows. The dining room was a paean to Van Gogh, with two walls abloom with sunflowers and the other two a starry, swirly blue.

Velda said two words over and over: "Oh, my."

After showing Velda to a bedroom filled with reproductions of soup cans, of portraits of Marilyn Monroe, Jackie Onassis, and Elvis, Eloise told her to "take a load off."

"I'm an afternoon napper—how's about we meet at 5:30 for cocktails?"

Velda, who couldn't remember the last time she'd taken a nap, drew a bath for herself in the large en suite tub and settled into a froth of bubbles, ignoring the portrait of *Black Lenin* scowling down at her.

Their cocktail hour was postponed by the doorbell ringing and gleeful shouts of "Trick or treat!"

Velda helped pass out big Snickers bars, earning an appreciative "Thanks!" from Spider-Men and *Frozen* princesses and ghosts and goblins whose bags held a majority of "fun size" (i.e., chintzy) candy bars. It didn't matter that the candy had almost run out by seven o'clock, as there were no more trick-or-treaters.

"Kids today," said Eloise as she turned off the porch light. "When we were young, we ran wild in the streets till at least nine."

"Us too," said Velda. "And where are the hooligans who soap windows or throw eggs at them?"

"Hooligans have my blessings," said Eloise, "as long as they stay away from my house. Now about that cocktail. Gin martinis okay?"

On the smoky mirrored surface of the walnut liquor cabinet, she measured gin and vermouth, and before pouring a dollop of olive brine into one glass, she asked, "Dirty okay?"

"Fine," said Velda, who didn't know the difference between a dirty martini and a clean one.

Eloise added the brine, and they carried their glasses to the living room's seating area.

"Put your feet up," said Eloise, settling herself gingerly on the couch. "I would myself, but my knees are stiff as plasterboard."

Watching Velda easily tuck her stockinged feet underneath her, she remarked on what good shape her old college friend had stayed in.

"I have?" asked Velda. It was in her nature to treat compliments like lint and brush them off, but she immediately felt silly, disputing something so obvious. "I have," she said with more conviction. "I've been lucky that I've always liked to exercise and that my body's always been up to the task."

She took a sip of her drink and tried—unsuccessfully—not to make a face.

"Oh dear," said Eloise. "Is it too strong?"

"I'm not much of a drinker, but let me give it another try." Gamely she took another sip, her eyes blinking as if she'd just taken a whiff of ammonia.

"Don't feel you have to finish it. How about some soda or water—or dinner!" She looked at her watch. "Oh my gosh, I'm so sorry, I was going to take you to this great little oyster bar down the—"

"I'm fine staying in," said Velda, not at all a fan of oysters. "And I'm not all that hungry. If you've got some little snack—"

"Snacks I've got!" said Eloise, and gripping the arm of the couch, she struggled to get up.

"No, no, please. Allow me. Just tell me where to look."

Gratefulness spread Eloise's smile wide.

"There's all sorts of stuff in the fridge. Dishes in the cupboard to the left of the stove. Silverware in the drawer by the sink. Crackers are in the pantry cabinet."

Finding an enameled tray propped near the toaster, Velda loaded it with a can of bubbly water, a jar of pepper jelly, and a plate filled with sausage, cheeses, sliced apples, and crackers and set it down on the coffee table.

"What a host I am, huh? Making my guest do all the work." Eloise surveyed the tray. "Very artful, by the way. I like how you surrounded the cheeses with sausage and apple slices, like a moat surrounding a castle."

"That's what I was going for," lied Velda, and they laughed.

"This reminds me of the kind of stuff we had in our dorm rooms," said Eloise, topping a wheat cracker with a slice of gouda. "When we used to eat saltines and that stuff in a can, that—"

"SPAM. I remember I couldn't believe you'd never had SPAM. I can't believe you can't even remember what it's called now—it's world famous!"

"You used to fry it up on a little hot plate. And then spread orange marmalade on it."

"Sweet and savory. I was ahead of my time."

The two women stared at one another: Velda, slim and wiry, her short hair like a white cap on her head; Eloise, large and soft, her iron-gray hair poking out of a drugstore scrunchy.

Eloise put down the cheese knife and sank back into the couch cushions.

"Tell me everything."

"That's exactly what I was going to say to you."

Eloise, like Velda, had married, but for a much shorter time—a year and a half—to a man who owned a heating-and-plumbing company.

"I was sure I'd always marry a doctor, a lawyer, someone who was . . . you know, a professional. The kind of man we college girls were supposed to marry." She shook her head. "I was in Philly for a couple years—remember I got that job as a social worker right after graduation—and the third winter I was there, Blake came to fix my boiler, and he was so nice, so courtly, so *non*condescending. He relit the pilot light and showed me how to bleed the upstairs radiators, and when he asked me if I wanted to have a drink sometime, I said, 'Sure.'"

Eloise spread a mound of pepper jelly on a cracker.

"Well, we eventually got married, but it didn't take long for us to realize that it just wasn't working."

In between bites of food, she explained that it was an amicable split—there were no children to consider, no real property to split, although Blake presented her with the keys to a used Chevy Impala.

"'For your escape,' he told me, which honest to gosh, Velda, made me think I should call off the divorce. Such a nice gesture, and one that showed me he really did understand me. He was a good man. Anyway, I quit my job and drove north and wound up living on a commune in New Hampshire for four years."

"You lived on a commune?"

Taking a sip of her drink, Eloise nodded.

"It was right when communes were booming in the late '60s, and I don't remember how I'd heard of it, but I did. And for those four years, it was great. I learned how to garden, how to cook, how to get along with people who didn't believe in deodorant." Here Eloise smiled. "But mostly, I learned that it was okay to be myself . . . to be a lesbian."

Hearing the word that scared, confused, and excited her, Velda couldn't help her quick intake of breath.

"You learned that all those years ago?"

The years had bracketed Eloise's smile with fine lines, but age didn't diminish its warmth or beauty.

"Well, I liked girls since I was a girl, but I was always trying to convince myself otherwise. Except when I couldn't—like when I was with you."

Velda took a swig of bubbly water, which took its time going down her throat.

"And it's true, a lot of people go through periods of experimentation, but I was never—and let me tell you, I tried!—satisfied when I experimented with men. I mean, to go so far as getting married . . . well, it wasn't fair to Blake or me. It was at Agape—the commune—that I really allowed myself to fall in love. Her name was Alice."

Now Velda reclaimed her barely touched martini and, taste be damned, took a big swallow.

"I was with Alice for twelve years, until she left me for another woman—and I thank God that she did, because a year later, Cath came into my life. The smartest—she taught chemistry at MIT!—most wonderful, lovely woman, who played the piccolo! I'd never met anyone who played the piccolo!" She gestured around the room. "Cath's the one who brought all the animals into the house. And oh, she loved hosting dinner parties—not only was she a great cook, but she'd always make up these really fun 'get to know one another' games to play. All strangers left as friends at our house." Eloise's voice faded, and when she spoke again, it was almost a whisper. "We were together for almost forty years."

After a long moment, she offered a "What are you going to do?" shrug.

"Of course, you know what it's like to be widowed. So tell me about Melvin."

"Mervin," said Velda. "And . . . well, he was the assistant principal at the first school I got hired at—"

"Oh, so you did use your teaching degree!"

Both women had fantasized about lives as artists, but practicality chose their majors.

"Not much. Mostly I just subbed." She shrugged, even though she wasn't sure why. "Anyway, after we got married, he was offered a position as a high school principal in a town south of the Twin Cities."

Her pause was long enough for Eloise to prompt, "And? You told me what he did, now tell me what he was like."

Either her drink had lost some of its bite or Velda didn't notice it as much, and she took another healthy sip.

"Oh, he was . . . very well respected. Knew what he wanted. One year he won 'Nicollet County Principal of the Year'!"

Velda shook the ice in her glass.

"He was a good provider . . ."

Eloise tilted her head, studying her. Nervous under her gaze, Velda rose, offering to refresh their drinks.

Following the host's instructions, the guest poured, mixed, and served.

"You're lucky," said Eloise, nodding her approval after her first sip. "I always wanted kids. You said on the phone that you had grandkids too?"

"My son, Wayne, has a boy. Pam married an older man and has two grown stepdaughters nearly her age. But I don't get to see them as much as I'd like—Wayne's in Montana and Pam lives in Hawaii—"

"Hawaii! Please tell me you at least spend your winters there."

Velda shook her head, embarrassed by the rise of tears in her eyes.

"I love my kids, but . . . we seem to get along better when we're not together." Not able to look at Eloise, she stared at the tray of half-eaten food on the coffee table. "I can't believe I told you that. I don't know that I've told anyone that."

"Oh, Velda," said Eloise, taking her friend's hand. "It's nothing to be ashamed of. A lot of people have complicated relationships with their children."

"When they were young, I was so invested in their lives! Because Merv had summers off, we'd take these long educational vacations, and during the school year, I was a Brownie leader, a Cub Scout Den Mother, Sunday school teacher, chairman of booster committees, room mother, president of the PTA, etc., etc. When I look back, I was just so busy! So busy making sure everyone would think I was such a wonderful mother!"

"Well, what about—"

"My friend Edie? Her daughter lives in England but the two of them are as close as can be, always emailing, Face-Skyping or whatever you call it, really in each other's lives, you know? And my friend Marlys, her sons and daughters-in-law are always calling her, and I can't believe the relationship she has with her granddaughter—they tell each other everything! Amelia—she's the granddaughter—she's even helping our church's erotica project!"

"What?" said Eloise, startled.

After Velda had told her about All Souls' rickety financial status and their idea to put out a "totally different kind of recipe book," Eloise leaned back and laughed, slapping one of her sore knees.

"What's wrong?" she said, noticing that not only was Velda not laughing with her but was fairly grim faced.

"Don't you see, thinking about the book—thinking what I might add to it—is why I'm here! Because the first thing I thought of when I thought of erotica was you and me!"

"Oh, Velda," said Eloise after a moment, "that's one of the nicest things anyone's ever said to me." She patted the couch cushion. "Scoot on over here."

Velda scooted and Eloise put her arm around her shoulder, drawing her near.

"Would it be all right if I kissed you?"

Her words were like the wave a water-skier gives to the boat's driver: *go!* Velda closed her eyes, trying not to let her disappointment show when she felt Eloise's lips on her cheek and not on her lips.

But why, she thought, *why try to hide my disappointment? Aren't I trying not to hide my feelings anymore?*

She opened her eyes. Eloise's face was just inches from hers.

"Is that all you've got?" she said.

Eloise laughed.

"That's what I always liked about you, Velda, your ability to ask for—no, demand—what you wanted."

"Are you kidding me? I feel like I haven't known what I've wanted for decades."

Velda sagged under the melodrama and the truth of her words.

"It's only since Merv died that I've felt I've been gradually coming back to myself, and then . . . seeing you. Because you always made me feel, well, like the real Velda." She reached for her glass, then shook it, the lopsided, melting ice cubes jittering inside. Her chest rose and fell in a deep sigh, and when she spoke again, her voice was a whisper, as if she didn't quite want to be heard.

"But you don't want to *really* kiss me, do you?"

Eloise patted her hand.

"Since Cath . . . well, I don't know if I'm ready for anything more after Cath."

"I appreciate your honesty." Velda rattled her glass again. "Can't say that I *like* it, but I appreciate it."

"And I appreciate you, Velda, and I'm thrilled we're back in each other's lives. And who knows? With more time . . ."

Velda didn't speak, but her hopeful expression did, and Eloise rewarded it with another quick little kiss—a peck—on the cheek.

If P is for Peck, thought Velda, *I'll take it.*

15

"I sure miss Johnny Carson," said Roger. "With his show, you used to feel like you were at a party you wanted to be at. With these shows, it's like you're at a party you don't want to be at."

Marlys, always a multitasker, looked up from her needlepoint kit. "That's because we're getting old, Roger."

"Ha! We're not getting old, we *are* old." Roger glared at the television. "But having a lip-synching contest with your guest? That's not entertaining—that's stupid."

"You laughed when Johnny Carson did stupid things."

"But he did stupid things funny."

Watching late-night television was a ritual they had shared since the kids were toddlers, when the evenings passed in a flurry of chaos, occasionally organized, but most often not. They had three boys, and Jim was only thirteen months old when his brother Peter was born, who was fifteen months when Eric came along. It was a marvel to Marlys that she'd stayed as sane as she had. Roger was a loving father, but like most fathers at the time, he was gone all day working (she wouldn't return to nursing until the boys were all in school). When he came home after a day of getting his insurance company off the ground, he was frazzled for different reasons, and by the time supper was eaten/uneaten/flung/spilled, baths taken (one tub, three boys, lots of splashing/crying/whining), and bedtime's goal of sleep successfully achieved, he and Marlys would collapse on the couch in front of the TV.

Leonard Amundsen, Roger's best friend at the University of Nevada, was from Kittleson, and having visited the small town during a winter and summer break, Roger had been convinced it was the place for him.

"It's so white in the winter, Marlys!" he'd told his fiancée in his campaign to move to Minnesota, "and so green in the summer! We don't always want to stay in the desert, do we?"

Marlys knew of no other clime but Vegas's hot, arid one, but if Roger had wanted to go to an uncharted Java Sea island during monsoon season, Marlys would've applied for a passport and packed a raincoat.

For the first three years, Leonard's wife, Sheree, had taken Marlys under her generous wing, introducing her to her friends, most of whom went to All Souls.

"I don't know how religious you are," she had said, "but it really doesn't matter—All Souls will take you as you are."

Neither Marlys nor Roger had been raised in a church, but far from home they'd found a welcoming community in the old brick building, a community that lost a member when Leonard abruptly left town.

"He's never coming back," wailed Sheree, showing Marlys the note he'd left her, in which he stated he'd fallen head over heels in love with a woman he'd met on a sales trip to Tampa.

Plus she's pregnant!!! he'd written, which was particularly harsh, as Sheree had struggled with infertility and more than anything had wanted to be a mother like Marlys, whose second baby's due date was just weeks away.

"A gold bar for your thoughts," said Roger now, their little joke acknowledging the value of each other's musings.

"Oh," said Marlys, who'd been staring at the lip-synched contest between the TV host and the breakout star of an action movie Marlys had never heard of. "I was just . . . who do you think that actress looks like?"

Roger claimed his sight was so good because carrots were good for the eyes, and he was a carrottop (or had been—what remained of his hair had turned a rosy gray). Just seventy, he was one of the rare people who didn't need glasses, even for reading, although he did narrow his eyes when focusing in.

He squinted at the television for such a long time that Marlys, a little irked, thinking he hadn't been listening to her, was about to repeat the question, when he said, "Why, she looks like Sheree Amundsen."

"That's just what I thought!" said Marlys, setting down her needlework and shifting the lever of her recliner (several years ago, they had replaced the TV-room couch with twin leather recliners, which she had to admit made up in comfort what they lacked in looks).

"Sheree Amundsen," said Roger. "I wonder whatever happened to her."

"I wish I knew," said Marlys, feeling bad that she didn't. The two women had kept in touch after Sheree left Kittleson and moved to Petoskey, Michigan, to be close to her family, but their letters faded in frequency, replaced by an annual Christmas card exchange that lasted nearly a decade. Sheree had landed in Detroit and married a General Motors executive, but the last Marlys had heard . . . well, she couldn't remember the last she'd heard.

"Do you ever wonder what happened to Leonard?"

"I don't have to wonder—he posts regularly on our alumni Facebook page."

"He does? Why didn't you tell me that?"

"Because I'm not really interested in what he has to say?" he said, his voice a question. "Because he's a guy I thought I really knew—and admired—but then he turned out to be a guy I didn't really know and sure as hell don't admire."

"Because of what he did to Sheree?"

"Because of that, sure." Roger took the remote off the small table in between the recliners and, after turning the TV and its lip-synching contest off, he turned to face Marlys. "Do you know that Leonard's on his fourth marriage?"

"No."

"He plasters up these pictures of his new wife—she's only forty-two, for God's sake! He gets a lot of comments, like, 'Atta boy!' and 'Way to go, Len!' but I—" Roger shook his head. "—I never leave a comment. I'm just sort of disgusted by it. He's like Charlie Kendrick, you know—gotta keep up with the new model."

"Well," said Marlys, "Charlie's got a car dealership, after all. It's not like he's hurting anyone when he gets a new car every year."

"That's true. Guess I'm jealous of his new Acura."

"But not of Leonard's new models?"

"Ha! I feel sorry that he never landed in that soft place of love."

They stared at one another.

"Did you just say, 'landed in that soft place of love'?"

Roger nodded, more a tenor than baritone giggle escaping out of him.

"I have no idea where that came from."

"Neither do I," said Marlys, reaching for his hand. "But I sure liked it."

Her phone rang, that is to say it played the first bar of Lionel Richie's "Lady," and looking at its screen, Marlys picked it up and with worry in her voice said, "Amelia? Are you all right?"

Marlys had pressed "speaker" so her granddaughter's voice was loud enough for Roger to hear.

"Sure, Grandma, why?"

"Well, it's so late!"

"Oh, sorry. But I knew you'd be up."

That was true—everyone in her family knew she and Roger were night owls who usually didn't get under the covers until after midnight.

"We are. So to what do I owe the honor of your phone call?"

"First of all, I want to know how the Halloween party went and if you were able to score any of that pumpkin popcorn for me?"

"We had a great turnout, and yes, I've got a bag for you."

"Oh, good—thanks. Second of all, I just wanted to tell you that I've got another letter for your erotica book! I was talking to my friend—"

Fumbling with her phone, Marlys turned off the speaker, and scrambling off her chair, she said weakly, "Sheesh."

Her slippers nearly raised sparks on the carpet as she hightailed it into the kitchen, where she felt free to hiss, "Amelia! Your grandfather was sitting right there next to me! He doesn't know anything about the erotica—"

Her stomach didn't exactly lurch, but there was some movement in her lower torso when she saw Roger, arms crossed, standing in the door's threshold.

"Amelia, listen, I really can't talk now—just email anything you or your friend have written. Love you, and see you for our Bake Day on Saturday, okay?"

Seeing her husband with that particular look on his face, the word her grandkids used when caught doing something they shouldn't be doing came into her head: *busted*. But not wanting to be busted, she turned to face the sink and pretended to do business there, even though there were no dishes in the rack, nothing to wash or rinse. Even so, she ran the water, just because turning on the faucet gave her something to do.

"What exactly," said Roger after a moment, his tone light, if confused, "is your 'erotica book'?"

Marlys looked out the window above the sink, seeing only a square of blackness and her flummoxed reflection in it. Still, she stared, hoping that like on a teleprompter, the answer would be spelled out for her.

When it was not, she turned around and smiled sweetly, before patting with her fist an exaggerated yawn.

"Whew, I'm beat. Think I'll turn in."

"Marlys," said Roger, his arms still a band across his chest. "I asked you a question. What did Amelia mean by your 'erotica book'?"

"So that's it," said Marlys finally, after telling her husband everything, from the Naomi Circle's discouragement after attending the Prince of Peace luncheon and seeing their Pulitzer Prize–worthy cookbook to their brainstorming about how to save All Souls and finally deciding to write about erotica.

"So Finn and Charlie know about this too?" said Roger, shaking his head. "I can't believe Finn didn't tell me—we ran the 'Treat Tree' game at the party tonight and he didn't say a word."

"I told Edie to tell him not to," said Marlys.

"Why?"

"Because we don't really know if it's going to happen. If it even could happen!" Marlys looked at her wedding ring, whose little chip of a diamond Roger had replaced with a much bigger stone for their tenth anniversary. "And . . . because I was embarrassed. I mean of course I was planning on telling you at some point, but I just thought you'd think the idea was either a joke . . . or a really bad joke."

They were both back in their recliners, but they were sitting on them rather than reclining, the seriousness of their discussion demanding a more alert posture.

"Why," said Roger, "because we don't have sex anymore?"

Feeling flushed, Marlys wished more than anything she'd let Amelia's call go to voice mail.

After a long moment, she said, "I'm sorry that we don't have sex anymore. But didn't we agree it was okay? I mean it being so painful for me, and you . . . well, you having a problem?"

Roger's smile was rueful. "They're not shy about saying it on TV, Marlys, so surely you can say it: erectile dysfunction. And yes, we did sort of agree that it was okay."

Nodding, Marlys said, "If God wanted older people to keep having sex, He would have kept our parts well oiled and in working order."

There remained a trace of ruefulness in Roger's laugh.

"They do say God works in mysterious ways . . ."

"But think about it, Roger—it's not as if we're not still physical. We hug and kiss all the time and neither of us can go to sleep unless we're spooning."

"All true. But I . . . don't you miss it?"

Marlys stared at the blank TV screen for a long moment. "Do you?"

"I think I'm supposed to, but in all honesty . . . not so much."

"Oh, honey, that's just how I feel! I mean, when we were young and . . . *active*, I loved it. I wanted you all the time! And I still want you, but not that way. I feel like I ran that race . . . and now I just want to stroll."

Roger chuckled.

"We're lucky, I guess, in that we're so compatible."

"Oh, I agree!"

"It's just the idea of people reading about our sex life, or lack thereof?" Roger's bottom lip bunched up. "Can't say that I'm a fan of that at all."

"You can read everything I write," she said, reaching for his hand. "And if you don't like something, I'll take it out."

"I'm not trying to be a jerk, I—"

"You couldn't be a jerk if you tried. It's not in your nature."

"It's just that this book . . . well, what are you going to write about if we're not exactly setting the bedroom on fire anymore?"

"Well, it's not as if I've forgotten all those fires we set."

"There were some pretty big blazes," said Roger with a smile, and on an invisible cue, they shifted the levers of their chairs and reclined.

For a long time, they sat back in cushioned leathery comfort, and when Marlys heard Roger's slight, guttural snore, she was about to nudge him and tell him it was time to hit the hay, but she was too content. Instead, she took the remote and turned on the TV, scrolling through dozens of channels with the mute button on.

"Oh, sorry, honey," she said, when Roger snorted awake.

"I was just dozing." Looking at the television screen, he asked, "What are you watching—*Planet of the Apes*?"

Pressing the guide button, words appeared at the top of the screen, and in the understanding and synchronicity that defined their marriage, they read the movie's title aloud.

"That's weird," said Roger. "It's like the TV was eavesdropping on us."

"Q is for Quest for Fire," said Marlys, with a laugh. "All kinds of fire."

~

When Bunny first met the Naomis and the usual information about family and children was exchanged, she explained that while she and her husband would have welcomed children, children were not to be.

Both had been noncommittal about being parents, although after they stopped using contraceptives and no pregnancies occurred, Bunny asked Burton if they should go to the doctor and check out what may be their problem.

"Do you think there's a problem?" Burton had asked.

"Not really. I just want to make sure you're still okay with just us as a family."

"I am if you are, although it's a shame not to pass down our good-looking genes."

Nodding somberly, Bunny said, "Probably be too much beauty for the world to handle anyway."

She had majored in math because she was good at it but had no particular career plans (Bunny doubted she would teach, having no patience for people who couldn't grasp that which she considered easy; she had to censor her impulse to shout every time Barbie Newsom, who sat next to her in sixth grade, asked her to again explain the difference between greater and less than signs). After their marriage, she put her math skills to work, serving as bookkeeper for the tailor shop, and it was Burton's wizardry with a needle and thread and hers with a pen and ledger (and later a computer) along with their mutual love of adventure that enabled them to work, live, and flourish in several American cities. Clients from all continents (except Antarctica) had suggested/implored Burton to open a shop in Rome, Bogotá, Lagos, Tokyo, and Sydney, but the couple was satisfied to travel abroad to silk and fabric factories, to trade and fashion shows, while keeping their home base at various times in Houston, Denver, or San Francisco.

They had been in New York for nearly ten years, and although Burton loved his Gramercy Park shop and its clients, at sixty he was beginning to think he might prefer to set his treadle to a slower speed, and it was at that time that Bunny's Uncle Maynard's estate was settled.

"How'd you like to move to Kittleson, Minnesota?" she asked her husband.

They were sitting on their small apartment terrace, and after Burton read the letter Bunny handed him, he stared for a long time at the East River.

"I don't know if we could live in a small town," he said finally.

"We could give it a try," said Bunny with a shrug. "I visited Kittleson a lot when I was a kid, and it *is* pretty. Lots of lakes. And you've been trying to figure out how to cut down your client list."

"Cut down," said Burton. "Not obliterate."

Four months later, after having been feted at dinner and cocktail parties thrown by grateful, well-dressed Wall Street brokers and Broadway impresarios, they had closed up shop on Irving Place and moved into the one they'd inherited on First Avenue, former home of Maynard's Lamps and Blinds.

"Burton," said Bunny now to her husband, reposed on his bed. "Burton, listen to this."

Cleaning out her file cabinet earlier that day, she had come across a bundle of cards he had given her over the years and brought them to "share" with her husband. Holding a birthday card in front of his face, she read its handwritten message.

"Fifty! You age better than wine, honey, better than cheese. Let's not even call it aging, let's call it shimmering, glowing, coming into your glorious—"

"Aww, that's pretty."

Startled, Bunny turned around in her chair to face the person looming in the doorway.

"I guess you didn't hear me knocking," said the attendant. Her languid drawl teased her vowels and consonants. "But the instructions are that Mr. B. is to be taken to the matinee movie."

Despite Burton's inability to participate in the many activities the facility offered, Bunny had requested that he be included in as many as possible, believing that it was good for him to be out among people playing bingo, making crafts, and watching the old movies that played every Tuesday.

"It's matinee time already?" said Bunny. Glancing at her watch and seeing that its digital numbers confirmed the woman's pronouncement, she added, "Whew! Time flies when you're sifting through the past."

"Mr. B. wrote those?" asked the attendant, coming into the room and standing at the foot of Burton's bed.

Gathering up the cards, Bunny nodded, not wanting to talk further.

"You are a soulful man, aren't you, Mr. B.?"

Touched by the attendant's accurate assessment of her husband, Bunny was also aggrieved by her intrusion.

"You're new here, aren't you?"

The big woman's smile was so broad, so full of gleaming white teeth that Bunny felt compelled to compliment it.

"Thank you," said the woman, with a slight bow. "And that white streak in your hair rocks."

"It's been like this since my early forties," said Bunny, her hand smoothing the side of her head. "I always wanted to color it, but Burton liked it."

She flushed, remembering how in his Pepé Le Pew accent, he'd call her "my sexy little skunk."

"And yes," said the aide. "I am new. New to your state and new to Belle Vista."

"Belle Vista, indeed," Bunny muttered.

Burton's window faced the parking lot, hardly a beautiful view, offering nothing more scenic than the circular driveway that curved into a wide, unimaginatively landscaped lawn.

"Shall we get you in your wheelchair and head down to the cinema?" said the attendant, wiggling one of Burton's slippered feet. "Today we are showing *Breakfast at Tiffany's*."

"Audrey Hepburn, Burton! She's one of your favorites, remember?"

There was no indication from her husband that he did.

"Listen, uh . . . ," said Bunny.

"Jolie," said the attendant, flicking several long beaded braids aside to reveal her name tag.

"Ahh. *Pretty*."

"That's right," said the woman, flicking her hair again and striking a pose. "Although Mr. B. calls me 'Très Jolie.'"

Giving credit to the attendant's audaciousness, Bunny smiled and said, "If he could talk, I'm sure he would."

"So is he going to the matinee? I already punched out, but I told Kay I'd bring him down," said Jolie, bending to pick up a card from the floor.

Bunny half rose from her chair to snatch it away.

"Sorry," she said, her face reddening. "It's just that—"

Sitting heavily back in her chair, she burst into tears, and the attendant retrieved the chair from the desk Burton never sat at and situated herself near Bunny, murmuring softly and patting the crying woman's shoulder.

"Sheesh," said Bunny finally, wiping her eyes with a tissue Jolie handed her. "I'm usually not so . . . expressive."

"It can't be easy . . . when your beloved closes down."

"No, it's not. And that's it *exactly*. Burton closed down, and I still need him to be open."

"How about if I make you some tea?" asked Jolie, to which Bunny invited the attendant to make herself a cup as well. The electric kettle was plugged in, and, as the strips of gray winter sky visible between the vertical window slats gradually darkened, lamps were turned on and Bunny and Jolie took turns reading aloud all the poetry, the claims of love Burton had written in those many cards.

Scrawled inside a birthday card were the words, *"Shall I compare thee to a summer's day?" Why not plagiarize Shakespeare? Because who but Shakespeare could so exactly, so precisely, with such long sighs, nods, and wonderment capture who my Bunny is? (And truth be told—if I'm thinking seasonally, you'd be autumn, Bun—golden days with red maple leaves and orange oaks and full blue skies, but wild too with gusty winds and bright cold nights, with silhouettes of migrating birds flitting across a full moon.)*

"Bunny is my honey," Jolie read from a Valentine's card, *"Oh I'm a lucky guy / to have this honey as my Bunny / What say we both get high?"*

Chuckling at the expression on Jolie's face, Bunny told her that occasionally she and Burton had enjoyed a toke or two, and that after smoking the rolled joint that had been tucked inside that particular card, they had devoured the box of Fanny Farmer chocolates Burton had also given her.

When they had read and commented on all the cards and eaten the vending machine packet of shortbread cookies Jolie retrieved from her smock pocket, Bunny said that okay, Jolie knew about her love life, now she should tell Bunny about hers, if she had one.

"I do," said Jolie with a solid nod. "And it's a good one. Hiram is—"

"Hiram? Is that still a name?"

"It is, obviously," said Jolie, batting her lashes as if trying to dislodge grit from her eyes. "It's a name that's been in his family for generations."

"Sorry, that was rude of me. It's just so . . . old fashioned."

"That it is, and so is Hiram. Now do you want to hear about him or not?"

Bunny avowed that she did, and after listening to the woman extol the qualities of this patient, kind, and accepting man, Bunny said that he sounded a lot like Burton.

"Oh, but my Hiram isn't a poet," she said, gesturing toward the stack of cards they'd read. "At least not with words. He does make me things, though. He's a master carpenter." Jolie's glimmery-white smile was wide. "That's why we came up here from Shreveport—he got a job at Selmer's Fine Furniture—"

"Selmer's? Oh, they make beautiful stuff."

Jolie nodded. "Hiram was a freelancer, and they saw some of his pieces online. Anyway, he makes more money now, and it helps pay for school—I'm finishing my nursing degree." She took a sip of her tea. "Plus I can get better treatment."

Worry puckered Bunny's forehead, and she was just about to ask if Jolie was all right when a realization dawned on her.

Taking in the woman's height, the span of her shoulders, her wide jaw and thick neck, Bunny said quietly, "Are you transitioning?"

There was a quiet clatter of Jolie's braids as her head bobbed up and down.

"Yes, although I prefer the word transforming." She made a face. "I've been taking shots up the yin-yang."

When Bunny blurted out a laugh, Jolie added, "Not literally, of course."

"I only asked because I just read an article in the paper . . . I never would have thought, I mean, I've never met someone going through a transition, or maybe I have and just didn't know it, but I don't mean to—"

Jolie waved her hand.

"It's a relief to talk about it. About who I am. Who I really am. No one in my family talks to me anymore—everyone *prays* for me, but no one talks to me—and Hiram, well, he fell in love with me when to the world I was a man, but he saw me first and foremost as a *person*."

Bunny opened her mouth to ask a question, but closed it again, not exactly sure what her question was.

"To have someone in your corner," said Jolie, studying one of her scarlet fingernails, "well, he's not just in my corner—he *guards* my corner—it's really something."

"Amen," said Bunny and wanting to underscore her agreement with something tangible, she dug in her purse. Finding a nearly empty roll of candy, she held it out to Jolie.

"Life Saver?"

Looking derisively at the battered roll of foil, Jolie said, "Lint Saver's more like it."

Bunny laughed and, tossing the stub of candy in the wastebasket, said, "Don't say I didn't try to bring anything to the party."

More time passed, and they were finishing their second cup of tea when another attendant poked her head in the doorway, expressing surprise to see Jolie.

"I thought you punched out."

"I did. I'm just chatting with my friend here and Mr. B."

"Oh." The attendant looked puzzled, as if trying to imagine mixing business with pleasure. "Anyhow. It's dinnertime. I gotta get Burton to the dining room."

Bunny looked to her husband, reclining in bed, eyes open but seeing who knew what.

"I should get moving too," said Jolie, standing, smoothing her smock with her big hands. "Hiram's making his famous jambalaya."

As the other attendant went to the bed and began hefting Burton up and into a wheelchair, Jolie asked Bunny, "You hungry?"

Bunny was and had to force herself not to slurp up the delicious spicy shrimp, sausage, and rice dish.

"Would you like a bigger spoon?" Jolie teased.

"Excuse her bad manners," Hiram said to Bunny. "I'm thrilled to witness your appreciation."

It was a small but lively dinner party, and laughter and conversation ricocheted around the finely crafted table the chef had built.

Hiram was shorter than Jolie by about five inches, and probably weighed fifty pounds less, but the inequality of their size did not reflect the equality of their relationship, which was one of back-and-forth teasing and of tooting the other's horn, as if it were a privilege to play that particular instrument.

"Your husband's a lucky man," Hiram said to Bunny at one point, "because there's nobody better with people who've been done in by age and its particular infirmities than my Jolie." He paused for a moment, before adding, "I know he's not lucky in some respects . . . but you know what I mean."

Bunny nodded; she did.

"So your husband . . ."

"Burton," prompted Jolie.

"So Burton," said Hiram. "How long has he been—"

"The way he is?" said Bunny, and her cheeks puffed out with air as she let loose a sigh. "About four years ago, he started forgetting things. It seemed pretty innocuous at first—you know, who doesn't forget their keys?—then he started getting lost coming home from the shop, and would ask me the same question ten seconds after I'd answered it . . . and then"—she took a sip of sweet tea—"and then—bam! In no time at all, he just started disappearing. Both physically and mentally."

The fog of that sad news settled on the trio for a while.

"Tell us about the Burton we didn't get to know," said Jolie finally, her voice gentle. "How did you two meet?"

Bunny hadn't told the story in a long time, and it was a pleasure to do so, especially for such a rapt audience.

"LSD!" said Jolie. "You were a wild thing!"

"Sometimes I think you baby boomers had all the fun," said Hiram.

"He's a Gen Xer," Jolie said to Bunny, and flicking her braids behind her shoulder with exaggerated insouciance, she added, "I'm a millennial."

Bunny basked in her hosts' attention and interest and told them about the big cities she and Burton had lived in and the awards and honors her husband had won—"*New York* magazine named him 'Tailor of the Year'!"

"Wasn't it hard moving to Kittleson after living in all those glamorous places?" Jolie asked.

"We were ready for a change."

"We were too," said Hiram, as he served them slices of a vanilla sheet cake. "But good Lord, this big a change?"

"We knew it was going to be a lot whiter than back home, but we didn't know it was going to be this *pale*," said Jolie. "Still, you can live among people who look like you and still feel like an outsider."

Hiram nodded.

"While you may have noticed I myself am of the Caucasian persuasion, Bunny, it's still very strange to be surrounded by so many of *my* own persuasion."

"Oh," said Jolie, "you mean gay white men who live with trans Black women?"

"Yes, that's exactly what I mean," said Hiram, with an elaborate eye roll. "Kittleson is absolutely *teeming* with them."

Laughing, Jolie asked if anyone wanted more cake, and Bunny lifted a hand in surrender.

"Everything was absolutely delicious, but I couldn't eat another bite. What I wouldn't mind, though, since I've told you how Burton and I met, is hearing your story."

"Whaddya, a cop?" asked Hiram.

"No, I, I—"

"Just messing with you. And I met my love," he said, "when she was playing football for the University of Louisiana as Jerome—oh, sorry, Jolie."

"My deadname," Jolie explained somberly. "I don't use it and prefer not to hear it anymore."

"Oh," said Bunny, taking in this new information, but not exactly sure how to comment on it, she asked, "So . . . you met at a game?"

"God no," said Hiram. "I hate football. We met in a little diner in Lafayette. We looked across the tables at one another and I knew, that's the one for me."

"I left school after my sophomore year—I wasn't doing the football team or me any favors and, well, we've been together ever since."

"Of course, it hasn't been easy," said Hiram, his smile less merry than wistful. "I am a gay man—the only woman I've ever been attracted to was Miss Bergeron, my first-grade teacher! And while I knew Jer—uh, deadname—was the one for me . . . I haven't always been so sure about Jolie."

"We've done a lot of soul searching. Of course, I've wondered, if it were reversed and he was really Helen instead of Hiram . . ."

"But as far as falling in love at first sight? I believe it, because it happened to me. And I believe, no matter how woo-woo it sounds, that what I first sighted—beyond this very enticing male specimen—was his essence, his soul. Now she's Jolie, but she still has the same soul that I first saw."

"Do souls have genders?" Jolie asked her guest.

"Well, I don't know," said Bunny, startled by the question. "I have to think about that one."

"That's what we find ourselves doing," said Hiram. "Giving things more thought."

"A lot more," said Jolie. "It's such a queer world . . . in so many respects."

It had been an evening Bunny wasn't in a hurry to end, but had to, as she was too old for sleepovers. Hiram and Jolie insisted on walking her to her car, which was parked in the driveway, a mere twenty feet from their front door, and when she got home and dressed for bed, she held her sweater to her face, smelling the dinner spices that lingered in the yarn.

As she climbed under her own bedcovers, faint with the milder scent of laundry detergent, she giggled, still buoyant from an evening of good food, laughter, and bold conversation.

Thinking of letters that would describe the couple, she was finally satisfied with *R*.

R is for Resilient, she thought. *Because whatever shocks and surprises come into your love story, you're resilient enough to bend with them, not break from them.*

16

The Jinxers, an improvisational troupe from the Twin Cities, billed their show as "3/4s Laughs and 1/4 Learning," and after entertaining the audience gathered in the college's newly renovated theater, the houselights went on and an actor named Danny stepped to the microphone and explained the "one-fourth learning" part.

"Even though we make it up as we go," Danny said, "there are rules that make the games work." He smiled and wiggled his eyebrows. "So, anyone willing to come up here and play by those rules?"

Amelia, who was minoring in theater, had invited Axel to the show, and when he stood up, she assumed it was to let her more easily pass by, but he followed her down their row and to the main aisle.

"You're coming too?"

Axel smiled. "He said, 'Anyone willing . . .'"

Their friendship had grown since their rained-out hike, and they attended campus events together, sometimes with Megan and other people and sometimes by themselves. Amelia occasionally found herself fantasizing that they might become something more than pals, but she honored the fact that he had a girlfriend, even if HanneLore was thousands of land and nautical miles away.

Onstage, they joined a dozen other students, almost all of whom Amelia recognized from theater classes. Danny and a troupe member named Melissa gave them some rules—"Don't negate!" "Stay in the moment!"—before leading them in several warm-up exercises. Audience suggestions were then asked for, and those onstage paired up, and scene work began: a postman delivering bad news to an acrobat, two convicts breaking out of jail and into another dimension, a lonely soldier flirting with her commander in chief.

When Melissa indicated that Amelia and Axel should step up, Amelia thrummed with either excitement or nervousness—she wasn't sure which.

"Okay, give me a location," Melissa asked the audience.

Words were shouted out.

"Okay, I heard 'zoo.' Now how about an emotion?"

"Lust!" was the word heard over the others.

Gesturing for Amelia and Axel to sit on stools, Melissa said in a hushed voice, "Good evening, Dr. Melissa Farner here, internationally renowned zoologist and real-life Dr. Dolittle who can not only talk to the animals but get them to talk back. With me here are two sub-Saharan lions—Simba and Nala!"

The audience laughed, recognizing the character names from *The Lion King*.

Amelia clawed the air with her hand, and Axel, stifling a laugh, copied her.

"Simba, Nala, welcome."

A loud *meow* came out of Amelia's mouth.

"Nala, remember," said Melissa. "You don't have to feel shy. I've told these nice people that we talk to each other."

"All right, then," said Amelia in an English accent. "If they won't freak out, neither shall I."

As the audience laughed, Melissa gave a slight nod, pleased with her student.

"And you, Simba, could you remind everyone how you and Nala met?"

Axel growled and, after leaping off his stool, he began crawling across the stage.

"He wants to protect our privacy," explained Amelia. "As King of the Jungle, he gets weary of the constant attention his love life gets."

"I'm sorry," said the "doctor," "but the personal lives of lions who talk is of great interest to the world."

Axel's growl was bigger, and, in answer, Amelia got off her stool and onto all fours.

Pacing in front of each other, growling and meowing, Amelia dipped her head against his shoulder and Axel pretended to lick her ear.

"Oh, dear," said Dr. Farner. "I hope I'm not interrupting anything."

"It's just that I find him so very attractive," said Amelia as they nuzzled like the big cats they were portraying.

"If you could just control yourselves a bit longer," said the doctor as the lions continued their pawing of one another, "I'd like to ask you—"

Axel raised his chest high and, tipping his head back, issued a loud and leonine roar.

Hooting and hollering, the audience broke into applause.

Walking back to their dormitory, Amelia and Axel were giddy, repeating funny lines said, opining on the differences between the scenes performed by the professional troupe and the students, and reliving their own time onstage.

"You were a total pro," said Amelia. "Talk about 'being in the moment'!"

"Yes," said Axel, "I may have to leave behind electrical engineering for a life on the stage."

Amelia laughed and bumped her hip against his.

Their building had an elevator, but because it was only five stories high, they took the stairs, and when Amelia opened the third floor door, she asked, "You want to come in? Cash in that hot chocolate rain check?"

Axel gave her a quick hug.

"*Danke*, but HanneLore will be up, and I want to tell her all about this evening."

On her dorm-room bed, Amelia stared up at the ceiling, wondering what Axel was saying to his girlfriend.

"HanneLore, HanneLore, HanneLore," she said aloud, her voice pinching into a curdled whine. "What's so special about HanneLore?"

The answer was immediate: Axel was what was so special about HanneLore.

Amelia pictured herself and Axel onstage, growling and cuffing one another, and how she'd felt when he'd raised himself up on his "haunches"—and issued that bellowing seductive roar.

She had been a jungle feline, had felt that basic animal instinct of seduction and excitement.

Sleepy, she yawned as she thought, *R is for Roar.*

~

"He should be here any minute," said Mrs. Schell for the third time. For the fourth time, she glared at her watch.

"No problem at all," said Pastor Pete. "I told him I'd stop by sometime late afternoon." In truth, they had agreed to 4:30, a time that had passed twelve minutes ago, according to her own watch, which she hoped she looked at a little less pointedly.

"Sometimes he gets carried away during a lesson," said Mrs. Schell. She shook her head, her blue-beaded chandelier earrings swaying. "If he charged for overtime, he'd make a fortune."

"How many students does he have?"

"Do you mind?" asked Mrs. Schell, reaching into her housecoat and tamping out a cigarette from a pack of Virginia Slims.

Obviously you don't care if I do, thought Mallory, but she shook her head as the woman lit up, inhaled deeply, and set the round cut glass lighter on the kidney-shaped coffee table.

While Tad Schell dressed like the tenor in a 1930s barbershop quartet, his mother had a fondness for the midcentury in decor, as well as in her attire and her habits. (Mallory didn't know anyone who wore housecoats, let alone smoked indoors anymore.)

"So," she said, nodding at the spinet piano in the room's corner, "do you play?"

"Just Tad. He's the only one of my kids who's the least bit musical."

"Oh, I'd say Tad's a lotta bit musical."

Failing to acknowledge Mallory's little joke (but true statement) with even a smile, Mrs. Schell instead squinted one eye, inhaled, and lifting her chin, sent a stream of smoke toward the popcorn ceiling.

"I'm an atheist, you know," she said, leveling her gaze at the young woman.

"Oh. No," said Mallory. "I mean, no, I didn't know. I mean . . . oh."

What she took as Pastor Pete's discomfort brought, finally, a smile to the woman's heavily lipsticked mouth.

"Does that bother you? I just thought you should know, you being a minister after all. Especially if you were here to solicit more money, instead of just apples."

Mallory was one part taken aback, one part offended, and one part amused, and it was the third part on which she decided to focus.

"Actually, I've been looking around, trying to find your purse, but I don't see it."

Mrs. Schell blinked several times, each time revealing the iridescent blue shadow her hooded eyelids hid.

"Of course," continued Mallory, "you can always mail a check later."

Taking another long drag of her cigarette, Mrs. Schell twisted her mouth, directing her exhale sideways, and when there was no more smoke to expel, smiled.

"Tad said you were a good egg," she said, "then again, he likes everyone. He failed to inherit my bullshit sensor."

"And did it go off with me?"

Stubbing out her cigarette, Mrs. Schell chuckled.

"Loud as a siren. The way it goes off every time I'm near anyone of the cloth." She reached for the lighter, flicking it on and off. "So what made you decide to be someone of the cloth anyway?"

"Wow," said Mallory, surprised. She watched the arrow of flame jump up and disappear. "I guess it's because I've always wanted to help people."

"You guess? Don't people who are called to be ministers *know*?"

"I . . . I'll bet many do. Could I trouble you for a glass of water?"

"Oh, all right," said Mrs. Schell, getting up from the armless couch. "Typical church person—ask, ask, ask."

It wasn't her put-out tone of voice that let Mallory know she was teasing, but the chuckle she heard as the woman went into the kitchen.

"First of all, I hate the words *faith journey*," said Mrs. Schell when Mallory had begun to tell her about hers.

"You do tell it like it is, don't you?"

"Wouldn't the world be better if everyone did? And wouldn't it be a better world if clergymen—and women, excuse me—told it like it is, not as they'd like it to be?"

"How do you know they're—we're—not?"

"Because the universe is a big mystery! And no one and no one religion has all the answers to it!"

Considering this, Mallory said, "I think it's the answers to some of the mystery that drew me to the church."

"Aha! *Some* of the mystery! What about all the rest?"

"I don't think we're capable of understanding 'all the rest.'"

"That doesn't sound like a preacher to me," said Mrs. Schell, lighting another cigarette. "Preachers like us to believe that they know all the answers!"

Mallory's index finger wrapped around a sheaf of her hair and began twirling it, but reminding herself it was a girlish habit, she placed her hands on her lap.

"You're right. Some preachers do like us to think they know all the answers. But not most of them. I think most of them are like me, using Scripture as a guide to help us figure out answers."

"Scripture!" sneered Mrs. Schell. "I hate that word! Bible verses my grandmother forced me to memorize!"

"Actually, the word refers to any sacred text."

"Well, that's just it, isn't it? With so many sacred texts, whose are you supposed to follow? Is one better—the real word, the truth, the light?"

After taking a puff off her friend Isla's cigarette in the seventh grade and feeling sickened by a wave of dizziness, Mallory had decided she wouldn't take up smoking—and never had—but at that moment, she had an urge to tap a Virginia Slim out of its pack, light it, and after a lung-filling inhale, blow a smoke ring and watch it waver into nothingness.

Not having a smoky disappearing circle to contemplate, Mallory said, after a long moment, "Believe it or not, I ask myself a lot of the questions you've asked me. But I think I'm too small to know what's the real world, the truth, the light. So I just have to follow what I can understand, what has meaning for me."

"No wonder my Tad likes you. He says you bring a seeker's soul to church."

Tears sprang to Mallory's eyes, but her unshadowed lids blinked them away. Feeling both complimented and busted, she said, "That's my problem. I think most people would like to have a minister who's found something."

Both women turned as a door slammed.

"Mom?" came a voice from the kitchen.

"Mom?" said Tad, entering the living room. "Pastor Pete! I knew that was your car in the driveway . . . Mom, didn't you get my message?"

"What message?"

Tad smiled in apology at Mallory, his palm gliding along the top of his oiled hair.

"The voice—and text—message I left on your phone telling you I was going to be late."

Mrs. Schell patted her housecoat pockets.

"I . . . my phone must be in the kitchen. Or maybe the bathroom."

"I'm so sorry, Pastor Pete," said Tad, touching the floor with his fingertips as the chair he sat down on swiveled in a wide arc. "Makayla, my student? Eleven years old? She's like a Schumann savant—I couldn't leave." Seeing the extent of his mother's hostessing—the aquamarine plastic water glass on the coffee table—he sighed. "I told Mom to tell you to take the apples I'd left in the truck."

"Like I said, Tad, I didn't have my phone with me. And besides, Madame Minister and I were having a very interesting conversation."

Tad was able to summon a weak smile.

"We did!" said Mallory. "The first of which I hope will be many!"

Mrs. Schell patted her salon-styled hair and said, "Anytime. But for now, let's get you those apples. The news is on soon, and I don't want to miss what El Bozo in Washington is doing."

"Nice truck," said Mallory.

"My grandfather's," said Tad of the 1942 red Ford truck on whose side was painted in cursive: *Schell Orchards*. "We park it by the farm's entrance in the summertime."

"Tad's father and I parked it in a lot more places than that," said Mrs. Schell, standing in the doorway leading to the attached garage. "And let me tell you, the back of that truck has held more than apples!"

Rolling his eyes, Tad lifted a box of Honeycrisps and objected when Mallory did the same.

"Oh, please," said Mallory. "It weighs a lot less than Soren."

Mrs. Schell gave a little wave and said, "Nice meeting you—nicer than I would have thought!" before ducking back inside the house.

"Sorry," said Tad as they walked to Mallory's car. "Mom's a little—"

"Tad, really. I had a lovely time with her."

"I'll bet. I just hope she didn't insult you. She's got very strong opinions about religion."

"Yes, she told me," said Mallory with a laugh, and as they shoved the boxes into her back seat, she thanked him for his contribution to the Thanksgiving baskets.

"These'll be a lot more appreciated than cans of jackfruit."

"Huh?" said Tad.

"I just mean that people are going to enjoy apples in their Thanksgiving baskets a lot more than stuff they don't know what to do with."

"Well, it's our pleasure," said Tad, "and I mean *our*. Despite all evidence to the contrary, my mother does have a charitable soul."

Although she paid careful attention as she drove with her brights on down the unfamiliar country road, Mallory's mind wandered, the scent of apples filling her car.

I wonder what Mrs. Schell would think of our erotica book?

She chuckled; surely if Tad had told his mother about it, she would have voiced her opinions to Mallory.

Seeing the railroad crossing sign indicating the train tracks ahead, she thought, *What would she come up with for those?*

She stopped and looked both ways, and driving forward—her wheels bumping over the steel bars—she said aloud, imitating Mrs. Schell's cranky, smoke-husked voice, "Why, 'RR is for Road Romps!' Had plenty of 'em in the back of the old Ford truck we'd drive into the orchard. Nothing like a little romping under a canopy of apple blossoms!"

17

"Kid wouldn't let me go," said Roger, climbing into the front seat of Finn's truck. "He said I'm just like Santy Claus!"

Finn and Charlie nodded; they had watched Roger laughing on the doorstep as the boy clung to his leg. Delivering boxes filled with a frozen turkey, stuffing mix, potatoes, canned and packaged goods, and Schell Orchard apples, they too had been received with exuberance, as well as occasional resentment.

A woman, whose weariness showed in the dark circles under her eyes and sallow complexion, had asked Finn, "Do you get off helping charity cases?"

"No ma'am," Finn said in the dank apartment corridor that smelled of rancid cooking oil and wet tennis shoes. He set the box on the floor, seeing as she didn't seem to want to take it from him. "But I do wish you a happy Thanksgiving."

"*Right*," said the woman.

Like other All Souls service groups, the Men on a Mission's membership had dwindled; from its 1980s peak of forty, there were now only thirteen men who participated and only six who'd been available to deliver the Thanksgiving boxes.

All the Naomis' husbands had been long-standing members and had reported for duty, and so would have Burton, had he not been in the nursing home, and Mervin, had he not been dead. It was the former rather than the latter the other men missed; Burton's sense of humor always lifted up their gatherings, whereas Mervin's imperiousness and know-it-allness dragged them down.

Now as Charlie checked the delivery sheet, he gave them the good news that there was only one more box to drop off and seeing as it was near the Belle Vista, what'd they think about stopping in to see Burton?

"Nice shot," said Roger, and after picking the ball off the floor, he added, "How about you put in a little more effort, Burt?"

The men were stationed at the rarely used ping-pong table in the facility's game room, Charlie and Finn on one end and Roger and Burton on the other. Although he was slouched in a wheelchair, oblivious to the game, his friends had nevertheless placed a paddle in Burton's hand, urging him to make plays.

"Twelve–nine," said Finn before serving.

Over the net the little celluloid ball skipped back and forth, and even without a sentient partner, Roger was a good player, but in the end, he lost by two points.

"Well, you threw that game away," he said to Burton, slamming his paddle on the tabletop in mock outrage.

Finn celebrated his and Charlie's victory by buying a Kit Kat bar from the vending machine, breaking it up into rectangles and distributing them to his friends.

"No?" he said, holding out a piece to the inert Burton. "Fine, more for me."

"That's why you've got a gut, Finn," said Roger, "and Burton doesn't. Now how about we take him for a spin?"

When Charlie first saw the Barones slide into a pew a few rows up from theirs, he whispered to his wife, "Who's that?"

Charlene shrugged, but her sister-in-law Nancy seated next to her, said, "Her name's Bunny—like the rabbit. I met her Thursday in the church parking lot when—"

Her whisper was momentarily drowned out by a heavy-pedaled blast of the organist's prelude.

"And we introduced ourselves," Nancy went on. "She and her husband just moved here, and I was at church to help with the flowers for Magda Wilson's funeral. In fact, Charlene, I expected to see you there as well."

"I . . . uh," began Charlene as Charlie leaned forward, directing his whispered comment to his brother, Rick.

"Sure is a nice suit the guy is wearing."

"He's a tailor of some sort," said Nancy, smug in her knowingness. "He's setting up shop in the lamp store on First Avenue."

"If he made what he's wearing," Rick said, "it sure is good advertising."

Charlie apparently agreed, becoming one of Burton Barone's first customers.

"I've never had a custom-made suit," he had said, standing in front of the three-sided mirror to admire the finished product. "And now I guess I'll have to order a half dozen more."

"My kind of customer," said Burton, brushing unseen lint from his client's shoulder.

That was nearly ten years ago, and while Charlie wouldn't claim that "clothes make the man," he could make a persuasive argument that "clothes make the *sales*man." Inspired by their boss's style, all of Charlie's salespeople had at least one suit made by Burton Barone, and while Charlie's hiring practice was to only bring aboard "people who believed in their product and knew how to sell it," that they looked like "class acts" (a common customer review) only helped sales, as evidenced by the number of repeat customers and "Dealer of the Year" plaques on the walls.

Charlie had joined Men on a Mission at Charlene's suggestion/insistence, but it was only after Burton came on board that he looked forward to their gatherings.

Burton Barone's joie de vivre invigorated the staid men's group, for whom innovation meant adding Christmas swags one year to their wreath sales. It was he who suggested the Halloween party ("Come on, it's about kids and candy and fun," he said when their then pastor had tsked about the holiday's pagan history), and every year put up for bid two beautifully crafted costumes (his princess gowns and faux-fur jungle-animal costumes bringing in the big money). His ideas inaugurated the summer carnival (Burton happily volunteering the group's members to sit in the dunking booth), as well as the pontoon-boat rides.

Charlie missed more than their church and business-affiliated camaraderie; he and Burton had forged a deep friendship, and in their long conversations—often in the back room of the tailor shop—Charlie had come to consider the older man his most trusted, and in some cases, only confidant. While he loved his brother, he didn't share his deepest thoughts and dreams with him—not after Charlie had told Rick he wanted to be a race car driver.

"He didn't just laugh," Charlie had told Burton. "He *howled*. And then he said, 'How far do you think that stupid idea is gonna take you?'"

"It didn't have to take you far," said Burton after a moment, "it only had to take you *fast*."

When Finn asked him what he was smiling about, Charlie said, "I was just thinking about all the things Burton did for Men on a Mission," not adding, *and for me*.

"I'll say," said Roger.

They were now in Burton's room, where an aide had instructed they bring him after their stroll through the facility's hallways. Setting the brakes on the wheelchair, Roger tapped Burton's shoulder.

"Remember that time you and Bunny gave dance lessons? I heard more people say that was the most fun they'd ever had in church."

"Which is why Reverend Wiggans shut it down," said Charlie. "Sure am glad he's not our pastor anymore."

"We could start them up again." No sooner had Finn made the suggestion than he shook his head. "Nah. It wouldn't be the same without Burton—he was such a good teacher. Made me think even my big feet could do something other than trip over themselves."

"I wonder what he'd think of our wives' moneymaking project?" said Charlie and, kneeling so that he was eye level with Burton, he said, "Any thoughts on erotica, Burt?"

"Ya, pick a letter," said Finn. "Like 'B is for Breast.' Or better yet, two letters: '*B*s are for *Big* Breasts.'"

"No," said Charlie, "that wouldn't be double *B*—that'd be double *D*."

"Good one," said Roger as the men laughed. "Give me a letter, Burton!"

Not waiting for him not to answer, Finn said, "How about—" Looking around the room, his eyes landed on the bedside lamp. "How about *L*?"

"Oh, I got this one," said Charlie. "Burt was a dancer, so I bet he'd say 'leg.' As in 'that lovely swooping curve from ankle to calf.'"

"Nice," said Finn. "But for me, the sexiest part of the leg is the thigh."

"You sound like Colonel Sanders," said Roger. "But I'd say 'L is for Lips,' right Burt? Because that's what you kiss with, and it's always the kiss that leads to things, right?"

"Especially a kiss on the thigh," said Finn.

The men were suddenly eighth graders, entertaining one another by their gym lockers.

"So *T* might be for thigh," said Charlie, "but it also could—"

A quick knock and a "Hello?" interrupted the men's juvenile frivolity.

"Time for our Mr. B. to get to the dining room," said the aide, a woman with a pile of dreadlocks cascading from her head.

"Already?" said Finn. "It's only 4:30."

"Dinner's early here," she said, going to Burton's wheelchair.

On the drive home, the men sat thinking their own thoughts, until Roger broke the silence by announcing, "Hey, there's Curtis!"

Responding to the blast of Finn's horn, Curtis Keeler, another Man on a Mission, looked up, his expression aggravated. Carrying a box, he was unable to return the men's wave and instead gave a terse nod.

"And there's Bill's van," said Finn, honking again at the vehicle parked curbside as they drove by it. The man in the driver's seat gave them a sour smile and a vague salute, the old man in the back seat a jaunty wave.

"Poor Evan," said Roger, "getting stuck with those two."

"I can't believe they're not done yet," said Finn.

"Well, Curtis probably includes one of his 'teachable moment' Bible stories with every delivery," said Roger.

"And Bill's probably soliciting votes for his mayoral campaign," said Charlie, and as the men laughed, he added, "If he wins, I'm moving."

~

"RACK-O!" declared Edie, a triumphant look on her face.

"Again?" said Finn, shaking his head as he surveyed his cards lined up in their plastic holder. "All I needed was something below a ten."

Edie gave the smirk of a satisfied winner and asked him his score.

"What does it matter?" he said, upending his card holder. "You won anyway."

Finn wasn't a sore loser, but he was the usual victor at RACK-O, and he knew his wife got a kick out of him pretending to take his loss hard.

"I'd challenge you to one more game," Edie said, tamping the cards into a neat deck, "but look at the time."

"All right," said Finn, with exaggerated weariness. He pushed himself away from the table. "So what are you having?"

"Surprise me."

Finn had become a mixologist after finding an old bar recipe book during one of his and Edie's many outings to garage/estate sales, and the book inspired not just a cocktail hour, but a real enjoyment of one. Neither had ever been much of a drinker; Finn was satisfied with the occasional beer out in the garage when he organized his tackle box or fiddled with a broken clock or toaster, and communion wine had taken up 90 percent of what Edie imbibed (the remaining 10 percent being the Irish coffee she'd treat herself to whenever they went to the Gold Leprechaun for their All-You-Can-Eat-Fish Fridays). For several years now, their dinner had been preceded by a cocktail hour, and Edie regretted that they hadn't initiated the ritual decades earlier, for while her cooking hadn't improved, a predinner drink made it seem as if it had.

"Mmmm," said Edie as Finn set on the table the glass, its rim gritty with sugar. "Good old sidecar."

While they had tried many of the more exotic recipes, it was too much of a bother to keep their liquor cabinet supplied with things like coconut crème or curaçao liqueur, and they had narrowed their focus down to a half dozen or so favorites.

Edie loved the little astringent zip of alcohol she got with a first sip and also the feeling that even at her age, she was doing something naughty—at least something her teetotaling parents would have considered naughty.

"So tell me more about Burton," she said, as Finn settled back in his chair. He had briefly mentioned that the Men on a Mission had stopped by to see their old friend after their basket delivery but hadn't provided many details; once their RACK-O game began, they were serious, nonchatty competitors. "How's he look?"

"Not there," said Finn, shaking his head. "Everything about him just sort of . . . sags."

His mouth pulled down and his eyes widened, an expression Edie had seen countless times before, one her gruff-on-the-outside/gooey-on-the-inside husband made as a usually unsuccessful attempt to stop his tears. She reached for his hand.

"Oh, Finn."

He dabbed under his eyes with his knuckled index fingers and gave a half smile.

"We pretended he was all-in with us—even had him hold a ping-pong paddle. I know Charlie visits him regularly, and I feel bad that I don't . . . but then I think, who are you showing up for? The Burton he used to be? Yourself, because it shows you care? Bunny, so she knows he isn't forgotten?" Finn stopped shaking his head and took a long sip of his drink, which seemed to slake both his thirst and his sadness.

"What?" asked Edie as he smiled.

"We . . . well, we told Burton about your erotica book and came up with some ABCs of our own."

Edie giggled.

"I'll bet you did. What were some of yours?"

"I said, 'B is for Breast,' and then I changed it to 'Two *B*s are for *Big Breasts*.'"

"Well," said Edie, nodding, "you do love my breasts."

Finn scratched his head.

"Yes, but here's the thing. All of us named a body part. Like it's the parts that are erotic." He studied the drink in his hand for a moment, and when he spoke again, his voice was soft. "And if that's true, then how are you going to find me . . . sexy? If my most important part doesn't work anymore?"

Edie got out of her chair and planted herself on his lap, ignoring the small *oof* Finn couldn't contain.

"Don't borrow trouble, Finn. You remember what the doctor said. And besides, you already know the answer." She settled her soft cheek next to his whiskery one. "What I find the most sexy is *you*. Whatever works or doesn't work, you will always be the one to get my motor running."

"Get your motor idling is more like it."

The kitchen timer beeped, and Edie rose to turn it off.

"Darn it," said Finn. "I was about to ask you to meet me in the boudoir."

After punching a few buttons on the oven's control panel, Edie turned and said, "So ask."

"What about supper?"

Hands on her hips, Edie said, "I guess it depends on what you're hungry for. The oven's off. The potpies'll stay warm." Pulling a dish towel off the oven door, she began twirling it as she sauntered across the room.

Following her into the bedroom, Finn said, "So, depending on your appetite, maybe 'S is for Supper,' huh?"

18

All Souls' holiday bazaar was an enormously popular community event, attracting crowds with its unusual combination of artistry and bargains.

"Of course my circle friends and I'll be there!" Nancy said. "Where else are we going to get our stocking stuffers at such ridiculous prices?"

Her tone of voice implied that she and her fellow Prince of Peacers were doing her sister-in-law's church a favor, but the message Charlene got and relayed to her fellow Naomis was: "We've got to charge them more."

"But isn't that why we get such a nice crowd?" Edie asked. "Because of our good deals?"

"I think Charlene's right," said Bunny, who lately, much to her surprise, found herself agreeing more and more with her. "We don't offer reasonable prices—like her sister-in-law said, we offer ridiculous prices. For *good* stuff."

"But what about all the people who come to the bazaar who *aren't* from Prince of Peace?" said Velda. "We're supposed to overcharge them too?"

"It's not about overcharging," said Charlene. "It's about believing in the value of what we're selling. After all, it is a fundraiser."

Marlys nodded.

"Exactly."

Her table, draped in a festive pine cone–printed cloth, was always a crowd favorite, laden as it was with her homemade bars, tarts, cookies, and dessert breads.

"You put the red stickers on these," said Marlys to her granddaughter, indicating a grouping of goodies wrapped in beribboned cellophane bags. To Amelia's friend, she instructed, "And you, Megan, put the green ones on these."

"Five dollars?" said Amelia, peeling off a sticker and pressing it onto a loaf of banana bread. "Didn't we charge three dollars for all bread and tarts last year?"

"We did," said Marlys with a little giggle. "But you know, inflation."

"Way to go!" said Amelia, seeing Megan's six-dollar stickers. "I always thought you undercharged."

"I'd pay ten dollars for these," said Megan, putting a sticker on a bag filled with a baker's dozen gingerbread cookies. "They're so *good*." Another sticker went on a bag containing a dozen blonde brownies. "Then again, so are these."

"See if you can sell everything by the time I get back," said Marlys and, thanking the girls once more for their help, she headed to her post at the door, where she'd volunteered to sell raffle tickets.

In tears, Megan had knocked on Amelia's dorm-room door the day before, claiming that Theo, her most recent crush, had ghosted her, not returning any of her texts.

"And I thought he loved me!" she had wailed, and although Amelia had heard this wail or variations on it before, she offered only sympathy. When Megan suggested they continue their wailing/sympathizing at the local watering hole, even though it was only three in the afternoon, Amelia recruited her to help her grandmother bake, and for hours, they helped Marlys, taking generous samples of whatever came out of the oven.

Full of sugary carbohydrates, Megan had groaned, "I'm definitely going keto tomorrow."

The Kids' Korner featured various games and activities, and Velda ran it briskly, accepting no whines or complaints about the small presents and favors dispensed there. Edie had a booth that sold her hand-sewn doll clothes and baby blankets; Bunny was the purveyor of the "All Souls Bookstore," which offered used books for sale; and Charlene presided over the collections of items subjectively called "Trash & Treasures."

Other tables and booths in the basement undercroft sold handmade jellies and salsas, sachets and soaps, hats and mittens. There was a lot of talent among the parishioners, and George Swenson and Denise Chelmers could always count on selling out their respective hand-carved tree ornaments and miniature oil paintings.

Every "vendor" was responsible for pricing their own items, and the Naomis had made phone calls to all of them, relaying the words of "a certain member of a wealthier church" who thought their own church bazaar prices were *ridiculous*.

"I'll tell you what's ridiculous," huffed Evan Bates. "Their lecture series. Last month I went to hear a missionary who claimed an angel saved her from a stampeding rhino. I paid ten bucks for the privilege, only to see she was speaking for free the next day at the mall bookstore!"

Evan the candy maker had marked up his popular maple sugar leaves and peanut brittle by 30 percent in response.

Church doors were opened at ten, and in no time, the basement was crowded with holiday shoppers toting empty bags they hoped to fill.

"You've got to get one of these, Bev," one woman said to another, holding up a loaf of Marlys's banana–chocolate chip bread.

"Ooh, and I do like snickerdoodles," said Bev, taking the bag of cookies and handing Amelia a twenty with her other hand.

"Oh no, you pay for everything at the door, when you're all done shopping."

"Might as well load it up then," said Bev, adding two pecan-pie tarts to her tote.

The few complaints about "higher prices" came from, of course, Charlene's sister-in-law.

"Seven dollars?" she said, lifting a lamp to see the price marked on its base.

"Oh, gee, Nancy," said Charlene, "That's *seventeen*. See the one next to the seven?"

That the vintage Leviton lamp was a steal at seventeen dollars mattered not to Nancy, who, failing to find the usual "ridiculous" prices, was getting fed up.

"I'll take it for twelve," said Nancy, reaching for the lamp.

"Sorry," said Charlene, although there was no apology in her voice. "Price is as marked."

Near the 3:00 p.m. close of the bazaar, the crowds had thinned out and Godfrey was showing Pastor Pete the colorfully illustrated book he'd scored for a dollar.

"Stan Lee's memoir! Guy created the best comics ever!"

Pastor Pete was reaching into her tote for her show-and-tell item—a knitted hat with bear-cub ears she'd gotten for Soren—when a loud, irritated voice rose up.

"Did I contribute to *what*?"

"Excuse me," said Pastor Pete, heading toward the nearby booth to investigate.

"Good, here's the one who can clear this up," said Bill Hall.

The minister looked to Marlys, who, standing behind the table, was slowly shaking her head.

"So please," said Bill, "please tell us that this young woman must be joking."

"Joking about what?" asked Pastor Pete, forcing herself not to copy Mr. Hall in spitting out every single word.

"About the sex book you guys are writing!" said a young woman whom Pastor Pete had never met and toward whom she felt an immediate uncharitable dislike.

"Hi, Pastor Pete. I'm Amelia, Marlys's granddaughter?" said the other young woman, extending her hand. "We've met a couple times? Last time at the Father-Daughter banquet when I went with my grandpa? And this is my friend, Megan, who's helping me and my grandma out and anyway, I think it's a big misunderstanding and—"

"It's no misunderstanding," said Megan, gesturing toward Bill. "When he asked how sales were going, Amelia said, 'Great'—and by the way, they are, we're just about sold out of everything—and I asked him if he went to All Souls, and when he said he did, I said, 'Well, I bet your erotica book is what's going to bring in the big bucks,' and then I asked if he had contributed anything to it."

Marlys and Amelia looked stricken. Bill's wife, Diane, looked bemused. Bill did not.

"What I want to know from you, our *church leader*," he said, "is what on earth is this erotica book, and why on earth would I want to contribute to such a thing?"

Pastor Pete laughed, or tried to—the sound coming out of her throat sounding more like a monkey gargling.

"Well," she said, finally, hoping her face didn't look as flushed as it felt, "in talking about fundraising, some of us came up with an idea to—"

"—to write a book about *pornography*?"

"Bill, dear, we're going to miss our flight," said Diane Hall, and turning to Pastor Pete, she reminded her, "We're spending the holidays in Florida."

"Oh yes," said Pastor Pete, nodding, never happier for a conversational segue. "Have a wonderful trip!"

"Believe me, I'll expect a full explanation when we return," said Bill as his wife pulled his arm.

"Which you shall have," said Pastor Pete.

As they all watched the couple depart, Bill Hall turned around to offer one final scowl.

"Well," said Megan brightly, "I guess he won't be adding anything to your book!"

~

On a Friday, Charlene brought her husband lunch at the dealership. It was something she had done early in their marriage but hadn't thought to do in years, and Charlie was so touched by the gesture that after they dined on egg-salad sandwiches and a thermos of cream of mushroom soup, he led her into the back seat of a new SUV.

"Let's neck," he said.

"Charlie," she whispered, "we can't—there's people—"

"Shh. Ed's in the office, writing up a purchase agreement. And besides," he said, kissing her, "the windows are tinted."

They were like two teenagers and might have been overtaken by lust had their deep kisses not been interrupted with fits of laughter caused by Charlie asking, "Can I feel you up?" When they emerged into the bright light of the showroom, still giggling, Charlene promised that next time, she'd let Charlie get to third base.

On Saturday, she'd drawn a bubble bath and invited him in, and on Sunday, she was on the phone with her daughter, writing down Tammy's flight information, when Charlie ambled into the kitchen wearing only briefs and stood in front of the dishwasher like a Mr. Universe contestant.

She was able to restrain herself during his first biceps-flexed pose, but when he struck his second stance—arms curved out like parentheses, fists touching in front of his stomach, grimacing and trembling, as if it were hard trying to hold back his mighty force—a giggle erupted out of her.

"What's so funny?" asked Tammy as Charlie readied his final beefcake pose, twisting himself as if he were about to throw a javelin, and Charlene could contain herself no longer, and in between hoots of laughter, she told her daughter, "See you in two days—love you!"

Going to her husband, she said, "My very own Charles Atlas," and pretended to swoon, allowing her strong man to catch her in his arms.

~

"'Skink'?" said Charlene, reading the elaborate cursive on the storefront window.

"They say it's short for 'Skin Ink,'" said Bunny.

"The lettering's like Burton's old sign," said Charlie, squinting. "Sort of."

Shopping on Main Street, the Kendricks had turned off on First Avenue to find Bunny standing in front of the former Barone's Tailor Shop.

"I'm sure I'll be getting an earful from some All Souls members," said Bunny, giggling. "But I just couldn't resist. Burton would *love* the idea of a tattoo parlor moving in. Besides, it's only a one-year lease."

Unable to look inside, as a black curtain was drawn across the window, Charlie asked when the store was opening.

"First week of the new year," said Bunny. "I'm their landlady, so I should get a good deal on some 'skink.'"

On Kittleson Bank's digital billboard, the temperature registered minus two degrees, but the trio stayed outside, huddling together as they talked about what tattoos they'd get and where they'd get them.

"'Don't tread on me,'" said Bunny, holding out her gloved fists. "Right across my knuckles."

"Me, I'd go old school," said Charlie. "A big red heart on my bicep with Charlene's name in it."

"I'm debating between a butterfly or a daisy on my ankle," said Charlene. "Or maybe a skull . . . on my face."

When the vaporized clouds of their laughter faded in the cold air, Bunny said, "What I'd really get is a little suit jacket." She tapped her chest. "Right here. In honor of Burton."

~

Coming in the back door, Charlene exclaimed, "Oh, honey, you've been wrapping presents!" as if it were a feat along the lines of discovering a planet.

Tammy looked up from the kitchen table cluttered with rolls of shiny paper, ribbons, tape, and scissors.

"Yeah, I ordered all of them online and had them delivered here. Figured it'd save me on packing and—"

"You should see downtown!" said Charlene as she and Charlie hung their coats and hats on pegs by the door. "It's so festive. I don't know where they got all the pine garlands and—"

"And we stopped at Gourmet Popcorn and got your favorite," said Charlie. "Caramel cashew." He held up two big shopping bags. "And," he added, his voice rising in a singsong, "there might be more goodies in here for you."

Reaching for something on the chair next to her, Tammy's voice was less a singsong than a taunt, as she said, "And I've got a goodie for you, Mom."

Charlene's bright, expectant expression faded to one of confusion to—when finally recognizing what it was that hung from her daughter's hand—deep embarrassment.

"What have you got there?" asked Charlie cheerfully, not quite sure what he was looking at.

Holding up a lacy red-and-black teddy by its straps, Tammy said, "That's what I was wondering! Like I said, before I left school, I ordered a bunch of stuff to be delivered here, and I guess I just assumed all the packages were for me—but I would *never* order anything like this." Now her voice turned snide. "Nope, this was a special delivery for Mom."

"That's, that's . . . ," said Charlene, two spots of pink coloring her cheeks.

She rushed out of the kitchen, unable to complete her sentence, and for a long moment, father and daughter stared at the door she'd exited. Finally Charlie held out his hand and said to Tammy, "I'll take that," and when she handed it to him, he dropped it into one of the shopping bags looped around his wrist and left the room.

Charlene took a long bath and, wearing the old velour robe her kids had given her for a long-ago Mother's Day, settled herself next to Charlie on the den couch when Tammy finally deigned to come down for dinner.

"We saved some for you," said Charlie, opening up the closed pizza box on the coffee table. "Your favorite—deluxe supreme, no black olives."

Tammy devoured nearly a slice before she spoke.

"The place I work at? We serve 'wood-fire' pizza and it's really popular, but it doesn't come close to the Norseman's."

It was a point of civic pride among Kittleson residents that many people claimed the pizza served at a joint opened sixty years ago by a Norwegian immigrant was the best they'd ever eaten.

"Well, you know what Old Man Lars said," Charlie said.

No one had to look at the printed napkins that came with the delivery, knowing the slogan by heart, which they all recited.

"It ain't no secret, it's my secret sauce."

As Tammy dug into her second piece, Charlene went to the kitchen, returning with a can of bubbly water, remembering that her daughter didn't drink pop anymore.

After finishing/inhaling the pizza, Tammy took a swig of water and leaned back on the couch, issuing forth a burp of considerable volume and length.

"Good one," said Charlie, and after the threesome laughed, Tammy gave her mother a look that made Charlene ask, "What?"

"It's just that you didn't say, 'That's disgusting.' You always say, 'That's disgusting,' after someone burps."

Charlene shrugged. "That's me. Full of surprises."

"I'll say," said Charlie. "Did you know your mother's thinking about getting a tattoo?"

"It'd just be a little skull," teased Charlene, drawing a circle around her cheek.

As the couple laughed, their daughter stared at them and said, "What have you done with my real parents?"

Charlene enjoyed the levity, but when she patted the couch cushion, her voice was suddenly serious. "Scoot a little closer."

With a sigh, Tammy obeyed her mother.

"I think it's time I say some other things," said Charlene, giving Tammy's knee a quick tap. "And *you* might find yourself saying, 'That's disgusting!' Either way, I'd appreciate you not talking until I'm finished. Understand?"

She told Charlie that he, on the other hand, could pipe in whenever he wanted.

"If I can add anything of value," he said with a wink, "I will."

Adjusting the lapel of her robe, Charlene took a deep breath and began.

"It all started when our Naomi Circle decided to write a book about erotica."

Tammy's mouth dropped open and stayed open as her mother told her how she had resisted the idea of such a book, which had led her to wondering why she was so resistant, which led her to exploring a difficult subject.

"See, my mother taught me that sex was a rigged game, one men always won.

"'If you give in, you're a slut, if you don't, you're a cold fish,'" she said, her voice harsh. "I cannot tell you how many times Mom told me that."

Evidently not able to stick to her gag rule, Tammy said, disbelief in her voice, "Grandma Ruth?"

"What I never told you, Tammy—what I didn't know myself until I was an adult—was that Grandma Ruth got pregnant in her sophomore year at college. She had wanted a career—she planned to go to law school after she graduated—but she dropped out to marry Dad and have me. I don't know if they would have ever married if she hadn't been expecting me; they certainly didn't seem to enjoy each other much. She resented him and he resented her. And boy, did she ever want me *not* to repeat her mistake."

Charlene took a steadying breath.

"The thing is, with your dad, I was able to rebel against those toxic lessons, but I guess ultimately I absorbed more of them than I knew. And I'm really sorry if I've passed on those lessons to you. Because I love your dad and I know he—"

"Mom, please, you don't have to say any more."

"I don't have to, but I want to. I want you to know that it's never too late to fix your mistakes, to throw out the bagged-out cotton underpants and order a skimpy little teddy for your—"

"Mom!"

"I know I didn't give you much guidance on the subject of sex—"

"—Uh, it was pretty much, 'Don't do it.'"

Charlene sighed.

"But like I said, it's never too late to fix—or at least try to fix—your mistakes. So my advice to you now is that when you're in a loving, respectful relationship . . . well, don't be afraid to go a little wild."

"Define wild," said Tammy, before quickly adding, "No, don't."

"I just mean it's okay to have a little fun with your partner. To tickle one another . . . in all sorts of ways."

Tammy stared at her mother with a look of concern bordering on alarm, but instead of reaching for her phone to call 911, she kissed her mother on the cheek and turning to her dad, she kissed his.

"As much as I'd love to hear more, I gotta go upstairs and throw up."

"Tammy!" said Charlene. "I only—"

"Mom, I'm kidding! But really, I've got a lot of stuff to do—like texting Tyler and telling him about all the sex ed he's missing out on."

Her brother, whose first job out of college wasn't adding much to his savings account but was depositing much into his worldview, taught English in Seoul, Korea, and had decided to stay there for the holidays.

The look on Charlene's face made Tammy laugh.

"Mom—*kidding!* Good night!"

After watching their daughter leave the room, Charlene sighed and said, "Well, so much for a good mother-daughter chat."

Charlie put his arm around her.

"Char, you did great."

"Ha! When I think of all that I could—" She cut off her words and shook her head. "Nope, I'm not going to do that anymore."

"Do what?"

"Agonize over all the things I should have done. All the things I did wrong."

Charlie squeezed his wife's shoulder.

"You forgave me," he said, his voice choked. "That was something you sure did right."

"It took me long enough."

The couple, married for twenty-seven years, stared into eyes that reflected back their long history. Their faces were a foot apart, then inches—then there was no space between them.

Their kiss began slowly, almost beseechingly, before becoming more urgent, as if their mouths, lips, and tongues were probing each other's for answers. When Charlie's hand found the opening of Charlene's robe and began to edge up the inside of her thigh, Charlene pulled herself back, her face flushed, her eyes shining.

"We can't do this here," she said, "Tammy might come down."

"Then let's go up," said Charlie, lifting her off the couch.

With his wife in his arms, Charlie climbed the stairs with a minimum of huffing and puffing, and Charlene, her head nestled in his neck, whispered, "My hero." When they were in the safety of their bedroom, he bumped the door shut with his backside.

"Put me down," said Charlene and nodding toward the bed, added, "and meet me over there."

Charlie obeyed and, propping himself against the pillows, watched as she slowly untied the belt of her old velour robe. Humming a classic stripper's ditty, she sashayed toward him, pulling open her lapels and flashing him. A foot from the bed, she let the robe fall off her shoulders, and Charlie, reaching for her in her red-and-black-lace finery, said, "I've got one, Charlene: 'T is for Teddy.'"

19

While many churches offered a midnight service on Christmas Eve, All Souls did not. Its second minister, Pastor Hacker, had taken a poll and discovered that congregants would prefer an earlier meeting time. That he only asked his wife, his mother-in-law, and two elderly ushers made for a skewed survey, but nonetheless one that emboldened him to announce that their candlelight service would be held at eight o'clock.

"Better for everyone," he decreed from the pulpit. "Including those who have a hard time keeping their eyes open past ten!"

The earlier hour did in fact work out well; regular members as well as those who claimed pew space only during Christmas, Easter, weddings, or funerals filled up the sanctuary, and there did seem to be fewer snores and bobbing heads.

Sitting in the back row, Godfrey recognized about two-thirds of the attendees. Bunny had waved to him as she rushed in with a couple he'd never seen before, and one that gave credence to the idea that opposites attract. The Black woman was over six feet tall and dressed in a faux-fur jacket dyed a neon pink, whereas the white man was compact and wearing a slightly big but well-tailored maroon wool coat. Charlene and Charlie were there and introduced their daughter, Tammy, to him, but the other Naomis were away visiting friends and family.

It pleased Godfrey that he knew this; it had been a long time since he felt part of a community and the comings and goings of its members.

Marlys had gifted him with a tin of homemade Christmas cookies and told him life and limb were risked for them.

"What do you mean?" asked Godfrey as he opened the tin to look at its bakery-worthy contents, arranged in rows of stars and trees and Santas decked out in colored icing, sprinkles, and sugar crystals.

"I sent Roger out to Jerdes to pick up more butter and sugar, and he slipped on our driveway! Broke one wrist and sprained the other! Fortunately, it was when he got home, when he'd already gotten my groceries."

His injuries were not serious enough to cancel plans to spend Christmas in Las Vegas with Roger's mother, Wilma, who was about to celebrate her ninety-fifth, and what she was convinced was her last, birthday. All her sons and their families would be coming—Peter from Albuquerque, Eric from the Twin Cities, and Jim from Chicago—"even though Wilma has been pulling this 'It's my last birthday' routine for about a decade," said Marlys.

She told Godfrey that she hoped he wouldn't be alone for Christmas, which was the same thing said by Velda, who was visiting her son in Montana, and by Edie, who was visiting her daughter in London.

"We take turns," Edie explained. "One year we fly over, and the next year Mary Jo and her husband, Nigel, come here. Do you have any family you'll be visiting?"

Godfrey shook his head.

"Not for Christmas, but my brother is planning a visit sometime in the new year."

He couldn't help his smile; it would be the first time he would be playing host instead of guest, and he was excited to show Chauncey his new life.

My new life, he thought near the end of the service, as the lights dimmed and Tad sounded several notes and Kathy Knudsen led the congregation in singing "Silent Night." Small, thin tapers had been passed out earlier, and ushers now lit the candles of the congregants sitting at the end of each row, who then lit their neighbors', until the sanctuary was filled with the glow of nearly two hundred candles (Godfrey always counted heads and gave the number to Dorrie Hillstead, the church secretary).

When the hymn ended, a hush, like a coda, filled the church before Pastor Pete held out her arms and ended the service by saying, "May the love and joy of this season live in your hearts and minds. Amen."

~

Although the snowfall was heavy, the temperature was mild, relatively speaking, and that there was no wind made the men's walk not just tolerable, but enjoyable.

"You know who that couple with Bunny Barone was?" asked Godfrey.

"Never saw them before," said Larry Donovan. "But I think the guy was wearing Burton Barone's coat."

"Really? What makes you think that?"

"I used to usher a lot. And Burton would come to church in that dark-red coat, and I'd think, 'Man, that's a good-looking coat.' Color choice wouldn't be mine, but Burton looked pretty suave in it."

"I never met him. But I've heard stories. All good ones."

"He's a nice guy. Damn dementia."

Of the forecasted seven to ten inches of snow, at least three had already accumulated on the ground. Behind the men were two lines of footprints, ahead of them, untrammeled white.

After his son's death, Larry didn't have the energy to serve on volunteer committees, but he continued going to Sunday services, sitting in the back row. It was there that he had struck up a friendship of sorts with another back-row denizen, Godfrey. The men had gone from exchanging nods to a few words to having a cup of coffee at Jerdes after they ran into each other at the deli counter, and now, when they'd both left the candlelight service, they'd made a sudden tacit agreement to take a walk in the falling snow.

"So," said Larry, after they surmised what the electric bill might be for the homeowners who had turned their yard and house into a Christmas light show. "I saw Bill Hall in the parking lot the day of the bazaar, and man, he was ranting to his wife about Pastor Pete condoning pornography . . . any idea what the hell he meant?"

Figuring he wasn't breaking any confidence now that the cat was partially and soon to be fully out of the bag, Godfrey filled Larry in on the Naomis' *ABCs of Erotica*.

"So someone writes, 'A is for . . . ,'" said Larry, stymied.

". . . Azure?"

He gave Godfrey a look that said, "That wouldn't be my first thought," but aloud he said, "Then someone else writes 'B is for . . .'"

"Buxom?"

The two men chuckled.

"I had a lady friend once whose eyes were azure blue and, well, she was pretty buxom," explained Godfrey.

"So you're writing something for it too?"

"God, no."

Tucking his scarf farther into the lapel of his coat, Larry asked, "I saw Bill Hall's reaction. You think other members'll get behind it?"

"I don't know. Pastor Pete is going to announce the whole project at the January meeting."

"That's a meeting I might just have to go to."

There was still no wind by the time they reached the Old Soldiers' Park at the west end of town, but the snow was falling with more force, and they agreed to head back to church.

"We had a blizzard one Christmas Eve," said Larry. "Zac was so worried. He asked me, 'How's Santa Claus going to be able to deliver presents?'"

"What'd you tell him?"

"I told him that in bad weather he fired up his 'super-duper sleigh rocket boosters.' And then Carol rapped it."

"What was there to wrap?" said Godfrey, confused.

"Zac was really into rap music, so Carol *rapped* about it. She'd make up rhymes—like Zac might ask if she'd make macaroni and cheese for dinner and she'd say something like, 'You want mac and cheese? First give me a squeeze.' Something like that."

"How'd the rocket-booster one go?"

"Can't remember. That was a long time ago. Zac was about five or six.

"Wait a second," said Larry, after they'd walked about a half block in silence. "Oh, don't you know," he said, clapping a beat with his gloved hands, "Santa loves the snow / And the harder it falls / to his reindeer he calls / let's fire up the super-duper sleigh rocket boosters! The super-duper, absoluper sleigh rocket boosters! Oh, yeah."

"Wow," said Godfrey, impressed.

"I have no idea where that came from," said Larry, shaking his head. "But you should have seen Zac—he was so excited, begging Carol, 'Do it again, do it again!' Which she did, and pretty soon we were all singing it."

He broke out in the biggest smile Godfrey had ever seen on his face.

"You won't believe it, Godfrey, but that's the first time I've thought of Zac without breaking down . . . or wanting to break something."

Feeling any words he might say would be inadequate, Godfrey merely nodded.

"You know what I'm going to do when I get home?"

Now Godfrey's head moved side to side.

"I'm going to write down the words to that song, and then I'm going to try to remember more of Carol's little raps—like that macaroni and cheese one. Then I'm going to picture how Zac would react to them."

"Sounds like a worthy endeavor."

"Like the 'Clean Your Room' song,'" Larry said with a laugh. "Oh my God, I just remembered that 'Clean Your Room' song! Zac hated that one!"

Now Godfrey laughed.

"Clean your room / Clean your room / 'Cause it's an awful mess, Zac / And that's an actual fact, Zac / I'll give you a half hour and a shovel / To dig out that hovel / Starting now!"

When they reached the church parking lot, Larry said, "You know, Carol sang me little songs too."

He pressed his key fob, and his car chirped.

"I usually take my time driving to my house . . . I'm never in a big hurry to go to that empty place. But tonight I'm going straight home. Home, where Carol would make up songs, including an adult-version one about boosting my rocket!"

Chuckling, he extended his hand to Godfrey and wished him a merry Christmas.

When Godfrey returned the sentiment, the handshake turned into a hug.

"And thanks," said Larry, getting into his car.

"For what?"

"For helping me remember."

Godfrey shrugged.

"I guess it's the Naomis you should really thank."

The handyman was almost to his truck when Larry, rolling down his window, said, "I will, Godfrey! I'll tell the Naomis I've got a *T* for them! 'T is for Thanks'!"

~

Two days after Christmas, Mallory dragged herself to the mudroom to put on her parka, her hat, her mittens, and her boots.

"Wait," said John, zipping Soren into his snowsuit. "What are you doing?"

"I'm going sledding with you and Soren."

"No, you're not. You're going to take a long nap."

"Are you sure, I . . . ," began Mallory, before her words were swallowed by a yawn.

"And I'm not talking about a little power nap," said John.

"Not a pow-a nap," said Soren.

"I want you to sleep all afternoon," said John. "And if you sleep through dinner, no problem. Soren and I can manage, right, buddy?"

"Wight!"

She moaned with a weary pleasure as she crawled under the flannel sheets and downy comforter, and it wasn't as a pastor but as a sensualist that she thought, *This is heaven.*

Having a good sense of when she needed to put forth energy and when she needed to pull back, Mallory paced herself, but during the church holiday season, energy was amped up and she tuned out signals that it was time to sit back and take a break. While she could never say she was happy with her sermons—wondering if her aim to teach, to inspire, to spread love had been reached—John had assured her that both her Christmas Eve and Christmas Day homilies had been full of joy and wonder, and as John just as easily (but far less often) would tell her when her words had fallen a bit flat, she believed him. And Tad had done wonders with the adult choir (if Kathy Knudsen were twenty years younger, she could be a winning contestant on *American Idol*). And had there ever been a dearer version of "Go Tell It on the Mountain" than that sung by their children's choir, and in particular, by the boisterous six-year-old Dylan Garcia, who didn't just tell it on the mountain, but with arms spread wide like a vaudevillian, shouted it?

And the beautiful banner Edie had shyly presented, replacing the one Mildred Wattrum had made—the one that for years had frightened children! *Had she made it freehand or from a pattern?* was the thought that slid Mallory into sleep.

"Oh, Mom, it's beautiful!" said Mary Jo, looking at a photo of the selfsame banner. "So much better than that scary old one!"

"Your mother's quite the artist," boasted Finn. "And she whipped it up in no time."

"I'd wanted to make one for years," said Edie. "But I didn't want to hurt Mildred's feelings."

Mary Jo magically enlarged the picture by moving her fingers on the screen of her father's phone.

"The detail! The little baby Jesus's face just beams!"

"Thanks, I used satin for it—so it would shine."

Flanking Mary Jo on the couch, her mother-in-law, Frances, leaned in to have a look.

"Lovely! Myself, I'm all thumbs when it comes to sewing."

"But you make an awfully good rum punch," said Edie.

"I agree," said Nigel, springing out of his chair. "Who'd like another?"

Seeing everyone was up for seconds, Mary Jo helped him refill the glasses at the punch bowl.

They were celebrating Christmas in the Mayfair home of Mary Jo's in-laws, and after dinner, they had adjourned to the living room to open gifts, the biggest one being two envelopes, which were presented to both sets of parents. Inside were itineraries for a two-week trip to Italy in February, all expenses paid for by their giggling children.

"We did pretty well this year," said Nigel, "and we'd love to share the wealth, so to speak."

"So to speak!" said Edie. "But we can't—"

"Mom," said Mary Jo, holding out her palm like a crossing guard. "Yes, you can."

A fire blazed on the hearth and an evergreen bough decorated the mantel; there was a plate holding the remains of ginger and shortbread biscuits on the coffee table, and in the corner of the room, lights twinkled on a silver aluminum tree decorated with gold crowns.

"It's naff, but it's tradition," Frances said. It was Finn and Edie's joke that it was also tradition that Frances repeated the story every time they visited. "We were married in December and Del's Uncle Stuart—he's a bit of an eccentric—thought it would make a wonderful wedding present!"

It didn't look naff (or as Mary Jo had translated, "tacky") at all to Edie, who admittedly suffered from Anglophilia and thought a simple tea cozy bordered on practical/decorative genius.

"Edie, I can't tell you what a brilliant gift these are," said Del, coming into the room and holding up a slim gift box. "Perfect to wear as I stroll down the Via Veneto!"

He had changed out of his cardigan and into a sport coat so that he could display one of the three pocket squares Edie had sewn for him.

"How'd you arrange it like that?" asked Finn, who was still old fashioned enough to wear a suit—or at least a sport coat—to church, but with an almost always empty breast pocket, although he did occasionally stuff a cotton handkerchief into it.

"Permit me," Del said, taking the remaining squares out of the box, and for a quarter hour, those assembled were given a tutorial on seven different ways to fold a pocket square, including the stairs, three-peak, and Dunaway folds.

"How'd you know to make these out of different fabrics?" Del asked Edie when he fashioned the piece of gold silk into a puff square.

"If you've sewn for as many years as I have, you get to know what your material will do."

Reaching out to touch the fluff of silk in her husband's pocket, Frances whistled and said, "D is for Dapper."

As Edie flinched in surprise, Nigel said, "We told Mum and Dad about your erotica book. They were quite taken by the idea."

"We were surprised to say the least that a church would endorse such a book!" said Frances.

"I don't know about endorsing," said Edie. "It's just an idea a few of us came up with."

"And believe me, when the whole church finds out," said Finn, "there'll be some opposition."

"Nigel and I decided we want to get in on the fun too," said Mary Jo, retrieving a small box from under the tree and shaking it. Her smile, matching her husband's, was mischievous. "In here are the letters of the alphabet." She set the box on the table. "We're each going to draw one and we have to come up with—in a minute or less—our ideas of erotica based on that letter!"

Taking off the lid, Mary Jo held the box out to her mother, but Edie, shy, waved her hand.

"I'll go," said Del, plucking a rectangle of paper from the box. Unfolding it, he said, "Oh, blimey." He rolled his eyes. "I've drawn the letter *U*." He cleared his throat and stared at the paper.

"Clock's ticking, Dad," said Nigel, looking at his wristwatch.

"All right, all right." Del looked up at the ceiling before casting his gaze around the room. "Got it! 'U is for Uncle'!"

After a moment, Finn asked, "As in 'cry uncle'?"

"No," said Del, chuckling. "As in my dear Uncle Stu and his abominable wedding present." He gestured to the shiny metal tree in the corner and explained—*again*—to Edie and Finn that he and Frances had been married in December. "Which is why, I suppose, Uncle Stu thought that an artificial Christmas tree would be the perfect present. When we were opening our gifts, he carried it in fully decorated, and when I saw the expression on my bride's face—which wasn't horror, but humor—I thought, *That's my girl!* That's why I married her; she knows how to have a laugh!"

Past midnight, the visiting Americans were in the guest room of Mary Jo and Nigel's home in Belgravia, Edie sitting on the edge of the bed and slathering her hands with rose-scented lotion.

"That smells nice," said Finn, hanging his cardigan on the clothes butler before plopping down on the corner chair with a contented sigh.

"Frances always gives such nice gifts," said Edie, who began giggling.

"And what about the kids? That's some vacation they've lined up for us!"

Edie agreed that being international jet-setters twice in one winter was pretty wonderful, but she was laughing about something else.

Slipping off his shoes, Finn looked up at his wife. It didn't take him long to surmise what she was finding so funny.

"U is for Uncle?"

"Well, that *was* a hard letter," said Edie, capping the bottle and setting it on the nightstand. "What would you have come up with?"

Finn considered the question for a moment before standing up.

"How about," he said, tugging his shirt free of his belted pants as he walked toward the bed. "How about 'U is for Unbuckle'?"

20

When Velda told her son she'd like to spend Christmas with him, he sounded surprised, and not in a good way.

"You want to what?" Wayne had said, his voice so loud that Velda had to hold the phone away from her ear.

She explained that she thought it would be nice to visit him and his family and then Pamela and hers.

"But Pamela said they had already had a house full of guests this year," she said, in a cheery voice she hoped disguised her disappointment.

"Yeah, well, that's Hawaii for you. You live there, you've got to expect company all the time."

He ended the call with the announcement that he and his wife had split up, but before Velda could ask for details, he said, "Text me your flight info, bye."

After a fairly short drive from the airport, Wayne turned into a parking lot behind a pale, peeling stuccoed building, assuring Velda that his living situation was only temporary and that he had a Realtor and was actively looking for a new house.

"When Anna said, 'Move out,' she meant, 'Move out *now*.'"

"I had no idea you were having marital problems," Velda said.

"Add them to a long list."

His apartment wasn't shabby so much as it was tired; it came furnished, providing if not any real comfort or style, at least places to sit and places on which to set things. Two wreaths had been placed on the complex's double glass doors, but any further holiday decor didn't make it up the thinly carpeted stairs and into 3B.

Wayne hadn't bothered to put out any holiday decorations either; the only thing adorning his living room wall was a picture of a generic mountainscape that looked, like the furniture, as if it had come from a motel-chain closeout sale.

The hard-cushioned couch was upholstered in a stiff and nubbly fabric that seemed closer to plastic than wool, and Velda thought if she moved too quickly something might ignite.

Carrying rectangles of folded linens and a pillow, Wayne emerged from the bedroom.

"Please," he said, setting the pile on the arm of the couch. "Take my bedroom."

"We've already been through this. I am not going to kick my son out of his bedroom and besides, I like sleeping on couches. It's good for my back."

"If you say so."

There was something in his voice that made Velda ask, "Wayne?"

That one word was like an arrow that reached its target, causing him to plunk heavily onto the couch.

"Wayne?" said Velda, scooting over to his side.

With a sharp intake of breath, he let loose a sob and collapsed into his mother's arms.

"Oh, Ma!"

Flummoxed, she sat frozen for a moment before she began patting his back.

"Shh, shh. It's all right, Wayne, it's all right."

Even though it obviously wasn't, that was her mantra, and Velda continued it until he at last sat up, shaking his head, his breath still staccatoed with little sobs.

"Sorry," he said finally, wiping his face with his hands.

"Wayne, don't be sorry, what's—"

Further surprising her, he stood up, with the announcement that he was going to bed.

"You're not going anywhere," she said, pulling his hand and forcing him back onto the couch. "Not until you tell me what's the matter!"

His sigh was both despondent and impatient.

"Just look around! Look around at this shithole, and then look at your son who lives in it."

Velda censored her urge to censor her son.

"It . . . I've seen nicer . . . but you said you're moving."

His laugh was like a bark.

"Of course I'm moving. But it doesn't matter if I move into a lodge up in Lolo—it'd still be a shithole because I'll live in it."

"Wayne." Her voice slid into a lower octave.

"I'm just such a loser! My wife—my soon-to-be *ex*-wife thinks I'm a loser—"

"Wayne, being a computer systems analyst is hardly a—"

"My son thinks I'm a loser—"

"I'm sure he thinks no such thing!"

Wayne's jaw unhinged, and he stared at his mother.

"What?" she said, the irritation in her question covering up for the discomfort she felt.

"How would you know what Ryan thinks? When was the last time you spoke to him?"

A heat wave roiled up Velda's neck and onto her face.

"Well, let me see, I'm not sure, I . . ."

"I'll tell you. On his birthday, last June."

“Has it been that long? And I sent a check, too, although I never did get a thank-you for that.”

“You keep tabs on things like that, don’t you?”

“No, of course not,” she said, feeling both offended and found out. “I can’t tell you how disappointed I was to find out he wouldn’t be spending Christmas with us.”

“I told you—he’d already made plans to spend the holidays with his girlfriend’s family in Sacramento.”

“You don’t have to yell at me, Wayne.”

“I wasn’t aware that I was,” he said, sounding startled. He took a deep breath before he went on. “Well, maybe it’s because I think you never listen.”

Even as she fought it, swallowing hard and blinking fast, this time it was Velda’s turn to cry. It wasn’t a half-hearted surrender either; her tears and sobs were an onslaught, and for a long while, Wayne was too stunned to do anything but sit on the petroleum product that was the couch upholstery and watch her. When he placed his hand on her shoulder, he did so tentatively, as if it were hot to the touch, and when she had finally quieted down, he said, “I thought you were being brave when you didn’t cry at Dad’s funeral, but when I think of it, I don’t ever remember seeing you cry.”

“Oh, I cried,” she said after blowing her nose. “I just went into the bathroom so you kids wouldn’t hear me.”

“What . . . what would you cry about?”

“Oh, little things, probably.”

“Come on,” said Wayne, not wanting her to dismiss the question.

“I could use some water,” said Velda, feeling parched.

Wayne sprang up, taking several strides over the gray-brown carpet to the nine-by-nine-foot square of linoleum that covered the kitchen floor. He returned with a glass of water, from which Velda took a long draw.

"Ahh, that's good water." She took another sip. "From a mountain stream, I'll bet."

When her son seated himself in the easy chair that didn't exactly fit its name, Velda positioned her trim body slightly to better face him.

"What came to mind first," she said, realizing she couldn't keep nattering on about the water and its possible origins, "is when we were at the dinner table, and Merv said maybe I should audit Mrs. Haugland's home ec class so I could pick up some pointers. He said he'd make sure she didn't grade me, because he didn't want me coming home with a D." Velda took another sip of water before putting the glass on a stack of computer magazines that served as the coffee table's coaster. "I had made what I thought was a pretty good meatloaf that night."

"He was always making snide jokes like that," said Wayne.

"You thought so?"

"*Duh!* He thought he was a real wit. I thought he was an asshole."

Wayne expelled a burst of air, a little surprised that his thoughts had become words.

"And I always thought you liked his jokes. You always laughed at them."

"But I cried afterward," said Velda. "Like I said, in the bathroom, usually."

"I'd cry up in my bedroom."

"Because of him?" she asked, and when Wayne nodded, she whispered, "I'm so sorry, I had no idea."

Wayne's words came after a derisive snort.

"I think you just chose what you wanted to see and hear. Like the jokes he'd make at *my* expense, as well as yours."

"But I . . . I thought you liked his teasing!" said Velda, slumping from the weight of shame and sorrow.

"Same here! You'd laugh when he made fun of you, so I thought, well, when he makes fun of me, maybe I just wasn't getting the joke. So

I'd laugh too. At least around him. Alone, I cried, at least when I was little. When I got older, I'd go in my room and punch stuff."

Velda couldn't stop shaking her head, and she repeated her apology.

"Once in my junior year," said Wayne, "I was talking to Sue Everly at her locker—I really liked Sue Everly—and Dad comes by, making his rounds, I guess, and says something like, 'Watch out for that one, Everly, he still watches Saturday-morning cartoons in his jammies.' Then he lets out one of his satisfied little chuckles, like 'Aren't I funny?' and goes strolling down the hallway, Mr. King Shit Principal who loves to embarrass his son."

"Oh, Wayne."

"Sue just looked at me with her big brown eyes, like she felt sorry for me and, I don't know, like she was kind of repulsed." He twirled the wedding band he still wore on his finger. "And I was just about to ask her to the junior prom, but not after she gave me that look." He sighed. "I heard she went with Mark Lenton."

From the next-door apartment, the music of Mariah Carey singing about what she wanted for Christmas seeped in through the thin living room wallboard, and they listened until it was over and "Do They Know It's Christmas?" began. Then they both began talking at once, and their conversation—interspersed with long pauses as they considered questions, blew their noses, or dabbed away tears—was the longest either could remember having with one another.

"So you really didn't recognize Dad was a bully?" Wayne asked at one point.

"I recognized that he thought he was always right and that it was easier for me to believe he was too," said Velda. "He was such a 'pillar of the community'—I thought maybe I wasn't seeing something everyone else was."

Wayne nodded. "Teachers would tell me all the time how much Dad did for the school and how lucky I was to be his son."

"I should have known you and Pamela were suffering too."

"Oh, not Pam. She couldn't do any wrong in Dad's eyes—don't you remember?"

Before Velda could reply, he added, "Her issues are mostly with you."

Velda flinched.

"But I . . . but I love Pamela!"

"You had a funny way of showing it. She thinks you were so hard on her because Dad wasn't."

As if all her bones were weakened by sudden fissures, Velda felt herself sinking into the couch, and as much as she felt she didn't deserve a reprieve, she couldn't stifle her yawn.

"Let's call it a night," said Wayne, obviously exhausted too. "We can talk more in the morning."

Velda didn't argue.

The difference between the ride back to the airport and the ride from the airport was immeasurable. The tenseness of people pretending to be family when they felt like strangers had been replaced by an ease and lightness. Having given each other the gifts of their honest selves, both of them were grateful and slightly awed.

"You call me when you get home," Wayne had said, after enveloping her in a hug.

"Will do," said Velda. "And you keep me posted on everything!"

Settling herself on the plane, she was unaware that she was humming, until her seatmate lifted her eye mask and snapped, "Do you mind?"

It had been an intense three days; every night Velda crawled under the covers on the couch (surprisingly comfortable for sleeping, if not sitting), thinking she'd replay and ruminate on everything she and Wayne had done and talked about, but sleep was quick to lasso and tie down any and all thoughts.

They had spent Christmas Eve day hiking up the M Trail; Wayne told her it was challenging, but Velda didn't have a problem keeping up.

They had dinner at a steak house and talked so long that when their server told them she was sorry, but they were closing, they looked up to find that the busy restaurant was now empty.

Velda was grateful that Wayne, not a churchgoer, obliged her desire to go to Christmas Day service. Sharing a hymnal, they sang one of her favorite carols, and hearing her son's surprising—and tuneful—harmonization, Velda thought, *Yes, joy to the world.*

Talk continued as they shared separate memories of the same events. Velda remembered the wonderment of seeing mighty Niagara Falls, while Wayne remembered asking his father if people could survive going over and Merv grabbing him as if he were going to toss him over and asking, "Shall we see?"

To Velda, family game night meant rousing tests of skill and knowledge, whereas to Wayne it meant a miserable evening of watching *both* his parents playing to win and their poor sportsmanship when they didn't.

"I'm so sorry, Wayne," said Velda, ashamed and embarrassed that it had been so important for her and Merv to beat one another, at the expense of showing their kids some fun.

Questions. Apologies. Promises to do better. And finally, Velda's confession that she thought she was in love with a woman; a woman she'd been in love with since college.

Wayne stared at his mother a long time before he spoke.

"I'm shocked . . . but then again, I'm not. I mean, it does explain a lot."

"It does?" Velda whispered.

"Well, sure. Lonely people aren't really happy people."

"I never really thought of it like that."

"Well, you forget, Ma, I majored in computer technology, but I minored in psychology."

They again shared something that had previously not been part of their relationship: laughter.

Later, Wayne put his phone on speaker and they talked to Ryan and to Pamela and one of her stepdaughters. Both conversations were awkward and hurried, but at least Velda had been able to tell her grandchildren and daughter that she loved them.

"It's a start," said Wayne, giving her a playful nudge with his elbow. "But next call you've got to tell them you're a lesbian."

On the day before her departure, Velda had cajoled her son, a committed nonshopper, into the strip mall thrift store across the street from his apartment building.

"Maybe we'll find you some nice dishes," said Velda. "You need more dishes. Or maybe a nice soft throw for your couch."

Once inside, they wandered up the aisles, past old *Reader's Digest* condensed books stacked on the top of a buffet with a cracked pane of glass; past racks stuffed with pilly Grizzlies jerseys and sweatpants with missing drawstrings; past shelves crammed with nicked knickknacks, yellowed linens, and scratched housewares.

"Do you have one of these?" asked Velda, who, having seen the bare interiors of most of his cupboards, was pretty sure he didn't.

"No," said Wayne, taking the blender. "And I actually could use one . . . for the tropical drinks I plan on mixing up for all the women I'll be entertaining."

Velda found his joke about his soon-to-be bachelor status encouraging—a step up from his previous moping.

"And here, maybe you could get those for your girlfriend."

Blushing at his words, Velda nevertheless had to laugh when she looked at what Wayne pointed to: a ceramic vase shaped like Cupid, whose raised white letters read, "Love Blooms."

Velda picked it up, but after pretending to consider it, said, “Nope, it’s chipped.”

“Like most relationships,” said Wayne, to which Velda replied, “My son, the philosopher.”

When they decided their browsing was complete, Wayne asked the cashier if there was an outlet with which he could test the blender.

The woman gestured with a shrug and half nod, and following her unenthusiastic directions, Wayne bent down next to a chest of drawers, gummy with partially peeled-off decals, and shoved the prongs of the plug into the socket.

Pop!

It wasn’t a loud noise, but one that shouldn’t come out of an electrical outlet, especially when accompanied by an arc of sparks.

“Whoa!” said Wayne, stumbling back.

“Wayne!” said Velda, rushing to him. “Did you get a shock?”

“Well, yeah,” he said, standing up and rubbing his hands together. To the cashier, he said, “Guess I won’t be needing that.”

Now on the plane, Velda giggled, and the woman with the eyeshade signaled her annoyance by shifting in her seat.

It wasn’t only the conversations with her son she had been enjoying; she and Eloise had been keeping up a text and email communication. In the latter, she had recounted the many shocks she and Wayne had gone through as they learned more about each other, and the literal one Wayne suffered with the thrift-store blender. She ended by writing that it had made her think of electricity.

So I’m thinking, maybe V is for Voltage, she had written. And that undeniable electrical current that runs between two people attracted to one another.

The captain's voice came over the PA system, announcing that they were next in line and would be taking off shortly, and before Velda turned off her phone, she read again the latest text from Eloise.

"V is for Voltage?" I'm starting to think it might be, "V is for Velda."

How could she not giggle again?

"Geez!" said her seatmate, and because she was wearing an eye mask, she couldn't see Velda stick her tongue out in reply.

21

"Have mercy. Oh, dear. Hang on!"

"We're fine, Hiram," said Bunny, steering into the slide. When the car righted itself, she said, "See?"

"Hiram's a terrible back seat driver," said Jolie, stating the obvious.

"That's because I'm rarely in the back seat!" said Hiram, who made it no secret that he would prefer driving.

Squeezing his hand, which had been holding hers in a death grip, Jolie said, "Settle down, hon. Can't you see Bunny's got this winter driving down?"

There were a few slight skids but no further fishtailing, and when they reached their destination, Bunny let her passengers off at an entrance.

"Fortunately, we can park in the handicap zone," she said. "I'll meet you inside."

Jolie's reaction was one shared by most first-time visitors.

"It's so big," she said, looking up at the three tiers.

"And those lights," said Hiram. "It's like a winter wonderland."

He hadn't been so enthusiastic about the glories of the season on the hour-and-a-half drive to the Mall of America. In the back seat, as Bunny negotiated the icy highway with a few slides and fishtails, Hiram had acted as if meeting his maker wasn't a far-off eventuality, but a present possibility. Now, out of the car and on solid tiled ground, with curtains of tiny white lights hanging from the ceiling, Hiram merely held, not crunched, Jolie's hand as they walked next to Bunny, who pushed Burton in a wheelchair.

"Look, he's smiling," said Jolie, and indeed there was a slight upward curve to Burton's lips.

"We used to come here just to people watch," said Bunny. "Burton always liked seeing what everyone was wearing."

It was New Year's Eve day, and while the mall's shops were still adorned in festive finery, the hordes of holiday shoppers were gone.

"Oh, look, there's a DSW!"

"She loves shoes," said Hiram as Jolie dragged him into the warehouse.

Apparently she loved hats, chocolates, and rides, too, pulling Hiram into the storefronts and the amusement park that offered them.

"Just one turn on the roller coaster," Jolie promised Bunny as they entered Nickelodeon Universe in the center of the mall.

Pushing Burton over to a bench, Bunny situated herself on it and smiled at her husband, who did seem more present, relatively speaking.

"Check them out," she said, nodding toward the group of adults and children dressed in matching green T-shirts that said, "Our Family Rocks!"

"I know what you'd say," she continued, and deepening her voice to imitate him, said, "'It's a fun idea and if one of them gets lost they'll be easier to find . . . but what T-shirts give in comfort, they take away in style and why, oh why, do those two women have to wear such tight jeans? I'm worried about their circulation!'"

She conversed with him, supplying his dialogue (mostly fashion critiques) as well as her own, until she pointed and said, "Oh, look, Burton, they're on the ride!"

They, or at least Bunny, watched the couple plunge down the dips and through the loops of the roller coaster, Jolie holding up her arms and laughing, her braids flying; Hiram was grim faced, his hands choking the safety bar.

After they got off the ride, Jolie was still laughing over the thrill, Hiram with relief. She was all smiles as she bent down to speak with one of the children in the green T-shirts, but when a green-shirted man lumbered over and said something, her expression changed.

"I wonder what they're talking about," Bunny said to Burton. She didn't have to wait long to find out.

"I can understand the ignorance of a child, but there's no excuse for yours!" Hiram said loudly, shaking his finger.

Towering over Hiram, the man laughed and, with a big hammy hand, waved away Hiram's finger.

There was a pause as the men sized each other up before deciding where to strike first, but Jolie and one of the women in the green T-shirt and circulation-snuffing jeans were faster, pulling them both away.

"Leave it be, Hiram!" said Jolie, holding onto his bicep like a bouncer escorting a troublemaker out of a bar.

"Whew," she said when they reached Bunny.

"What was that all about?"

"Let's get out of here," said Jolie, and she began pushing Burton through the amusement park, with Bunny and Hiram loping after them.

They took a glass-car elevator up to the third tier and walked along a great hall of restaurants.

"I love that guy!" said Jolie, steering Burton into a bakery named after a television cake maker.

She bought two cupcakes swirled high with frosting, and after handing one to Hiram, she leaned down to give Burton a sample.

"Come on, Mr. B., I know you like strawberry," she said, and when he opened his mouth slightly, she held the cupcake to it.

When his mouth closed around the pink peak and he gave his version of a smile, Bunny said, "How do you know strawberry's his favorite flavor?"

"It's my job," said Jolie, and trading cupcakes with Hiram, she told him to take Burton on ahead.

"Hiram's always ready to go into combat in defense of me," said Jolie, watching as her boyfriend pushed Burton's wheelchair past a gaggle of teenage boys and girls. "He forgets that I could take care of myself physically, if need be, although I'd rather the need *not* be."

"What made him so mad?"

Peeling the paper wrapper, Jolie took a generous bite of the cupcake and held it out to Bunny, who declined the offer.

She chewed for a while and patted her bottom lip with her finger, whose long nail was the same color as the frosting.

"Well, like he said: ignorance. Not of the child—he asked me two reasonable questions, which I was happy to answer. The first was, 'Why are you so big?' And I explained to him that people come in all shapes and sizes. The second was, 'Why does your hair look like snakes?' And I was about to give him a similar reply, that hair, too, comes in different shapes, different textures, but then the kid's big galoot of a father had to come along and offer his two cents'—his nasty two cents'—worth."

She took another bite of cupcake, and when she was done chewing, she swallowed hard.

"Which were, 'Jeffrey, get away from that freak!'"

Bunny sighed, feeling as if she were expelling some air, but mostly weariness.

"I'm sorry."

Jolie shrugged. "It's hardly the first time something like that has happened, and it'll hardly be the last. Still, it doesn't help when Hiram wants to get into fisticuffs."

"Especially with guys who're about twice his size."

"Hiram's little, but feral," said Jolie and although her words weren't meant as a one-liner, it struck them as funny.

"And speaking of that crazed wombat," she said, "look how far he's gotten with Mr. B."

They caught up to the men at a popcorn stand, where Hiram was helping himself to samples in little paper cups and Burton was snoozing.

"He was wide awake until I started telling him my life story," joked Hiram.

The sampling of caramel popcorn did its intended job, and Jolie bought a bag.

"I always like to end the year on a sweet note," she said, and as she held the bag open for the others, the deep puffs of a tuba filled the air.

"Oh, good, there's a concert!" said Bunny.

As they quickened their pace, she explained they were headed toward the rotunda, or at least a view of the first floor rotunda, where concerts and events were held, but when they got to the circular third floor railing, they looked down to see no stage, risers, or chairs assembled for an audience. There was, however, a tuba player keeping a simple five-note melody.

"Hey, look there," said Jolie as a snare drummer and trumpeter strolled toward him from different directions, followed by a clarinetist, a flautist, and a guitarist all playing the same five notes.

"What the . . . ," Bunny muttered and was about to surmise that all the good talent had been used up for the Christmas concerts, when a dozen young men and women emerged out of several storefronts.

Forming a half circle around the instrumentalists, they began singing the five notes that were a teasing introduction to Prince's "1999."

"It's one of those flash mob things!" said Jolie.

The young singers, their voices harmonizing well with the odd assembly of instrumentalists, moved and swayed to the music.

"Oh," said Bunny, pointing at a young woman wearing a tasseled stocking cap and a joyful expression. "That's Marlys's granddaughter!"

Burton was roused from his slumber by the music, and the foursome took the elevator to the first floor to be closer to the concert, listening to songs pertaining to the holiday, including "What Are You Doing New Year's Eve?," which caused Bunny to bend down and whisper to her husband, "Remember how much you loved Ella Fitzgerald singing this song?"

"He was quite the dancer," she told her friends, and taking the handles of her husband's wheelchair, she twirled him slowly around. Inspired, Hiram held out his arms to Jolie, and the two couples danced, Bunny getting teary eyed over how much the graceful couple reminded her of herself and Burton.

"Remember, honey?" she said to her seated partner. "I asked you if you wanted me to wear flats so there wouldn't be much of a height difference?"

As a college girl, sophisticated dates hadn't been a part of her social life (although once a guy from her international-studies class did take her to a restaurant that served cheese fondue), but when Burton began taking her out dancing, she wore dresses (mostly borrowed) and heels that made her several inches taller than her dance partner.

"Be proud of your height," he'd tell her anytime he caught her slouching. "I am!"

Bunny spun and glided his wheelchair to a more up-tempo song by U2, and when the clarinetist announced that their final number would be "Auld Lang Syne" and asked everyone to sing along, Bunny, Hiram, and Jolie took up the invitation, along with the clumps of people gathered on all floors.

The applause was enthusiastic at song's end, and when the performers shouted, "Happy New Year!" audience members returned the good wishes. As people began to disperse, Amelia, grabbing Axel by the arm, rushed over to Bunny.

"Mrs. Barone! So cool to see you guys here!"

"Likewise," said Bunny. "I didn't have any hopes of hearing a concert today and then you all show up!"

"We kinda just threw together the idea of a flash mob a couple days ago. A lot of kids were on winter break—I just got back from Las Vegas; my great-grandma turned ninety-five! Anyway, at the last minute we got together a good enough group, don't you think? And this, by the way, is Axel."

After complimenting him on his tuba prowess, Bunny introduced her party.

"I very much enjoyed your dancing," Axel said to his elders. "You motivated the crowd!"

"Yeah," Amelia said. "After you guys started dancing, there were people on the second and third floors dancing too."

"Axel, Amelia, come on!" called a young man carrying a guitar case.

"That's Noah—his parents are having a party for us at their house." Amelia's voice lowered to a whisper. "They only live a couple miles from here . . . and they're rich."

"They have an indoor pool!" said Axel.

"Sounds fun," said Bunny, and the older group bid goodbye and "Happy New Year!" to the younger, who did the same.

Like Burton, Hiram fell asleep on the drive home, relieving Bunny of his nervous back seat driving. A light snow was falling, but rising temperatures had melted the road's ice and treachery, and Bunny turned on the radio, asking Jolie if she had any music preference.

"Classical would be nice."

The notes of a pianist leading an orchestra through a Brahms concerto filled the vehicle, and they listened to it for a few minutes until the soft "wow" Jolie whispered to herself was apparently not as soft as she intended.

"What?" asked Bunny.

"I just realized," said Jolie, leaning forward from her position in the middle of the back seat, "this was the third time I've gotten into a fight on New Year's Eve."

"Wow is right," said Bunny, turning down the radio. "Care to elaborate?"

Jolie stared out the windshield and described not the snowy environs, but what she was seeing in memory.

"The second time was when I was seventeen, in New Orleans. I'd been exploring the French Quarter and I was on this little side street by the Voodoo Museum when these two guys jumped me and hauled me—or tried to—into an alleyway."

"Oh, jeez," said Bunny.

"I was still presenting as a man, and I easily took care of one punk, but the second punk knew how to throw a punch, a couple of which landed. But not like the right cross I delivered to his jaw, which sorta ended the skirmish."

"Jeez!" Bunny reiterated, looking at her friend through the rearview mirror.

"That fight was a lot easier to take than the one that happened when I was a kid. And yeah, I was physically hit, but it didn't come close to the emotional wallop . . ."

She told Bunny when he was eleven years old—and "my deadname" to the world—his sister Merigaye had snatched away his notebook and how her screams and giggles as he'd given chase were loud enough to cause their father to put an end to their shenanigans.

"I think his curiosity was piqued by how outraged and panicked I was, because he *demanded* that Merigaye hand over the notebook. Not to me, but to him."

Jolie sighed. "When Daddy saw that I'd been writing out my New Year's resolutions, he thought it would be funny—funny to *him*—to read them aloud, mimicking my voice. Most of them were simple things like, 'I resolve to beat Danny Broussard in the one-hundred-yard dash,' and to 'eat more of my MawMaw Dora's beignets,' but there was one that ended his little comic recitation."

"Which was what?" asked Bunny, putting on her blinker to move into the slower lane.

"Which was—and this I'd written in capital letters no less—'I resolve to one day really and truly be the woman I am!' There was this dead silence, then he's staring at me with this, this *fury* and I'm just paralyzed with fear . . . until he slapped me so hard I fell to the floor."

"Oh, Jolie."

"I claimed, well, hollered actually, that it was just a joke, that my teacher had given us the assignment to write real *and* funny resolutions. Daddy said that was a damn fool assignment if you asked him, and then he ripped the page out of my notebook and crumpled it up. I fished it out of the wastebasket later—he had squeezed it to about the size of an acorn—and I read it over every year. And by the way, I did beat Danny Broussard in the one-hundred-yard dash."

Jolie looked at Hiram, softly snoring, his head leaning against the window.

"And then today, whoo! I almost got in another fight. Well, Hiram did." She studied him for a moment. "But on this New Year's Eve day, I also got to dance with the man I love and no one said a word about that. At least that I heard. And then we got people at the Mall of America to follow our lead and dance along with us. Imagine that."

"And look at you," said Bunny. "You kept that resolution you made when you were eleven."

"Why, yes I did," said Jolie, a smile blooming on her face. "So you know what I say? I say, 'W is for Woman.' The woman I really and truly am."

22

"Charlene, these egg rolls are delicious!" said Edie.

"Thanks. I got the recipe from Price of Peace's *Table Blessings*."

"Oh," said Edie, not as enthusiastically.

"I didn't *buy* it," said Charlene with a laugh. "Nancy gave it to me for Christmas, although I would have preferred some of her employee-discount bath salts."

"And who made this artichoke dip?" asked Bunny.

Marlys raised her hand.

"One minced clove of garlic," she said, "two small jars of drained artichokes, cup of mayo, cup of parmesan cheese. Mix it all together and bake about forty-five minutes at 350."

"We definitely have to include this recipe," said Bunny, spooning the dip on a crescent of french bread, "if we ever do a regular cookbook."

"Or we could include it in our irregular one," said Velda. "A is for Aphrodisiacs, like Artichokes."

Except for Marlys and Edie, who were good friends, the Naomis rarely saw each other in social settings outside of All Souls—that they all gathered together for a New Year's Eve party was a first.

The invitation had been spontaneous, issued by Marlys the day before when she ran into Bunny at Jerdes's meat counter.

They were exchanging pleasantries when a gruff voice behind them said, "Get that rib eye out of your pocket or I'm calling the manager!"

Startled, they turned around, and were doubly startled to face a Naomi not known for kidding around.

"Charlene!" they said in unison, and Bunny, recovering first, held up her hands and, shaking her head at Marlys, said, "Caught over a lousy rib eye—I told you, take the filet mignon."

Amused by their repartee, they browsed the aisles together, and it was while reaching for a bottle of cranberry juice that Marlys said, if they didn't have plans, why not come over to her house tomorrow night?

"Edie and Finn are already coming, and I can ask Velda too. It'll be a Naomi party!"

"We could do a potluck," suggested Charlene.

"Good idea," said Marlys. "Maybe everyone bring an appetizer?"

"In that case," said Bunny, pointing her cart toward the deli section, "I'd better shop for my contribution."

When Marlys's boys were growing up, the large finished basement was their own private clubhouse / indoor gym / band studio as well as a place to host parties (including a particularly memorable one held without permission while their parents were out of town). In reclaiming the space after their youngest son left home, Marlys had ferreted out every last athletic sock, every broken CD case, and an odd pair of tweezers that Roger informed her was a *roach holder*, "and one that doesn't catch bugs." She replaced the carpet and the battered furniture, took down the posters featuring sports heroes as well as *Sports Illustrated* models, and hung family photos, making an inviting space for hosting gatherings and the jam sessions Roger had with any visiting relative or friend willing to join him.

When everyone was done snacking on homemade egg rolls, artichoke dip, and Swedish meatballs, as well as Jerdes's grocery store turkey-and-cheese roll-ups and antipasto plate, they retired to the seating area by the fireplace, drinking champagne and joking about days gone by, when a New Year's Eve party meant staying awake until at least midnight.

"Well, I'll still be up," said Bunny, whose insomnia fairly guaranteed it. "Just me and whatever eighty-year-old movie they're playing on TCM." Shrugging, she stared at the champagne flute in her hands and began to cry.

Surprised as anyone—maybe more so—by her outburst, Bunny apologized to those who had gathered around like EMTs to offer assistance.

"It's just that Burton and I—well, we had some wild New Year's Eve parties! And I felt so bad dropping him off today after we got back from the Mall of America, bad that I feel *relieved* I'm not there with him, ringing in the new year . . . even though for him, it'll be the same as the old year."

Charlene, next to Bunny on the large sectional couch, patted her knee and said, "I'd like to hear about one of those wild parties."

When Bunny's face crumpled again, Velda thought, *Oh, good one, Charlene*, but her inner scolding disintegrated when Bunny's expression shifted into a sly smile.

After a sip of her drink, she said, "Well, let's see . . . there was that one on Nob Hill where a Getty showed up . . . no, no, I would have to say the one in Aspen rang in the new year the loudest.

"We had friends in Denver who had a cabin, well, a chalet really, in Aspen and we were invited out there for the holidays. Along with about a hundred other people."

Bunny proceeded to tell the group about the huge sauna built into the house's lower level and how all night, people would use it and then run outside in their swimsuits or nothing at all to roll in the snow.

"They had a big bonfire going and at midnight, there was a choir of about two dozen brave and naked and half-naked souls surrounding it, linking arms and singing 'Auld Lang Syne'!"

"And you and Burton were part of the choir?" asked Edie, and when Bunny nodded, she added, "And were you—"

"Let's just say Burton and I didn't like to do things in half measure."

The room erupted in laughter.

"That should be in you gals' book," said Finn. "S is for Sauna—"

"—and Serenading in the Snow," added Roger.

"*Sans* clothes!" said Velda, thinking how she and Eloise would have fit right in with that crowd.

Roger, whose right wrist was still in a cast from his driveway fall and whose left was wrapped in an elastic bandage, asked Charlie if he'd mind refilling glasses.

"My pleasure," said Charlie, holding up a champagne bottle. In a French accent that was more appreciated for its effort than its acuity, he asked, "Anyone need a top off?"

"I'll keep mine on for now," said Charlene. "But ask me later."

The unexpected remark caused another round of laughter, and Charlene blushed with pleasure.

"I tell you what," said Charlie, as he circled the room refilling glasses. "You've got to hand it to these women and Pastor Pete for coming up with this ABC idea."

There were calls of "hear, hear!" and "amen!" followed by a moment of silence, as if everyone was pondering that which had just been toasted.

"It's certainly made me think a lot," said Velda quietly. "I would say it even changed me . . . in more ways than you can imagine."

"We're all ears," said Bunny at the same time Edie giggled and said, "Do tell!"

And Velda did. She told them about her outwardly successful but inwardly destructive marriage and how it had made her into someone she felt she was not. Her audience was too riveted to even sip at their drinks, but when Velda finally paused to wet her whistle, Charlene said, "I had no idea."

"It's sad to think I could have won a Best Actress award for how I've lived my life." Her voice was resigned, but when Velda began speaking of how the letter *E* came into her head, her whole mien changed.

Her excellent posture and trim, athletic figure had always belied her years, but it was now her beaming face that made her appear if not ageless, then at least like a person whose vibrancy shone past any number.

"'E is for Eloise,' of course! Eloise was the girl I'd fallen in love with in college."

Looks of surprise were exchanged as Velda told of their affair and, after trying hard to forget Eloise all these years, finally contacting her.

"And?" said Bunny.

"That's why I wasn't at the Halloween party—I went to see her. I was hoping for fireworks . . . there were fireworks on my part, but not on Eloise's." Her smile combined hope and ruefulness. "She recently lost her life partner and isn't ready for another romance yet . . . but we've certainly got a friendship going. We're even talking about taking a vacation together this spring." She made a face that was both scared and excited. "Hope springs eternal."

"I'm happy for you, Velda," said Finn, and his words and the nods, smiles, and "me toos" of the others brought tears to the confessor's eyes. "That was real brave of you to share with us."

Now Velda's gratitude for his kindness and support was tinged with guilt; how many times, in her mental shorthand, had she referred to Finn as "that big lug"?

Edie, sitting so close to her husband she was nearly on his lap, sensed he wanted to say more, and she squeezed his hand.

He understood her encouragement and cleared his throat.

"I myself have something to tell you."

As he revealed his prostate-cancer diagnosis *and* his fear of what eventual treatment might mean regarding his sex life, Bunny wondered,

Is there something in the champagne? while Charlene thought, *Sheesh, what's next?*

Oh, no, was the thought that followed when she saw Charlie looking at her with an expectant expression. She gave a quick shake of her head.

"Phew! Hope I didn't bring you all down." A smile nudged aside Finn's sheepish expression. "But actually, it kinda feels good to get that off my chest." He looked to his friend Roger. "Now here's where you'd usually bring up the mood with some music."

Holding up his bandaged/casted wrists, Roger said with mock mournfulness, "I would if I could." It was the rare gathering that didn't include a quick jam session, or, if there were no musicians to join him, at least a drum solo.

Marlys sprang up and, surprised, Roger watched as she strode across the room—not in the direction of the bathroom or the stereo—but to the "music stage" in the corner of the room, which held Eric's old electric keyboard, one of Jim's guitars, and Roger's drum kit.

He and their guests watched her with a mixture of curiosity and confusion, the way a jury might watch a juggler interrupt a trial attorney's closing argument.

Planting herself on the padded stool, Marlys picked up a pair of sticks from the holder underneath the high hat and twirled one expertly in her right hand before bringing both down on the snare and tapping out a drum roll. She stepped out four loud beats on the bass pedal and proceeded, like a choreographer, to make her sticks dance over the toms, the snare, the cymbals. She played double time beats, cross-stick beats, and dance beats, handling the sticks with a bold assurance, a smile breaking through her pressed-together lips.

I . . . am . . . flabbergasted, thought Edie. She had heard Roger play dozens of times, but never in their yearslong friendship had she any idea that Marlys knew what to do with drumsticks that had nothing to do with fowl.

It's Buddy Rich, thought Bunny of Burton's favorite drummer.

Marlys could have played on and on, but as proud as she was to have acted on the impulse that had led her to the drum kit, she wasn't about to milk it.

After a final riff that had the toms and the crash cymbal crying for mercy, she returned the sticks to their holder, stood up, and brushed the front of her skirt as if she had just served her guests a plate of lemon bars instead of a rocking drum solo.

She plopped down on the arm of the couch next to Roger, who looked dazed, and answered a barrage of questions.

"Well, my dad got me a little drum set when I was five years old—he said he could tell I had rhythm from the way I tapped my spoon on my high chair!

"Well, I played all through school—in fact the first thing I wrote about for our ABC book was about playing in band class with Roger!

"Well, in college, I was in an all-girl band—the Corduroy Window—but I don't know, I just sort of gave it up when the kids were little.

"Well, it was early November—Roger had gone to a hockey game with our son Eric—and I was ironing some shirts in the laundry room, and I don't know, I just felt compelled to come in here and sit at his drums. And now every time he leaves the house, I head down here to play!"

"But honey," said Roger, whose exhilaration hearing her drum was tempered by bewilderment and a little bit of hurt, "why did you keep it a secret from me?"

Marlys took a tiny sip of her champagne—she liked the bubbles but not the sour taste—and shrugged.

"It wasn't a question of keeping it a secret from you . . . it was figuring out why for so long I had kept it a secret from myself." Her voice wavered, but deciding a hostess's tears were unseemly, she cleared her throat. "When I played drums as a girl, I felt so . . . me. But then after we married and the boys came along and everything got so busy, I just sort of forgot about that part of me." She looked to the group. "Not that Roger didn't encourage me to keep playing—he did—but I guess I didn't think it was that important to keep up. But I think it is now." She reached out to touch her husband's face, her fingers running along his faintly bristly jawline. "And I was planning to give you a private concert when I thought I had my chops down." The expression on her flushed face was half-apologetic/half-jubilant as she said, "I really don't know what came over me just now."

Roger had been staring at Marlys, transfixed, seeing both the gray-haired woman whose bad perm hadn't quite grown out as well as the girl he had fallen for all those years ago. Now he turned to the others.

"She was really the best percussionist in high school," he said. "She blew away the rest of us in band class."

"Oh, I did not," said Marlys, and then, feeling as if far too much attention had been given her, she stood up.

"I made a red-velvet cake for dessert. And who wants coffee?"

As expected, the party broke up before midnight, and Charlene and Charlie, who only lived three blocks from the Severtsons, walked home arm in arm under a clear, star-filled sky that seemed a celebration itself. Blue shadows fell across the snowdrifts, and scallops of Christmas lights still looped around bushes and hung across roof eaves.

Slipping as her boots caught an icy patch, Charlene was steadied by Charlie tightening his grip on her arm, and a moment later, she was his ballast when more ice threatened his balance. Their laughter spilled out in vaporous clouds.

"Some party, huh?" said Charlie. "Marlys on drums—*whoa*."

"Everything was whoa! A party and a therapy session, with everyone getting something off their chests, like Finn said." She paused and they walked for a while, snow crunching under their feet. "But I just couldn't."

"In case you could've, though, I wanted you to know it was okay with me."

"You telegraphed that perfectly, and that's why I got so scared. I thought, *If it's all right with Charlie, what's to stop me?* And who knows, I probably will tell the Naomis at some point—which is so strange that I feel they're now my confidantes!—but I thought there was only so much drama we could take in one evening."

"Drama there was," agreed Charlie.

He pushed his glove up to look at his watch when Charlene asked what time it was, and when he said, "Eleven forty-three," Charlene suggested they hurry as she wanted to see the new year begin at home, on the couch, watching the mirror ball drop.

The couple had met in a gas station, when twenty-three-year-old Charlene approached the handsome young man filling up his Ford Mustang to ask if he could help her check the air on one of her tires.

"My first thought," Charlie told her later, "was I'd do anything this beautiful blonde babe asked me to do!"

He checked not just one but three tires and then showed her how to use the gauge so she could check the last one.

"Just in case I'm not around next time," he said, "although I hope I will be."

They lobbed flirtatious lines back and forth, but when a man at pump three swore as gas spewed out his car's fill spout, Charlie suggested they "blow this joint" and asked if he could take Charlene to the Kittleson Café for a cup of coffee.

"Oh, I've got a long drive home," said Charlene, "but if you're ever in Decorah, give me a call."

Charlie took her number, and even though the Iowa city was 150 miles away, he drove there that weekend and called her from a phone booth on College Drive.

That romantic gesture—not only did he take her out for coffee, he brought her a bouquet of gladioli—began what really was a whirlwind courtship, considering that three months later they were married.

Charlene was an inexperienced but eager enough partner in the bedroom . . . until she wasn't. She couldn't really remember when she stopped opening her arms for Charlie when he reached for her, let alone when she stopped reaching for him first. Charlie pleaded with her to tell him what was the matter—was it him? The kids? Household responsibilities? But as time went on, he accepted her indifference. As more time passed, they still had a sex life, although one with a weak pulse, and then came the incident that nearly sent it to the morgue.

~

Five years earlier, Charlie had come home one brisk autumn evening and presented Charlene with two surprises. One was a big bouquet of her favorite flowers, which she accepted with delight, chattering happily as she filled a vase with them. The second ended all delight, let alone happy chatter, as it was Charlie's mournful confession that he'd been having an affair.

"I'm so sorry," he said, wringing his hands. "But this woman, this crazy woman, well, she said she was going to call you tomorrow and 'spill the beans,' so I . . . well, I thought you should hear it from me first."

Charlene's knees were suddenly rubber, and she sat heavily on the kitchen chair, staring at him, wanting to ask him to repeat his words because they made no sense to her, because how could they?

"She came into the dealership," said Charlie, his words rushing out as if he were auditioning for a radio announcer's job. "She was real flirty, she said I should be selling Ferraris or Mercedes the way I was dressed. She said she'd like to look at some minivans, so I took her around the showroom, had her sit in one of our new Odysseys."

He went on and on, as if he were confessing to a police detective who knew how to draw out every cliché and tawdry detail.

When Charlene realized her mouth was hanging open, she closed it, not allowing egress for the shocked, snide, and hurt commentary that screamed in her head.

How could you?

Her name is LaRee? As in whee? Tee-hee?

How much younger is she than me? How much prettier?

You met five times in a "shabby little motel in Mankato"? Too bad it wasn't a Best Western—you could have used your rewards points!

One night you came home—you said you'd had a staff meeting—and you smelled like microwave popcorn. Was that after you'd been with her? Was that your after-sex snack?

"I'm so sorry, Char, so sorry and ashamed. I wish to God I could have spared you finding out, but then she wanted money—can you believe it? And if I didn't give it to her, she said she was going to call you! And I called her bluff, I said, 'Go ahead, I'll give you her phone number,' and she yelled at me to get out, but I don't know, maybe she'll make good on her threat. And Burton said—"

"*Burton*?" said Charlene, the first word she'd spoken. *"Burton knows about this?"*

"Well, yes, I was just at his shop. He's my friend, Char, and I thought he could give me some good advice. Plus he's partly responsible for making me look so good. I mean I was wearing the gray pinstripe when she came in—"

His face fell, mirroring the look on his wife's.

"That might be the stupidest joke I ever made," he said, shaking his head. "It's just that, well, like I said, I was hoping Burton could give me some good advice—the woman was trying to extort me, for God's sake!"

"And now he'll probably tell Bunny."

"Oh, no," said Charlie. "Burton understands what I told him was in confidence. In fact, we both—"

"You both what?" said Charlene, her voice shrill. "Made a pinkie promise?"

She swept her arm across the table, knocking the heavy glass vase filled with gladioli to the floor, and ran out of the room just as the kids, in high school at the time, came through the back door and helpfully pointed out the obvious: "Dad, there's broken glass and flowers all over the floor!"

~

"A minute to go, Charlie," said Charlene now. They had made it home in time and were snuggled in front of the TV.

"Thank you for everything, Charlene."

"Thank you for everything, Charlie."

The two stared at one another, knowing all that "everything" was.

"Let's count!"

And together they did, and after the jubilant shout, "Happy New Year!" they kissed like the battle-weary/war-won lovers they were.

23

"'Don't make waves.' That was what the senior pastor kept telling me at my first church." Tucking in her chin, Mallory deepened her voice. "'Oceans can make them, beauticians can make them, but ministers should *not* make them.'"

"He really said that?" asked Godfrey.

"Really said that and thought he was pretty clever saying it. So I said, 'What about Martin Luther? What about Martin Luther King Jr.?'"

"And his response?"

Adding a wagging finger to add to her imitation of the pastor, Mallory said, "'You're not Martin Luther and you're not Martin Luther King Jr.'"

"What a putz."

"I was so glad I was only hired on a six-month interim basis."

"Their loss," said Godfrey, shaking his head.

The church custodian was not quite in a somber mood, more a melancholic/grateful one, having just taken his brother to the airport after spending four wonderful days introducing Chauncey to the sights, sounds, and people of Kittleson.

In the RV park where Godfrey lived, they'd made a six-foot snowman they called Dad, pelting it with snowballs before building it up again, gently patting its sides and setting an old felt hat on its head at a jaunty angle.

They'd had coffee with Evan Bates, who gave Chauncey a bag of his homemade peanut brittle, and gone to karaoke night at the Gold Leprechaun with Larry Donovan. They'd howled when Godfrey sang—or tried to sing—"You're So Vain" by Carly Simon, and further laughed themselves into near sickness when Chauncey added what he thought was some smooth choreography to his rendition of Lionel Richie's "Three Times a Lady."

"I'm glad you're here," older brother had said to younger. "It seems like you're in the right place."

"Who'd a thunk it, huh?"

On their last night, Pastor Pete invited them over for dinner.

Among the rudimentary set of dishes and appliances the church parish furnished were two Crockpots, of which both Mallory and John made good use, especially in the fall and winter months.

"I've got to get me one of those," said Chauncey Kowalski, accepting his second bowl of a chicken-tarragon stew.

"It'd be perfect for you on the ranch," said John, that night's chef. "You stick everything in in the morning and when you come home, dinner's ready."

"Yes, man should not live by TV dinners and frozen pizzas," said Godfrey. "Course you'd have to learn how to chop vegetables and stuff. And get a spice cabinet."

"What's a spice cabinet?"

While the men joked about the paucity of Chauncey's kitchen contents and what he could possibly make with salt, pepper, and a freezer-burned hunk of venison a hunter friend had given him, Mallory got up from the table and, when she returned, said, "This'll help." She handed him a Crockpot recipe book. "It'll tell you everything you need to do, step by step."

Touched, Chauncey tried to maintain a stoic expression, but it was foiled by a busy tongue that revolved inside his closed mouth, poking out his lower lip and the sides of his cheeks. For a long moment, he riffled through the pages, finally jabbing a finger at the splayed-open one.

"There," he said. "That's what I'll make first: Connie's Crappie Chowder."

He was the kind of man who didn't mind a joke at his own expense, and after realizing he'd mispronounced the fish *crap-ee* instead of *craw-pee*, he laughed with the rest of them.

It immediately became one of Mallory and John's code phrases—with Chauncey's original pronunciation—to describe anything that surprised or delighted them.

"Connie's Crappie Chowder," John said late that night, when Mallory had emerged from the bathroom, letting the towel she'd wrapped around her slip to the floor.

~

Inside All Souls now, Godfrey was helping prepare for the State of the Church meeting, and it was while setting up folding chairs that Pastor Pete further expounded on the waves that might be made that night.

"John was even hoping for a blizzard so we could cancel the meeting."

"Where is John anyway?"

Usually he came early along with his wife.

"He'll be here as soon as our babysitter, who's great, but not exactly punctual, shows up."

"Well," said Godfrey, clenching his fists, "I'll be your bouncer if any fights break out."

Mallory's laugh was weak, but sincere.

The church had a snowblower, which Godfrey had kept busy earlier, clearing out the sidewalks and parking lot, and while the snow had lessened in ferocity as people began to arrive, flakes still flew like feathers, as if impish angels were winding down their hours-long pillow fight.

Mallory and John (the babysitter's excuse this evening had been that it had taken longer than she thought to shovel out her driveway) welcomed people into the undercroft; all of the Naomis were in attendance, as well as three of their husbands. Pastor Pete was heartened to see the new members Tamara and Carlos Garcia, who were the type of go-getters who had remodeled their attic into a main suite, started a neighborhood dinner club, joined the PTA of their sons' elementary school, and volunteered to serve on the committee to "Dazzle Main Street" all within four months of moving to Kittleson. They were the type of young professionals Mallory thought would have been more attracted to Prince of Peace, and she considered it a coup of sorts that they had joined All Souls. There were about two dozen other members, including Art Chelmers, the treasurer, as well as some Men on a Mission and their wives.

After Velda read the minutes of the last meeting at the podium, Pastor Pete stood behind it to discuss "old business."

"Sharon Krueger wants to thank everyone for their help with costumes for the Christmas pageant and—"

"I still haven't gotten my bathrobe back," said Evan Bates, raising his hand. "It's not the greatest, but it's got sentimental value—it's the robe the hospital gave me when I went in for my hip replacement." He turned to Bunny, seated next to him. "Can't recommend that operation highly enough. Wish I would have gotten it years ago."

With a brisk nod, Pastor Pete assured him he'd get his robe back, before turning to the choir director.

"Tad, I believe you want to say a few words?"

The man who looked like he might stand behind a counter and fill a paper sack with horehound candies stood, and Edie wondered if there was a vintage website from which he ordered his matching suspenders and bow ties, these particular ones patterned with snowflakes.

"I just wanted to remind everyone that if you have a voice, our choir could certainly use you." He smiled and rolled his eyes, acknowledging that it was the line with which he began all his church addresses. "And I also want to extend my thanks to all the Christmas concert participants, especially to Tamara Garcia for her flute solo."

The new member smiled even as her eyes filled with tears; she had been inspired to play the instrument by her recently deceased father, who had been a big James Galway fan.

Pastor Pete was reading the final tally of the monies brought in during the Christmas bazaar when Bill Hall, whose simmering impatience was now at full boil, spoke up.

"I'm sure we'd all like to hear how many doilies and crocheted dish towels were sold, but criminy—when are you going to tell us about your little sex book?"

Here we go, thought Godfrey, standing in the back.

Pastor Pete cleared her throat, not because she wanted a clearer passageway through which her words could travel, but because there weren't any words at the ready. Or at least ones she really wanted to say.

"Ahem."

More seconds to collect both her thoughts and the right words passed, but she was given even more of a reprieve when Velda stood up and, hands on hips, said, "First of all, Bill, it's not a sex book. It's not any kind of book. We haven't even gathered up the submissions yet." She wiggled her eyebrows, which were mostly penciled in, owing to the fact that age did a number on a lot of things, including eyebrow hair. "Although I personally have been working on some."

"Me too," said Bunny, rising. "I mean *come on*; you all know All Souls' cash flow has hit a logjam. We thought writing about erotica would be a . . . well, a unique fundraiser."

"Who thought that?" demanded Bill, his big fleshy face growing pink.

"We all did," said Marlys, standing.

"That's right," said Edie, one hand braced on Finn's shoulder to give her better leverage as she stood.

"Well, you ladies can't go ahead with something like this!" said Curtis Keeler, who wasn't about to remain in his seat. "It's . . . it's blasphemy!"

"Blasphemy and pornography!" said Bill. "And I want nothing to do with smut peddling!"

"The Naomis are hardly smut peddlers," said Charlie, rising. "Granted, I haven't read any submissions except for Charlene's, but from what I've heard, they're writing more about love and romance than erotica." He smiled as Charlene rose from her chair and took his hand. "And there's nothing the matter with love and romance, is there?"

"Charlie Kendrick!" Bill Hall said. "What has gotten into you?"

Diane Hall tugged at her husband's sleeve, but he shook off her hand, as well as her suggestion that he calm down.

"I demand that you put a stop to this nonsense right now!"

"I second the motion!" said Curtis Keeler.

"Is it up for a motion?" Evan Bates asked.

As the voices crescendoed and Pastor Pete asked that everyone please, *please* sit down, two young people entered the room, and Marlys and Roger, feeling taps on their shoulders, turned to see their granddaughter in the row behind them. They whispered greetings, and Amelia whispered back an introduction of her friend Axel.

Having been told by her grandmother of the upcoming meeting and the inevitable sparks that were going to fly, Amelia had decided to lend her support by attending and invited Axel along.

"*Ja*! I'd like to see, as you say, these sparks fly!"

Loud voices continued to jostle over one another and, wishing she had a gavel, Pastor Pete instead clapped her hands.

"People, please! One at a time!"

"I'll tell you what," said Bill Hall, "I have not been a member of this church to have its good name embarrassed, besmirched, and made a mockery of. There are plenty of good fundraising ideas that we can employ instead."

"Great," said Pastor Pete. "I'd love to hear them."

Bill Hall heard a sarcasm in her voice that wasn't there.

"Well," he stammered, "the pontoon and hayrides bring in money, and the Hot Dish Jamboree *would* bring in more if people would stick to simple recipes and not try to outdo one another with oddball ingredients!"

This did not sit well with those who had contributed year after year to that particular fundraiser.

"You're always welcome to bring in a casserole or two yourself," said Marlys sweetly.

"Well, what about the Christmas bazaar and the Halloween party?" said Curtis. "They always bring in money, so why don't we have more events like those? I mean the year's full of holidays."

"Sure, we could have an Ash Wednesday sale," said Bunny and after a moment added, "and sell charcoal."

"Or maybe we could celebrate Ascension Day," said Velda with a wink toward Bunny. "And sell ladders."

"Thank you for giving some thought to new fundraisers," Pastor Pete told Curtis, who was shaking his head in disgust at the women's unhelpful wisecracks, "and to everyone, I really do want to hear your further ideas. But for now, let's get some sort of consensus on this current project."

"Well, what are the children of All Souls—never mind the world at large—supposed to think about this?" said Bill, practically shouting. "I for one vote absolutely no."

"I think we should know what we're voting on," said his wife, Diane, ignoring the look her husband gave her. "What do you mean by erotica? Is it going to be something tongue in cheek, or a romance-novel kind of erotica, or will it be on the smutty side?"

"I'll give you an example," said Edie. "The first letter I chose was *A* and I said it was for 'Acting' because sometimes pretending to be someone you're not, or feeling something you're not feeling, helps to . . . well, you know, helps you to put a little *oomph* back in your relationship."

"That's my girl," said Finn to his wife, whose rosacea was compounding the intensity of her blush.

"And I wrote about gallantry," said Charlene. Nervousness had softened her voice to almost a whisper, and clearing her throat, she repeated herself. Charlie taking her hand gave her confidence, which increased her volume. "I wrote about my husband standing up for me, for being gallant."

"That's not my idea of erotic!" said Gene Palmer, a Men on a Mission member.

Maybe it should be, thought Charlene, who, before the meeting began, had noticed that Gene didn't help his wife, Rita, out of her coat the way Charlie had helped her, but dashed out of the cloakroom after hanging up his parka.

Charlene was, of course, perfectly capable of getting out of her own coat, but appreciated these small gestures from her husband that said, "Here, let me help," or better yet, "You're cherished," and from the wistful expression she saw on Rita's face, Charlene gathered she would have welcomed a small gesture of her own.

"Believe me," said Marlys. "When we first talked about this, I got so agitated I accidentally broke Edie's glasses. But what we've learned—and remember, we haven't even collected or read all the submissions—is that everyone has a different idea of what erotica is."

"Like my old roommate," said Amelia. Looking around at the assemblage, she rose as she introduced herself, reminding the older members that she was the Severtsons' granddaughter and had grown up in All Souls until her family moved.

"When my grandma told me about the idea, I thought it was really . . . weird, but then, just for fun, she and I had a little writing session and, well, what she wrote told me things about her and my grandpa I didn't know." She flushed, not as hard as Edie, but her facial capillaries were getting a definite workout. "I mean, it was really sweet. So I don't think you have to worry about a bunch of raunchy stuff, although who knows?" After a nervous laugh, she said, "Okay, sorry, I'm rambling. Anyway, my grandma and I thought that the book should have some young people's takes on the subject—like my friend Axel here—"

Axel cheerfully waved a hand.

"—and, so we wrote some stuff. I wound up writing about my first college roommate, Jewel, and the bad stuff she was involved in. She and I had some issues, but I was able to track her down and—" Here she looked at Bill Hall. "—well, maybe an ABC book like this one would have helped her." She took her phone out of her back pocket and looked at Pastor Pete for permission. At the pastor's nod, she began reading off her screen.

Hey Amelia,

Very surprised to hear from you, and when I read the first part of your email, not "happily" surprised. It just brought up a lot of bad shit.

Amelia looked up, shrugged, said "sorry," and went back to reading.

I won't bore you with the details of why I thought so little of myself that I craved any attention, even violence—still working through all of that with my therapist—but I will tell you that I look at sex a lot differently than I did a couple years ago. Thank God! It hurt me to read about that girl you wrote about in your "J is for Jewel" piece, just as it hurt me to be that girl who got hurt by that—here Amelia chose to censor content—M-effer. That's why I left school all of a sudden—with two cracked ribs, two broken teeth, a black eye, and more fear and shame and anger than I knew what to do with. But I got help and am back at school—UC Berkeley. And not to brag—okay, to brag, because why not?—I won the Bruehling Award, which is the top math prize here, so I'm not completely worthless!

I almost erased that last part because it makes me sad how much of my sense of self that "M-effer" took away, but I'm leaving it in because I'm trying to be honest about stuff I used to lie about.

Anyway! Thanks for thinking "J is for Jewel!" You're right; in love, in sex, our partner should be valued. We should all be valued.

~

Evan Bates's mother had grown up on a farm and didn't visit a big city until she was twelve years old. With her mother, she explored and shopped in downtown Topeka, and while there were plenty of sights and sounds that awed her, one in particular was a standout: buskers on a street corner, a shawled woman in a bright skirt playing a concertina while a tiny monkey in a fez skittered around her, clapping its hands.

The sight impressed Evan's grandmother as well, who had seen this particular type of entertainer but never a female one, and whose whispered comment became the family's expression, passed down through the generations, whenever something left them almost expressionless.

"Well, I'll be a lady organ-grinder."

They were the words that came out of Evan Bates's mouth, breaking the long silence following Amelia's recitation, and considering the topic being discussed, those words were racier than Evan had ever intended.

Nervous laughter, confused looks, and mutterings followed, and then Bill Hall sputtered an irate, "I've had enough!"

Curtis Keeler was clearly in agreement, getting up in a huff that nearly knocked his chair over as he followed his friend out of the undercroft. Both men's wives were slower to exit, Diane giving Pastor Pete a thumbs up and Patrice tight lipped, which was either a sign of disapproval or a means to hold back a smile.

Art Chelmers rose and, shaking his head, stated his opinion of the women's project.

"An X-rated church fundraiser? I'd say 'X is for *X* It Out' and come up with something better!"

"I'd say 'X is for *XOXO*,'" countered Tamara Garcia, "as in lots of hugs and kisses. And as far as voting on it? I say 'Y is for Yes.'"

24

The highway was plowed and snow-free, and LeAnn drove fast, passing the truckers who obeyed the speed limit and keeping up with those who pushed it. She passed two deer carcasses lying crumpled on the road's shoulder, a sad but not uncommon sight while driving through Wisconsin, and like a tennis referee, she constantly looked left and right, watching for any flicker of movement from the bordering trees.

She had the radio on but couldn't listen to an entire song without banging on the steering wheel with the heel of her hand or shouting a wide range of expletives.

Waking up that morning, she had been in the midst of a luxurious stretch when a great idea propelled her to throw off the covers and bound out of bed.

Why not surprise her man, whom she hadn't seen for three days, who had flown in late from a team scouting trip to Boston? If he were on one of his morning runs, she could at least offer him high-carb pastries as well as further cardio in bed.

At the bakery, she bought two chocolate-covered donuts, two blueberry muffins, and a coffee to go, and as she drove several miles to Owen's condo, she debated letting him know she was coming (What if he were still sleeping or had already left for his run?) or surprising him.

She chose surprise. She *was* surprised.

Having just turned the corner and a third of a block away from his building, LeAnn saw him come out the front door. Endorphins rushed through her body—how handsome he was in his UW sweats (although she was going to have to scold him for not dressing warmer)—but her feel-good hormones were shoved aside by a less sanguine one: adrenaline. Seeing that he had not exited the door alone, LeAnn gasped and pulled to the curb. He was with a woman. She squinted. *Was that his assistant, Gina?*

So what if it is, the voice inside her head said, struggling to sound reassured. *Maybe they were just getting some work done.*

The backpack the woman was carrying certainly wasn't cause for alarm, stuffed no doubt with office files and not a change of clothing, and that his arm was around her—it was cold out, after all—and the kiss . . . well, LeAnn couldn't explain away that kiss. The kiss that Owen, *her Owen,* was sharing with his assistant—she was pretty sure it was his assistant—was a long kiss that had him pressing her against the blue Audi parked in front of his building.

After the woman got in the car, she rolled down her window and Owen bent to kiss her again, and when she drove off, he stood watching her, blowing her a final kiss with a swoop of his arm before he began to run.

LeAnn was shaking so hard her hand slipped off the gear shift, bumping her coffee in the cup holder and sloshing some onto her hand. Wearing gloves, she didn't feel the hot liquid, at least not on her fingers. Inside her, an inferno raged.

She managed to put the car in drive, and began to do so, slowly, like a narc following a worm of a dealer on his way to the school playground.

The forward movement calmed her, and her shaking dulled to a tremble. It was after she had followed him about a mile, and as he turned a corner that would lead him into the park, that she sped up and, pulling to the side of the road, honked her horn.

Owen turned around and saw her, his face registering confusion and a trace of alarm.

"LeAnn!" he said, readjusting his features into a wide smile. He jogged over to her car, and, as she rolled down the passenger-side window, he squatted and said, "Baby! What a nice surprise!"

LeAnn forced her own mouth into a smile.

"You said it, baby!"

He casually leaned into the open window.

"I was just going to call you after my run—brunch at DeLano's sound good?"

"I'd *love* brunch at DeLano's, but I already stopped at the bakery!" Her voice was perky as a morning talk show host. "I got us some yummy pastries and was just bringing them over to you—but I didn't have enough for your guest!"

Owen's cheeks, reddened by the weather and his physical efforts, paled.

"LeAnn, look—"

"No, you look." Tearing open the bakery bag, she grabbed a donut and threw it at him.

A smear of chocolate blotched his forehead, but his reflexes kicked in and, jumping back, he was able to dodge the second donut and the first blueberry muffin.

"LeAnn, I can explain everything!"

"No, you can't," she said, hurling the last muffin, which, much to her satisfaction, clipped his ear. "Because your explanation would just be a lie!"

She pressed the button that rolled up the passenger-side window, and after checking her rearview mirror, hit the gas pedal.

At home, she could only think to splash cold water on her face, charge her phone, stuff some clothes (not work files—ha!) into her own backpack, and get into her car.

"Asshole!" she hollered now, over Katy Perry singing about being chained to the rhythm.

She had driven over a hundred miles when she realized her phone hadn't beeped/chirped or vibrated, and after frantically patting every pocket of her coat and jeans, she dragged her backpack across the front seat, preparing to rummage through it with the hand not on the steering wheel. It was then she saw in her mind's eye a picture of her phone on her kitchen counter, tethered by its charger cord.

The car was filled with more expletives and pronouncements of what an idiot she was. *How could she have forgotten her phone?* The thought of turning around flamed out almost as soon as it arose—she had driven too far—and she forged ahead, ignoring the trucker in the next lane who ogled her from on high in his cab, tooting his horn and wagging his tongue.

It was just after four o'clock when she pulled up in front of the church parsonage and four fifteen when she finished pounding on the front and back doors. It hadn't occurred to her that Mallory might not be home, and she was consumed with defeat, as well as an urgent need to empty her bladder.

"Hey!" she cried, seeing the custodian emerging from the church's back door.

Keys in hand, Godfrey looked up to see a woman race from the Petersons' backyard and onto the parking lot. His first thought was how fast she ran without slipping or sliding (then again, he was a thorough shoveler); his second thought was *why* was she running toward him so fast?

"Hey, Godfrey," said the woman, leaping up the steps, "could I please use the bathroom?"

Not sure how she knew his name, he nevertheless said, "Be my guest," and pushed open the door.

It didn't take long for him to remember that the woman with the panicked look on her face was Pastor Pete's friend—Lou Ann? Lorraine?

"I'm LeAnn," she said, offering him her hand several minutes later. "Mallory's friend? I met you a couple months ago?"

"I remember meeting you, just didn't remember your name."

"You don't happen to know where Mallory is, do you?"

"Matter of fact, I do," said Godfrey, locking the church door. "She and John and Soren are down in Hogeboom—"

"Hogeboom?"

"Town about thirty miles southwest of here. A parishioner's mother is celebrating her one hundredth birthday and they went down to help celebrate."

"Any idea when they might be back?"

Godfrey shrugged and said, "I suppose you could call and ask her."

"Well, that's just it. I left my phone at home."

"Oh."

"Maybe you could call her?"

"I don't have a phone, myself."

"You don't have a phone?"

Godfrey shrugged again. "Doesn't seem that necessary. But we could call her from the church landline."

LeAnn thought for a moment.

"Nah. I don't want to interrupt someone's one hundredth birthday party." She looked at her watch. "I guess I'll just wait till they get home."

"Where?"

"Where what?"

"Where will you wait for them? I mean, it's pretty cold."

As if to lend credence to his forecast, a stiff wind pushed a dusting of snow off the roof, and when Godfrey asked if she was hungry, LeAnn realized she was.

"So you haven't eaten anything all day?" Godfrey asked, squirting mustard on his bratwurst.

"I know," said LeAnn, salting her french fries. "I should have saved at least one of those donuts."

In Godfrey's truck, she had relayed the events of her day, enjoying the driver's low chuckle as she told him how she'd pelted her boyfriend, her *former* boyfriend, with pastries.

He had told her that Kittleson wasn't Madison when it came to dining options, but the bowling alley had good cheap food, and since it might be a while before the Petersons got back, why not try their luck in a game or two while they were at it?

The friendly teenager who wore a pin reading "Notorious RBG" checked back midway through their meal to inform them that anyone who bowled three strikes won either a free beer or an order of nachos.

"Well, considering this'll be the first game I've bowled since middle school," said LeAnn, "I guess I should order my beer now. Godfrey? Can I buy you one?"

Shaking his head, he told the server, thanks, but he was fine with water.

"I had a bit of a drinking problem," he said after the teenager left.

LeAnn nodded. "Oh, yeah. Mallory told me, but I forgot." She dragged a fry through a puddle of ketchup. "I hope you don't think she's betraying your confidence. We . . . we tell each other a lot."

"I don't mind. That's what friends do." He wiped his mouth with a square of napkin and surveyed the triangle of pins at the end of the lane. "So, ready?"

"As ready as I'll ever be."

In the second frame, Godfrey bowled a strike.

In the second frame, LeAnn got two gutter balls.

In the fifth frame, she threw her ball so hard that it bounced before careening down the lane and knocking down, barely, the ten pin.

"It must be these," she said, looking down at her rented red-and-yellow bulbous shoes. "How am I supposed to do anything in something so ugly?"

"I think it's more your approach," said Godfrey with a laugh. "Or your swing. Or maybe you should try a different ball."

In the sixth frame, he bowled another strike and LeAnn managed, much to her surprise and with a lighter ball, to knock down a total of seven pins.

In the seventh frame, Godfrey bowled his third strike.

After the game, the free nachos were delivered.

"Are you like, really into bowling?" asked LeAnn.

"Not really."

"Not really? You bowled three strikes!"

"I just wanted these," he said, twisting a chip to loosen it from its mooring of melted cheese. He chewed for a moment and added, "I do like sports that make a lot of noise, though, so bowling's good. The thunk of the ball on the wood, the roll of it down the alley, the crashing of pins."

"Or the glug-glug when the ball goes in the gutter," said LeAnn, whose score was a woebegone fifty-seven.

"But mostly, I come here for the food."

"So you're a gourmand, huh?"

"Only the best bratwurst and nachos for this guy."

"Can I see how long your hair is?"

Coming out of nowhere, the question momentarily fazed him, but he shrugged and, after pulling off the elasticized band from his ponytail, shook his head as if he were in a shampoo commercial.

LeAnn laughed. "Now you look totally heavy metal."

"Not a fan," said Godfrey, corralling his hair back in the rubber band.

"No? What kind of music do you like?"

"I like . . . I like pan flutes and recordings of whales."

"Maybe we should see if Mallory's home yet."

"I was kidding."

"So was I," said LeAnn, her smile broad.

"But they are probably home by now," Godfrey said, "unless you'd like to bowl another game?"

"I think I've been shamed enough today," she joked / didn't joke.

Back in the truck, LeAnn asked Godfrey how old he was.

"Forty-one. How old are you?"

"Same age as Mallory. Thirty-six."

"Sometimes I feel like I'm about seventy. And sometimes about seven."

"I felt about fifteen today, when I saw Owen with . . ." LeAnn's voice trailed off, as if she didn't have the energy to finish the sentence.

"Let's see if we can find some whale music," said Godfrey, turning on the radio dial, and for the short ride back to the parsonage, they listened to Mick Jagger sing about wild horses followed by Maria Muldaur singing about midnight at the oasis followed by the voice of a DJ crediting the singers and reminding listeners that he didn't play oldies, he played goodies.

"Looks like they're home," said Godfrey, pulling behind a car parked in the Petersons' driveway.

"Thanks for rescuing me, Sir Godfrey."

He bowed his head and put his hand on his chest.

"Thanks for being a witness to my bowling wizardry, Lady LeAnn."

Mallory was happy to see her friend, but not happy about the circumstances that led to her surprise visit, and she patiently listened and offered just the right questions and murmurs of sympathy. Still, after seeing Mallory surreptitiously check her phone for the third or fourth time, LeAnn sensed that something other than her own problems was occupying the minister's mind.

When she said as much, Mallory apologized.

"It's just that I haven't quite finished tomorrow's sermon. And I'm nervous about it."

She began to tell LeAnn what had happened at the recent church meeting.

"I mean, people are outraged—outraged and disgusted! I just thought this was going to be a fun little thing that might raise a little money, but it might be what finally does us in!"

"I'm sure—"

"I'm not sure of anything!" said Mallory. "And as much as I'd love to—"

"No worries. Get to work. I know where the guest room is."

25

In her church office, Mallory found on her desk a note written in John's much-better-than-her-own handwriting.

> *Y is for You, darling Mallory, and all you've done for me as your lover, your husband, your coparent (yippee!), and your absolute biggest fan. Y is for You, who works to make this world of ours a loving, peaceable, and celebratory one. Y is for bold, beautiful You. Remember who You are, honey, and go get 'em.*

She folded the paper into a small square and tucked it into the left side of her bra.

Seated at the organ in the choir loft, Tad had been softly playing the prelude, but putting the pedal to the metal, he signaled his singers, who began the first several bars of "Joyful, Joyful, We Adore Thee," and the congregation, hymnals in hand, rose and joined in. The church service settled into its routine: the recitation of the Nicene Creed, a choir solo, Scripture readings, and the Peace. After the parishioners shook each other's hands, Mallory climbed the four steps to the pulpit.

She took a long general view of the congregation, at the people who had invited her into their homes or sat in her office as they asked for advice, forgiveness, help. People who had shared with her their triumphs and sorrows, fears and hopes . . . and occasional sermon critiques. To them all, she sent out a silent message of love before narrowing her focus to those in the front row. Bunny and Finn both winked at her, and John mouthed the word, "You." Nodding slightly, she breathed in all the air her lungs could hold, and began.

"I type up my sermon on my computer, but I always write the first draft by hand, feeling that my thoughts take the journey from my head, take a left and wander into my heart, back out to my arm, and finally into my hand holding the pencil. My wastebasket is filled with crumpled beginnings of this sermon—I wanted to have the perfect beginning, but perfection is an ideal rather than a reality, at least when it comes to my sermons."

She smiled, grateful for the smattering of laughter.

"This church, our church, is nearly one hundred years old and has a storied history. It fed and sheltered people during the Great Depression. It held funerals for soldiers who lost their lives in World War II, in Korea, in Vietnam, in Afghanistan."

Penny Tyler bowed her head; her beloved son had been killed eight years ago in the Parwān Province.

"It's been a place of worship, a sanctuary, a gathering spot for many, and when I came last spring, my goal was to be the kind of pastor that would continue those traditions of inspiring, of guiding, of welcoming. Lately, I feel I've been failing."

There were scattered murmurs, and Vonnie Vozniak, up in the choir loft, coughed as a Tic Tac nearly lodged in her throat.

"In my short time as your minister, I have had conversations with some of you about your struggles with faith—"

Her eyes sweeping over those gathered, she saw Glenda Parks, who'd spent several hours in Mallory's office asking why God would abandon her, just as her husband—"the lying, cheating conniver"—had; she saw Tad up in the choir loft, who'd once made the offhand, but seemingly genuine, comment that sometimes he wondered if music was his real God.

"—and what I've always counseled is that faith is big enough to be struggled with. Faith can stand to be tested, that is if you believe your faith is worth fighting for, even when doubt is pinning it to the ground.

"My own faith is a solidly rooted sequoia . . . when it's not a weak little sapling, ready to tip over in the slightest wind. In John, chapter fourteen, verse six, Jesus says, 'I am the way, and the truth, and the life . . . ,' and yet there are times I wonder, 'What if you're not? What if Muhammad is, or Buddha or Krishna or Mother Nature? Or what if it's all of them at the same time?'"

Mallory was aware of her audience, aware of the uncomfortable shifts in posture, the looks of consternation and perplexity passed around the congregants like hot potatoes. She took another deep breath.

"But I believe my faith is ultimately strong enough to handle these questions, *wants* me to ask these questions. What I wonder about is, is it fair to you to have a pastor with a faith like this?"

"I'd say it is!" said Velda from the front row, and in the shock of the moment of someone responding aloud, Pastor Pete ad-libbed, "Well then, can I get an amen?"

She couldn't help but hear Curtis Keeler's loud whisper, "What is this, a comedy club?" but was pleased that more than half of the parishioners responded by whispering/saying/shouting, "Amen!"

When laughter, the ultimate easing of tension followed, Pastor Pete felt tears come to her eyes. She looked to her husband, whose smile and barely perceptible nod helped her resolve to not dissolve.

"The thing is," she continued, "and I don't know if you'll want to hear this either—is that while my faith is strengthened by prayer, by studying the Bible, it really grows because of all of you."

Pastor Pete's blonde hair was pulled back in a low bun, and her pastoral robe was zipped up to the center of her clavicle, and she wore a purple-and-gold satin stole.

Her husband would later tell her she seemed to be "aglow with a dewy radiance" and laugh when Mallory dismissed the over-the-top compliment, claiming the only thing she'd been aglow with was flop sweat.

"What I mean is," the pastor said, walking toward the middle of the chancel, "in you, I see daily the wonder and beauty of God's creation, and I want to do right by you."

She continued talking, not sermonizing, about what she had hoped to bring to All Souls and how much she wanted to be up to the task of overseeing the flourishing and growth—spiritual and in numbers—of the congregation.

"I won't hold you in suspense any longer. Several days ago, I sent out an email telling you I had something controversial to talk about today, something that had caused some *concern* at our State of the Church meeting." She scanned the congregation carefully. "Just making sure all minors are in Sunday school."

She continued, telling them of the Naomis' fundraising idea, grateful that the congregation's whispers never rose to the level of heckling.

"But it seems word has already spread about *The ABCs of Erotica*, as I have received—unsolicited—twenty of these sorts of entries, some of which I'd like to share with you now."

From the deep pockets of her robe, she unfolded a piece of paper.

"This person asked to remain anonymous," she said, announcing that *L* was for love.

Charlie nudged his wife and whispered, "While I totally agree, I didn't write it."

"It's true you don't need an emotional attachment to be turned on—the body definitely does have a mind of its own. I myself spent much of my youth, my teens, my twenties, my thirties, even my early forties, with sex underlined and at the top of my to-do list. With girlfriends, with my wife, with myself—it really didn't matter. Being turned on by cleavage or a passing backside—"

"Passing backside," Godfrey, in the back row, whispered to Larry, "sounds like a sports term."

"—is the easy sort of erotica, and while there's nothing wrong with easy, sometimes the things that are harder earned are the more satisfying. Being turned on by someone you argued with earlier in the day about changing the oil filter or by watching her vacuum the drapes—that's the kind of erotica that takes in the history of your love story—a story you want to keep going, a deeper, harder-won kind of erotica.

"Anyway, that's my take on this whole thing. 'L is for Love.'"

Pastor Pete looked up, and while some expressions on congregants' faces were not pleasant ones, at least she had everyone's attention.

"Here's another one," said Pastor Pete, "also signed, 'Anonymous.' 'S is for—'"

The faces of her congregants were expectant, like students waiting to hear if their own answers—Soft, Silky, Sex (duh!)—were the ones Teacher cited.

"'—Soul.' When as hard as you try to be cool and not let anybody in, but a certain woman insists that you do by being kind and patient and telling you how lucky she is to be with you. When that woman doesn't think showing your feelings makes you less of a man but more of one and that woman cradles you in her arms and lets you cry like a baby when you're hurting so bad and the funny thing is, you don't feel like a baby in her arms, after you've wiped your face of tears and snot, you feel not so much like a whole man, but a whole person. When that woman knows your secrets and doesn't run off screaming but tells you some of her own and both of you see so much more than each other's faces when you look into one another's eyes—you see each other's souls or at least feel each other's souls, which is a pretty amazing thing."

With a smile, Bunny acknowledged Jolie's slight nudge in her side, a reminder of the conversation about soul she'd had with her and Hiram.

"So there I was," she'd tell Burton later, "sitting in the pew of a church called All Souls, listening to someone's idea that soul was erotic!"

The final anonymous one Pastor Pete read was titled "P is for Private."

"As in, that's what the sex act should be—private! I am not a prude—I realize that God didn't create sex only for procreation, but I don't feel writing about it has a place in our church. Sure, it may raise money because of its shock factor, but do we really want to be shock peddlers? Aren't there enough of those in the world already? Instead of catering to people's baser instincts, aren't there better topics we can explore to raise money for our church?"

If she didn't know he was dead, Velda would have been certain Mervin had penned that particular entry.

"Next week I promise a more traditional sermon," said Pastor Pete, with an apologetic shrug. "I so want to do right by our church and our community—I have so many plans for this big new year!—but I want to *lead*, not trample. That's why in continuing today's rather unorthodox service, I'm asking all members to vote. We've put slips of paper in the pledge-card holders so please write 'yes' or 'no' on them and the ushers will collect them along with the offering."

As collection plates were passed down the rows, Tad directed the choir in singing "Beautiful Savior," a song that would probably win a number of votes if one were taken for "favorite hymn."

There had never been a Coffee Hour more crowded than the one that followed the service.

"Seems like everyone who was upstairs is downstairs," Godfrey said to the Severtsons, who stood behind the serving table.

"I know," said Marlys. "I'll have to cut smaller pieces of my Kringle."

"Although we might just run out of coffee," said Roger, handing Godfrey a cup.

"Heaven forbid," said Marlys, recognizing a true All Souls catastrophe.

The undercroft buzzed from both the fluorescent lights and the conversations of people situated around tables and standing in small groups.

"I texted my parents," said Axel, looking at his phone. "And they wrote back, '*Wir stimmen ja!*'" He smiled. "That means they vote yes."

"We're not members yet," said Jolie. "But we're thinking of joining. Any church that would even *think* of putting out a book about erotica gets my vote."

"So you voted?" asked Amelia.

"No, I decided to play by the rules."

"First time ever," said Hiram.

"My mother?" said Tad. "I told her what was going on, and she said she might actually have to come to a service. And she's an atheist!"

"How's Burton doing?" Rita Palmer asked Bunny.

"Oh, you know. The usual."

"Those your friends?" asked Rita's husband, nodding at the nearby group.

"They certainly are," said Bunny, not liking Gene's tone.

"Wonder how a gal like that got so big."

"Funny," said Bunny before excusing herself, "I was wondering how some people get so small."

Finn joined a small cluster of Men on a Mission, wanting to swat away the finger Bill Hall waved in their faces.

"However this goes down, I've got to tell you, we're both thinking of moving on to Prince of Peace."

"Sorry you feel that way, Bill," said Charlie, although he didn't sound particularly sorry.

"Don't know why anyone would want their church to become a laughingstock," said Curtis Keeler, every word a tsk.

"I don't want All Souls to become a laughingstock," said Finn. "I also don't want it to go under." He looked at his fellow Men on a Mission. "And our hayrides and wreath sales just ain't cutting it, fellas."

"You know, we hold you sort of responsible for all this trouble," Velda said.

"What?" said LeAnn. "I didn't—"

"She's teasing you," said Edie. "If anything, we're grateful to you."

"That we are," said Velda. "We needed help thinking outside the box, and you definitely helped us do that."

Edie giggled.

"Outside the room, outside the house, outside the town, outside the *county* that the box was in!"

A half-dozen children raced around the perimeter of the room, but most of the older kids, not wanting to hang around Sunday school any longer than necessary, had walked or driven home, taking their younger siblings with them.

A natural hostess, Marlys circulated through the room, tray in hand.

"Last four pieces," she said, offering the Kringle to two young women watching their children chase one another.

"We were just talking about you Naomis and what you did," said Tamara Garcia, taking a piece of the pastry.

"Yeah, neither one of us ever thought much about joining a circle," said Carla Holtz, who like Tamara was fairly new to All Souls. "But if we did, it'd be one like yours."

"Then do!" said Marlys. "We'd love to have you!"

"You don't have to be on Social Security to join?" teased Carla.

Laughing, Marlys said, "You're going to fit right in."

~

When Pastor Pete, Art Chelmers, and Dorrie Hillstead entered the undercroft, people suddenly quieted, moving themselves to either side of the room.

"Like Moses parting the Red Sea," whispered John to Godfrey and Larry Donovan.

"Well," said Pastor Pete, waving some paper. "The votes have all been counted—three times."

"We just wanted to make sure," said Art Chelmers, his officious voice reminding people he took his role as church treasurer seriously.

"And the results are," said Pastor Pete, reading, "ninety-eight for and forty-two against."

A brief silence was broken by scattered cheers and whistles.

Evan Bates, who had just finished his second piece of Marlys's Danish Kringle, brushed his suit lapel with his hand (he was very conscious of not being the Old Guy with Crumbs All Over His Shirt) and said, "Pastor Pete?"

Nerves seemed to halt his voice, and, after clearing his throat, it became gruff.

"Pastor Pete?"

Steeling herself—she had expected some protests but was surprised that the first of them came from him.

"Yes, Evan?"

"I was waiting for the vote to come in," said the nonagenarian, making his way carefully to where the trio stood.

"Now I don't usually like to make a big show of things," he said, gently nudging Dorrie Hillstead aside so that he could stand next to the minister. "But today I thought, maybe it's about time I did."

The old man began to cackle, amused by a joke no one else was in on.

Pastor Pete looked to her husband; his shrug answered her own.

"New years are always exciting and new years that start a new decade, even more so!

"Now, I could have put this in the collection plate," said Evan, taking an envelope out of his breast pocket, "but then it might have been the last time we saw Art Chelmers."

The treasurer opened his mouth to protest but was silenced by more of the old man's laughter.

"Just pulling your leg, Art. I know you're an honest treasurer, but for ceremonial purposes, I'd like to hand off this particular gift to Pastor Pete."

"Happy 2020!" he said, cackling again as he gave her the envelope with instructions to open it.

Mallory unfolded the rectangle of paper inside and stared at it, seeing numbers but not comprehending them.

Leaning in to get a look, Art Chelmers gasped.

Dorrie Hillstead craned her neck to get a look, and when she did, her hand flew to her mouth.

The crowd was silent, staring at them. Finally, Bunny called out, "What is it?"

"It's," said Mallory, ". . . it's a check."

"My brother Eldred, the one who chose to pass right upstairs in church?" Evan said to the crowd. "Farmed in North Dakota? Farmed in Williston, North Dakota, on land that—whee-doggy—"

Quite a few parishioners wondered, *Did he just say whee-doggy?*

"—land that happened to sit on top of quite a bit of oil! He's been making hand over fist off that land, which is a good thing, because he was never much of a farmer."

He cackled again.

"In his will, he was mighty generous to our two nieces and one nephew and mighty generous to me. And so *I* decided to be generous because I believe in our frisky pastor and the fresh air she's brought to All Souls." He turned to Pastor Pete and said, "No offense, I mean frisky in the best sense."

"No offense taken," she said.

Evan looked out at the crowd. He was a decades-long church member but couldn't remember if he'd ever felt so . . . tickled. Maybe that one Palm Sunday when, during the processional, Pastor Wiggans's delinquent son waved his palm with so much force that it knocked off Mildred Wattrum's hat?

"Now what if the vote had gone the other way and you had proven to be a bit more closed minded than I'd like to think you are? Honestly, ask yourselves: What ideas do closed minds ever come up with anyway?" He began rocking back and forth on his old but neatly shined dress shoes. "Would I have withheld this gift to punish you? Guess you'll never know."

His cackle rose, and a radiator clunked, and Bunny, unable to stand the suspense called out, "How much is it for?"

John later told his wife she looked as if she were about to break out in a dance, but LeAnn said no, she thought Mallory looked like she might throw up.

"It's," said Pastor Pete, looking again at the check in her trembling hand to make sure she saw what she thought she'd seen. "It's for a million dollars."

Air was inhaled in one great communal gasp.

"There're just two small caveats," said Evan, and Mallory thought, *Here it comes,* but the old man didn't demand that the church be renamed in his honor or that sunrise services be added not just at Easter but every other Sunday. Instead, he said, "First, a headline, or in this case, a title. Title is very important."

He unfolded from his pocket his church program filled with his notes, and, scanning it, the old newspaper man said, "And from the submissions you read this morning, they didn't match your title. They were less *shouts* about the whole complicated brouhaha about sex and love than *suggestions* about how to make both better."

"Exactly," whispered Marlys to Roger. "That's what we've been saying all along."

"We don't want the word *erotica* turning off people." The old man's cackle rose up again. "Excuse the unintentional play on words! But yes, let's give this worthy endeavor a worthier title."

"We can do that," said Pastor Pete and, to the congregants, said, "All ideas are welcome."

"Excellent. The second caveat is I'd like to put my dibs on the letter *Z*."

"You can take any letter you'd like. You can write about the whole alphabet if you like!"

"Oh, I doubt I'd know what to do with all those letters. I just need the *Z*."

Always ready to celebrate with music, Tad said, "I think we need a song!" and sitting at the old upright, proceeded to play "For He's a Jolly Good Fellow," which, although secular, was almost holy in the way it was sung, with grateful, exultant voices.

"So what does *Z* stand for?" asked Pastor Pete, leading Evan toward the cloakroom for a private moment.

"You'll find out when I send you the piece," he said, but seeing the minister's disappointment, he added, "All right, I'll give you a teaser: 'Z is for Zinnia.'"

"The flower?"

"A bloom that doesn't get its deserved attention, but no. Zinnia was the name of the woman who taught me how to make candy. The teacher who helped me understand the alchemy of sweetness."

"I can't wait to read the rest," said Mallory, and moved to tears by all the old man had given her and the church, she had a sudden impulse to share something of her own.

Leaning close to whisper in his ear, she said, "We're not telling anyone just yet, but I'd like you to know. I'm pregnant."

Evan Bates beamed at Pastor Pete.

"This is shaping up to be a bang-up year."

In the undercroft, everyone hugged one another in celebration, which to many of those claiming Scandinavian ancestry, was as exhausting as a triathlon.

After making the rounds and participating in the hug fest, the Naomis found themselves in their own little huddle.

"Well, we did it, ladies," said Bunny. "It looks like 'Operation Save All Souls' is a success—especially now that we have a little money to back up our project."

"Look out, world," said Velda, "*The ABCs of Erot* . . . I mean *Title to Be Determined* is on its way!"

"Maybe now we can even afford colored pictures," said Edie. "Like Price of Peace's *Table Blessings*!"

"Pictures!" said Marlys. "That might be pushing the envelope a little too far."

"Did you know," said Velda, "that the idiom 'pushing the envelope' comes from the aviation world?"

Bunny laughed. "Well, thanks to you, I do now."

"I can't wait to tell my sister-in-law Nancy about this," said Charlene. "She loves reminding me that the Naomis are the last circle of All Souls and that 'sooner or later they'll both come to an end.'"

"That's mean!" said Edie.

"Also not true," said Velda crisply. "With Evan's gift, All Souls will be around for a long time."

"As will the Naomis!" said Marlys. "Besides, last doesn't mean we're losing, last means—"

Her friends helped her out.

"Surviving!"

"Remaining!"

"Enduring!"

Raising their hands in a Styrofoam-coffee-cup toast, the Naomis proclaimed, "To the last circle!"

Their boisterousness had attracted the attention of others, most of whom were compelled to echo the toast.

"To the last circle!" shouted the grateful parishioners, and it wasn't clear who in the crowd, in a deep Barry White bass, added, "Of love!"

Acknowledgments

I wonder what both my parents—long gone from our temporal world—would have thought of this book and what letters they would have come up with. Thinking of their relationship, I'd say "S is for Shampoo." I can see my dad perched on the toilet (lid down!) of our tiny bathroom and my mother sitting at his feet as he shampooed in her Lady Clairol. They would joke and laugh as he washed the gray away, and I always saw that home–beauty salon ritual as loving and playful.

So here's to their memory; I miss them.

Hats off to my first readers, Renee Albert, Wendy Smith, and Greg Triggs; I appreciate your enthusiasm, humor, and excellent taste.

To my related-in-every-way-except-blood sisters, Las Chicas, thanks for all the fun and support. And for their excellent hosting of us, gracias to Lee Duberman and Richard Fink of the fabulous Casa Papaya in San Miguel, Mexico. Long may sunset margaritas on rooftops reign. Also to Sue Krieg, who graciously let the Real Housewives of Ahwatukee run wild in her house. ("I don't feel a thing!")

To WWW—glad to have the camaraderie of writer friends like you.

To the women of Lakselaget—I enjoy swimming against the current with you. And Linda Jo Stuckey—I miss our craft dates!

Bouquets of gratitude to the Lake Union team, to my editor Alicia Clancy for starting everything, to Megan Westberg and Lauren Grange for your laser-sharp eyes, to Christine Lay for the education, and to

Jen Bentham for corralling. Another bouquet to Philip Turner for your advice and counsel.

As always, I'm grateful for my family—my husband, Charles, who makes me laugh, says I'm a fox even when I feel like a mangy cougar, and always turns my books cover out in bookstores; for my daughters Harleigh and Kinga and their absolute grooviness and the accompanying grooviness of Gabe and Calvin . . . and my little pie, my granddaughter, Leika.

We need food and shelter and good walking shoes, but the Beatles were pretty close when they sang about love being our only necessity. It's always an honor/revelation when characters take over and tell me what's what, rather than vice versa, and their ideas of what "got their motor running" and kept it running surprised and tickled me.

Deep thanks to Sheila de Chantal and her amazing Brainerd Friends of the Library crew, who for the past ten years have invited me to emcee Wine & Words, and wide thanks to Pamela Klinger Horn for bringing together readers and writers in Literature Lovers' Night Out—if awards were given out for literary events, these two would bring home the gold.

To Stephen Borer and Brian Motiaytiz, thanks for all the years of support of me both on stages and in pages.

And to my readers! I'm honored to be a part of your reading life.

Book Club Questions

1. If you were to pick a letter to write about in the Naomis' book, what would it be and what would you say?
2. How does the ABCs project change the Naomis? How does it change their partners? Which character do you think changes the most?
3. Pastor Pete questions her own faith at times; do you think this makes her a stronger or weaker minister?
4. If you're part of a faith community, how do you think the Naomis' project would be received in your place of worship?
5. Did any of your mothers/grandmothers belong to a church circle? What would you say they got out of it?
6. Did you have a relationship with a grandparent as close and supportive as the one Amelia shares with Marlys?
7. Pastor Pete struggles with her own judgments on age. Godfrey initially can't relate to a "group of old bags" like the Naomis. Have you been on the receiving end of ageism/sexism? Have you found yourself making judgments about people based on their age and sex?
8. What do you think young adults might include in a book like the Naomis'?